THE SHADOW CHILDREN

Among the Hidden

Among the Impostors

BY MARGARET PETERSON HADDIX

SIMON & SCHUSTER BOOKS FOR
YOUNG READERS

NEW YORK LONDON TORONTO SYDNEY

SIMON & SCHUSTER BOOKS FOR YOUNG READERS
An imprint of Simon & Schuster Children's Publishing Division
1230 Avenue of the Americas, New York, New York 10020
This Simon & Schuster Books for Young Readers paperback edition May 2009
Among the Hidden copyright © 1998 by Margaret Peterson Haddix
Among the Impostors copyright © 2001 by Margaret Peterson Haddix
All rights reserved, including the right of reproduction in whole or in part in any form.
SIMON & SCHUSTER BOOKS FOR YOUNG READERS is a trademark of Simon & Schuster, Inc.
Also available in a Simon & Schuster Books for Young Readers
hardcover edition and Aladdin paperback edition.
Designed by Lucy Ruth Cummins
The text of this book was set in Elysium.
Manufactured in the United States of America
10 9 8 7 6 5 4 3 2 1
The Library of Congress has cataloged the hardcover editions as follows:
Haddix, Margaret Peterson
Among the hidden / Margaret Peterson Haddix.
1st ed.
153 p. ; 22 cm.
Summary: In a future where the Population Police enforce the law limiting a
family to only two children, Luke has lived all his twelve years in isolation and
fear on his family's farm, until another "third" convinces him that the government is wrong.
[1. Science Fiction] 1. Title.
PZ7.H1164 Am 1998
[Fic] 21
97033052
ISBN-13: 978-0-689-81700-7 (hc)
Haddix, Margaret Peterson
Among the impostors / Margaret Peterson Haddix.
1st ed.
172 p. ; 22 cm.
Summary: In a future where the law limits a family to only two children, third-born
Luke has been in hiding for the entire twelve years of his life, until he enters
boarding school under an assumed name and is forced to face his fears.
[1. Science Fiction] 1. Title.
PZ7.H1164 Ap 2001
[Fic] 21
00058325
ISBN-13: 978-0-689-83904-7 (hc)
ISBN: 978-1-4169-9027-7

Also by Margaret Peterson Haddix

The Missing
Found
Sent

The Shadow Children series
Among the Hidden
Among the Impostors
Among the Betrayed
Among the Barons
Among the Brave
Among the Enemy
Among the Free

Dexter the Tough
Say What?
Because of Anya
The Girl with 500 Middle Names

Palace of Mirrors
Uprising
Double Identity
The House on the Gulf
Escape from Memory
Takeoffs and Landings
Turnabout
Just Ella
Leaving Fishers
Don't You Dare Read This, Mrs. Dunphrey
Running Out of Time

For John and Janet

Among
the Hidden

CHAPTER *ONE*

He saw the first tree shudder and fall, far off in the distance. Then he heard his mother call out the kitchen window: "Luke! Inside. Now."

He had never disobeyed the order to hide. Even as a toddler, barely able to walk in the backyard's tall grass, he had somehow understood the fear in his mother's voice. But on this day, the day they began taking the woods away, he hesitated. He took one extra breath of the fresh air, scented with clover and honeysuckle and—coming from far away—pine smoke. He laid his hoe down gently, and savored one last moment of feeling warm soil beneath his bare feet. He reminded himself, "I will never be allowed outside again. Maybe never again as long as I live."

He turned and walked into the house, as silently as a shadow.

"Why?" he asked at the supper table that night. It wasn't a common question in the Garner house. There were plenty of "how's"—*How much rain'd the backfield get? How's the planting going?* Even "what's"—*What'd Matthew do with the five-sixteenth wrench? What's Dad going to do about that busted tire?* But "why" wasn't considered much worth asking. Luke asked again. "Why'd you have to sell the woods?"

Luke's dad harrumphed, and paused in the midst of shoveling forkfuls of boiled potatoes into his mouth.

"Told you before. We didn't have a choice. Government wanted it. You can't tell the Government no."

Mother came over and gave Luke's shoulder a reassuring squeeze before turning back to the stove. They had defied the Government once, with Luke. That had taken all the defiance they had in them. Maybe more.

"We wouldn't have sold the woods if we hadn't had to," she said, ladling out thick tomatoey soup. "The Government didn't ask *us* if we wanted houses there."

She pursed her lips as she slid the bowls of soup onto the table.

"But the Government's not going to live in the houses," Luke protested. At twelve, he knew better, but sometimes still pictured the Government as a very big, mean, fat person, two or three times as tall as an ordinary man, who went around yelling at people, "Not allowed!" and "Stop that!" It was because of the way his parents and older brothers talked: "Government won't let us plant corn there again." "Government's keeping the prices down." "Government's not going to like this crop."

"Probably some of the people who live in those houses

MARGARET PETERSON HADDIX

will be Government workers," Mother said. "It'll all be city people."

If he'd been allowed, Luke would have gone over to the kitchen window and peered out at the woods, trying for the umpteenth time to picture rows and rows of houses where the firs and maples and oaks now stood. Or had stood—Luke knew from a sneaked peek right before supper that half the trees were now toppled. Some already lay on the ground. Some hung at weird angles from their former lofty positions in the sky. Their absence made everything look different, like a fresh haircut exposing a band of untanned skin on a forehead. Even from deep inside the kitchen, Luke could tell the trees were missing because everything was brighter, more open. Scarier.

"And then, when those people move in, I have to stay away from the windows?" Luke asked, though he knew the answer.

The question made Dad explode. He slammed his hand down on the table.

"Then? You gotta stay away *now*! Everybody and his brother's going to be tramping around back there, to see what's going on. They see you—" He waved his fork violently. Luke wasn't sure what the gesture meant, but he knew it wasn't good.

No one had ever told him exactly what would happen if anyone saw him. Death? Death was what happened to the runt pigs who got stepped on by their stronger brothers and sisters. Death was a fly that stopped buzzing when the swatter hit it. He had a hard time thinking about himself in connection with the smashed fly or the dead pig, gone stiff in the sun. It made his stomach feel funny even trying.

"I don't think it's fair we've got to do Luke's chores now," Luke's other brother, Mark, grumbled. "Can't he go outside some? Maybe at night?"

Luke waited hopefully for the answer. But Dad just said, "No," without looking up.

"It's not fair," Mark said again. Mark was the second son—the lucky second, Luke thought when he was feeling sorry for himself. Mark was two years older than Luke and barely a year younger than Matthew, the oldest. Matthew and Mark were easily recognizable as brothers, with their dark hair and chiseled faces. Luke was fairer, smaller-boned, softer-looking. He often wondered if he'd ever look tougher, like them. Somehow he didn't think so.

"Luke don't do nothing nohow," Matthew jeered. "We won't miss his work at all."

"It's not my fault!" Luke protested. "I'd help more if—"

Mother laid her hands on his shoulders again. "Hush, all of you," she said. "Luke will do what he can. He always has."

The sound of tires on their gravel driveway came through the open window.

"Now, who—" Dad started. Luke knew the rest of the sentence. Who could that be? Why were they bothering him now, his first chance all day to sit down? It was a question Luke always heard the end of from the other side of a door. Today, skittish because of the woods coming down, he scrambled up faster than usual, dashing for the door to the back stairs. He knew without watching that Mother would take his plate from the table and hide it in a cupboard, would slide his chair back into the corner so it looked like an unneeded spare. In three seconds she would hide all evidence that Luke existed, just in time to step to the door and offer a weary smile to the fertilizer salesman or the Government inspector or whomever else had come to interrupt their supper.

CHAPTER TWO

There was a law against Luke.

Not him personally—everyone like him, kids who were born after their parents had already had two babies.

Actually, Luke didn't know if there was anyone else like him. He wasn't supposed to exist. Maybe he was the only one. They did things to women after they had their second baby, so they wouldn't have any more. And if there was a mistake, and a woman got pregnant anyway, she was supposed to get rid of it.

That was how Mother had explained it, years ago, the first and only time Luke had asked why he had to hide.

He had been six years old.

Before that, he had thought only very little kids had to stay out of sight. He had thought, as soon as he was as old as Matthew and Mark, he would get to go around like they did, riding to the backfield and even into town with Dad, hanging their heads and arms out the pickup window. He had thought, as soon as he got as old as Matthew and Mark, he could play in the front yard and kick the ball out into the road if he wanted. He had thought, as soon as he got as old as Matthew and Mark, he could go to school. They complained about it, whining, "Jeez, we gotta do homework!" and, "Who cares about spelling?" But they also talked about games at recess, and friends who shared candy at lunchtime or loaned them pocketknives to carve with.

Somehow, Luke never got as old as Matthew and Mark.

The day of his sixth birthday, Mother baked a cake, a special one with raspberry jam dripping down the sides. At supper that night she put six candles on the top and placed it in front of Luke and said, "Make a wish."

Staring into the ring of candles—proud that the number of his years finally made a ring, all around the cake—Luke suddenly remembered another cake, another ring of six candles. Mark's. He remembered Mark's sixth birthday. He remembered it because, even with the cake in front of him, Mark had been whining, "But I wanna have a party. Robert Joe had a party on his birthday. He got to have three friends over." Mother had said, "*Ssh*," and looked from Mark to Luke, saying something with her eyes that Luke didn't understand.

Startled by the memory, Luke let out his breath. Two of his candles flickered, and one went out. Matthew and Mark laughed.

"You ain't getting that wish," Mark said. "Baby. Can't even blow out candles."

Luke wanted to cry. He'd forgotten even to make a wish, and if he hadn't been surprised he would have been able to blow out all six candles. He knew he could have. And then he would have gotten—oh, he didn't know. A chance to ride to town in the pickup truck. A chance to play in the front yard. A chance to go to school. Instead, all he had was a strange memory that couldn't be right. Surely Luke was thinking about Mark's seventh birthday, or maybe his eighth. Mark couldn't have known Robert Joe when he was six, because he would have been hiding then, like Luke.

Luke thought about it for three days. He trailed along behind his mother as she hung wash out on the line, made strawberry preserves, scrubbed the bathroom floor. Several times he started to ask, "How old do I have to be before people can see me?" But something stopped him every time.

Finally, on the fourth day, after Dad, Matthew, and Mark scraped back their chairs from the breakfast table and headed out to the barn, Luke crouched by the kitchen's side window—one he wasn't supposed to look out because people driving by might catch a glimpse of his face. He tilted his head to the side and raised up just enough that his left eye was above the level of the windowsill. He watched Matthew and Mark running in the sunlight, the tops of their hog boots thumping against their knees. They were in full sight of the whole world, it seemed, and they didn't care. They were racing to the front door of the barn, not the side one off the backyard that Luke always had to use because it was hidden from the road.

Luke turned around and slid to the floor, out of sight.

"Matthew and Mark never had to hide, did they?" he asked.

Mother was scrubbing the remains of scrambled eggs out of the skillet. She turned her head and looked at him carefully.

"No," she said.

"Then why do I?"

She dried her hands and left the sink, something Luke had almost never seen her do if there were still dirty dishes left to be washed. She crouched beside him and smoothed his hair back from his forehead.

"Oh, Lukie, do you really need to know? Isn't it enough to know—things are just different for you?"

He thought about that. Mother was always saying he was the only one who would ever sit on her lap and cuddle. She still read bedtime stories to him, and he knew Matthew and Mark thought that was sissified. Was that what she meant? But he was just younger. He'd grow up. Wouldn't he be like them then?

With unusual stubbornness, Luke insisted, "I want to know why I'm different. I want to know why I have to hide."

So Mother told him.

Later, he wished he'd asked more questions. But at the time it was all he could do to listen to what she told him. He felt like he was drowning in the flow of her words.

"It just happened," she said. "You just happened. And we wanted you. I wouldn't even let your dad talk about... getting rid of you."

Luke pictured himself as a baby, left in a cardboard box

by the side of a road somewhere, the way Dad said people used to do with kittens, back when people were allowed to have pets. But maybe that wasn't what Mother meant.

"The Population Law hadn't been around long, then, and I had always wanted lots of kids. Before, I mean. Getting pregnant with you was like—a miracle. I thought the Government would get over their foolishness, maybe even by the time you were born, and then I'd have a new baby to show everyone."

"But you didn't," Luke managed to say. "You hid me."

His voice sounded strangely hoarse, like it belonged to someone else.

Mother nodded. "Once I started showing, I didn't go anywhere. That wasn't hard to do—where do I go, anyway? I didn't let Matthew and Mark leave the farm, for fear they'd say something. I didn't even say anything about you in letters to my mother and sister. I wasn't really scared then. It was just superstition. I didn't want to brag. I thought I'd go to the hospital to give birth. I wasn't going to keep you secret forever. But then..."

"Then what?" Luke asked.

Mother wouldn't look at him.

"Then they started running all that on TV about the Population Police, how the Population Police had ways of finding out everything, how they'd do anything to enforce the law."

Luke glanced toward the hulking television in the living room. He wasn't allowed to watch it. Was that why?

"And your dad started hearing rumors in town, about other babies..."

Luke shivered. Mother was looking far off into the distance, to where the rows of new corn plants met the horizon.

"I always wanted a John, too," she said. " 'Matthew, Mark, Luke, and John, bless the bed that I lie on.' But then I thank the Lord that I have you, at least. And it's worked out, the hiding, hasn't it?"

The smile she offered him was wobbly. He felt he had to help her.

"Yes," he said.

And somehow, after that, he didn't mind hiding so much anymore. Who wanted to meet strangers, anyway? Who wanted to go to school, where—if Matthew and Mark were to be believed—the teachers yelled, and the other boys would double-cross you if you didn't watch out? He was special. He was secret. He belonged at home— home, where his mother always let him have the first piece of apple pie because he was there and the other boys were away. Home, where he could cradle the new baby pigs in the barn, climb the trees at the edge of the woods, throw snowballs at the posts of the clothesline. Home, where the backyard always beckoned, always safe and protected by the house and the barn and the woods.

Until they took the woods away.

CHAPTER THREE

Luke lay on his stomach on the floor and idly ran the toy train back and forth on the track. The train had belonged to Dad when he was a little boy, and his own father before him. Luke could remember a time when his greatest longing had been for Mark to outgrow the train so Luke could have it all to himself. But it wasn't what he wanted to play with today. There was a beautiful day unfolding outside, with fleecy clouds in a blue, blue sky, and a mild breeze rustling the grass in the backyard. He hadn't left the house in a week now, and he could almost hear the outdoors calling to him. But now he wasn't even allowed in the same room as an uncovered window.

"Are you *trying* to be discovered?" Dad had bellowed at Luke just that morning, when he'd held the shade a few inches back from the kitchen window and peeked out longingly.

Luke jumped. He'd been so busy thinking about running barefoot through the grass that he'd half-forgotten there was anyone or anything behind him, in the house.

"No one's out there," he said, glancing again to be sure.

He'd been trying not to look beyond the ragged edge of the backyard to the bulldozed mess of branches, trunks, leaves, and mud that had once been his beloved woods.

"Yeah?" Dad said. "Did it ever occur to you that if there is, they might see you before you see them?"

He grabbed Luke by the arm and jerked him back a good three feet. Freed from Luke's grasp, the bottom of the shade banged against the windowsill.

"You can't look out at all," Dad said. "I mean it. From now on, just stay away from the windows. And don't go into a room unless we've got the shades or curtains pulled."

"But then I can't see anything," Luke protested.

"Better that than to get turned in," Dad said.

Dad sounded like he might feel sorry for Luke, but that only made things worse. Luke turned around and left, scared he might cry in front of Dad.

Now he gave the toy train a shove, and it careened off the track. It landed upside down, wheels spinning.

"Who cares?" Luke muttered.

There was a harsh knock on his door.

"Population Police! Open up!"

Luke didn't move.

"That's not funny, Mark!" he shouted.

Mark opened the door and bounded up the stairs that led to Luke's room proper. Luke's room was also the attic, a fact he had never minded. Mother long ago had shoved all the trunks and boxes as far as they could go under the eaves, leaving prime space for Luke's brass bed and circular rag rug and books and toys. Luke had even heard Matthew and Mark grumble about Luke having the biggest room. But they had windows.

"Scared you this time, didn't I?" Mark asked.

"No," Luke said. Nothing would force him to admit that his heart had jumped. Mark had been playing the "Population Police" joke for years, always out of their parents' earshot. Usually Luke just ignored Mark, but now, with Dad acting so skittish...What would Luke have done if it really had been the Population Police? What would they do to him?

"Matt and me, we've never told anyone about you," Mark said, suddenly serious, which was strange for him. "And you know Mother and Dad don't say anything. You're good at hiding. So you're safe, you know?"

"I know," Luke muttered.

Mark kicked the toy train Luke had crashed. "Still playing with baby toys?" he asked, as if to make up for slipping and being nice.

Luke shrugged. Normally, he wouldn't have wanted Mark to know he played with the train anymore. But today everything else was so bad that that didn't matter.

"Did you come up here just to bug me?" Luke asked.

Mark put on an offended look.

"Thought you might want to play checkers," he said.

Luke squinted.

"Mother told you to, right?" he asked.

"No."

"You're lying," Luke said, not caring how nasty he sounded.

"Well, if you're going to be that way—"

"Just leave me alone, okay?"

"Okay, okay." Mark backed down the stairs. "Jeez!"

Alone again, Luke felt a little sorry he'd been so mean. Maybe Mark had told the truth. Luke should apologize. But he didn't really feel like it.

Luke got up and started pacing his room. The squeak of the third board in from the stairs annoyed him. He hated having to duck under the rafters on the far side of his bed. Even his favorite model cars, lined up on the shelves in the corner, bothered him today. Why should he have model cars? He'd never even sat in a real one. He never would. He'd never get to do anything or go anywhere. He might as well just rot up here in the attic. He'd thought about that before, on the rare occasions when Mother, Dad, Matthew, and Mark all went somewhere and left him behind—what if something happened to them and they never came back? Would someone find him years from now, abandoned and dead? He'd read a story in one of the old books in the attic about a bunch of kids finding a deserted pirate ship, and then a skeleton in one of the rooms. He'd be like that skeleton. And now that he wasn't allowed in rooms with uncovered windows, he'd be a skeleton in the dark.

Luke looked up automatically, as if to remind himself that nothing lit the rafters but the single bulb over his head. Except—there was light at either end of the ceiling, leaking in under the peak of the roof.

Luke stood up and went to investigate. Of course. He should have remembered. There were vents at each end of the roof. Dad grumbled occasionally about heating the attic for Luke—"It's just like throwing money out those vents"—but Mother always fixed him with one of her stares, and nothing changed.

Now Luke climbed on top of one of the largest trunks and looked down through the vent. He could see out! He could see a strip of the road and the cornfield beyond, its leaves waving in the breeze. The vent slanted down and limited his view, but at least he was sure nobody would ever be able to see him.

For a moment, Luke was excited, but that quickly faded. He didn't want to spend the rest of his life watching the corn grow. Without much hope, he stepped down from the trunk and went to the other end of the attic, the portion that faced the backyard. He had to slide boxes around and drag an old step stool from the opposite end of the attic, but finally his eyes were level with the back vent.

The view was not of the backyard—it was too close— but of the former woods. He'd never realized it before, but the land there sloped away from his family's house, so he had a clear view of acres and acres that once had been covered with trees. The land was abuzz with activity now. Huge yellow bulldozers shoved brush back from a rough road that had been traced out with gravel. Other vehicles

Luke couldn't identify were digging holes for huge concrete pipes. Luke watched in fascination. He knew tractors and combines, of course, and had seen his dad's bush hog and manure spreader and gravity wagons up close, in the barn. But these machines were different, designed for different jobs. And they were all operated by different people.

Once, when Luke was younger, a tramp had walked up to the house and Luke had only had time to hide under the sink in the mudroom before the man was in the house, begging for food. The door of the cabinet was cracked, so Luke had been able to peek out and see the man's patched trousers and holey shoes. He'd heard his whiny voice: "I ain't got no job, and I ain't et in three days.... No, no, I can't do no farmwork for my food. What do you think I am? I'm sick. I'm starving...."

Other than that tramp and pictures in books, Luke had never seen another human being besides his parents and Matthew and Mark. He'd never dreamed there was such variety.

Many of the people running the bulldozers and shovel contraptions were stripped of their shirts, while others standing nearby even wore ties and coats. Some were fat and some were thin; some were browned by the sun and some were paler than Luke himself, who would never be tan again. They were all moving—shifting gears and lowering pipe, waving others into position or, at the very least, talking at full speed. All that activity made Luke dizzy. The pictures in books always showed people still.

Overwhelmed, Luke closed his eyes, then opened them again for fear of missing something.

"Luke?"

Reluctantly, Luke slid down from his step stool perch and scrambled over to recline innocently on his bed.

"Come in," he called to his mother.

She climbed the stairs heavily.

"You okay?"

Luke dangled his feet over the side of the bed.

"Sure. I'm fine."

Mother sat on the bed beside him and patted his leg.

"It's—" she swallowed hard. "It's not easy, the life you've got to live. I know you'd like to look outside. You'd like to go outside—"

"That's okay, Mother," Luke said. He could have told her then about the vents—he didn't see how anyone could object to him looking out there—but something stopped him. What if they took that away from him, too? What if Mother told Dad, and Dad said, "No, no, that's too much of a risk. I forbid it"? Luke wouldn't be able to stand it. He kept silent.

Mother ruffled his hair.

"You're a trooper," she said. "I knew you'd hold up all right."

Luke leaned against his mother's arm, and she moved her arm around his shoulders and hugged him tight to her side. He felt a little guilty for keeping a secret, but mostly reassured—loved and reassured.

Then, more to herself than to him, Mother added, "And things could be worse."

Somehow, that wasn't comforting. Luke didn't know why, but he had a feeling what she really meant was that things were going to get worse. He snuggled tighter against Mother, hoping he was wrong.

CHAPTER FOUR

Luke found out what Mother meant a few days later when he came down for breakfast. As usual, he opened the door from the back stairs to the kitchen only a crack. He could remember barely a handful of times in his entire life when someone had dropped by before breakfast, and each time Mother had managed to send Matthew or Mark up to warn Luke to stay out of sight. But he always checked. Today he could see Dad and Matthew and Mark at the table, and knew from the sound of frying bacon that Mother must be at the stove.

"Are the shades closed?" he called softly.

Mother opened the door to the stairs. Luke started to step into the kitchen, but she put out her arm to keep him back. She handed him a plate full of scrambled eggs and bacon.

"Luke, honey? Can you eat sitting on the bottom step there?"

"What?" Luke asked.

Mother looked beseechingly over her shoulder.

"Dad thinks—I mean, it's not safe anymore to have you

in the kitchen. You can still eat with us, and talk to us and all, but you'll be...over here."

She waved her hand toward the stairs behind Luke.

"But with the shades pulled—" Luke started.

"One of those workers asked me yesterday, 'Hey, farmer, you got air-conditioning in that house of yours?'" Dad said from the table. He didn't turn around. He didn't seem to want to look at Luke. "We keep the shades pulled, hot day like today, people get suspicious. This way is safer. I'm sorry."

And then Dad did turn around and glance at Luke, once. Luke tried to keep from looking upset.

"So what'd you tell him?" Matthew asked, as if the worker's question was only a matter of curiosity.

"Told him of course we don't have air-conditioning. Farming don't make nobody a millionaire."

Dad took a long sip of coffee.

"Okay, Luke?" Mother asked.

"Yes," he mumbled. He took the plate of eggs and bacon, but it didn't look good to him now. He knew every bite he ate would stick in his throat. He sat down on the step, out of sight of both kitchen windows.

"We'll leave the door open," Mother said. She hovered over him, as if unwilling to return to the stove. "This isn't too much different, is it?"

"Mother—" Dad said warningly.

Through the open windows, Luke could hear the rumble of several trucks and cars. The workers had arrived for the day. He knew from watching through the vent the past few days that the caravan of vehicles came up the road like a parade. The cars would peel off to the side and unload the nicer dressed men. The more rugged vehicles pulled on in to the muddiest sections, and the people inside would scatter to the bulldozers and backhoes that had been left outside overnight. But the vehicles barely had time to get cold, because the workers were there now from sunup to sundown. Someone was in a hurry for them to finish.

"Luke—I'm sorry," Mother said, and scurried back to the stove. She loaded a plate for herself, then sat down at the table, beside Luke's usual spot. His chair wasn't even in the kitchen anymore.

For a while, Luke watched Dad, Mother, Matthew, and Mark eating in silence, a complete family of four. Once, he cleared his throat, ready to protest again. *You can't do this— it's not fair—* Then he choked back the words, unspoken. They were only trying to protect him. What could he do?

Resolutely, Luke stuck his fork in the pile of scrambled eggs on his plate and took a bite. He ate the whole plateful of food without tasting any of it.

CHAPTER *FIVE*

Luke ate every meal after that on the bottom step. It became a habit, but a hated one. He had never noticed before, but Mother often spoke too softly to be heard from any distance, and Matthew and Mark always made their nasty comments under their breath. So they would start laughing, often at Luke's expense, and he couldn't defend himself because he didn't know what they had said. He couldn't even hear Mother saying, "Now, be nice, boys." After a week or two, a lot of the time, he didn't even try to listen to the rest of the family's conversation.

But even he was curious the hot July day when the letter arrived about the pigs.

Matthew brought the mail in that day from the mailbox at the crossroads a mile away. (Luke had never seen them, of course, but Matthew and Mark had told him there were three mailboxes there, one for each of the families that lived on their road.) Usually the Garners' mail was just bills or thin envelopes carrying curt orders from the Government about how much corn to plant, which fertilizer to use, and where to take their crop when it was harvested. A letter from a relative was a cause to celebrate, and Mother always dropped whatever she was doing and sat down to open it with trembling hands, calling out at intervals, "Oh, Aunt Effie's in the hospital again...." or, "Tsk, Lisabeth's going to marry that fellow after all...." Luke almost felt he knew his relatives, though they lived hundreds of miles away. And, of course, they didn't even know he existed. The letters Mother wrote back, painstakingly, late at night, when she'd saved up enough money for a stamp, contained plenty of news of Matthew and Mark, but never once had mentioned Luke's name.

This letter was as thick as some from Luke's grandmother, but it bore an official seal, and the return address was an embossed DEPARTMENT OF HUMAN HABITATION, ENVIRONMENTAL STANDARDS DIVISION. Matthew held the letter at arm's length, the way Luke had seen him hold dead baby pigs when they had to be carried out of the barn.

Dad looked worried the minute he saw the letter in Matthew's hand. Matthew put the letter down beside Dad's silverware. Dad sighed.

"Can't be anything but bad news," Dad said. "No use ruining a good meal. It can wait."

He went back to eating chicken and dumplings. Only after his last belch did he turn the envelope over and run a dirt-rimmed fingernail under the flap. He unfolded the letter.

" 'It has come to our attention...,' " he read aloud. "Well, so far I understand it." Then he read silently for a while, calling out at intervals, "Mother, what's 'offal'?" and, "Where's that dictionary? Matthew, look up 'reciprocity.' " Finally, he threw down the whole thick packet and proclaimed, "They're going to make us get rid of our hogs."

"What?" Matthew asked. More serious than Mark, he had talked for as long as anyone could remember about, "When I get my own farm, it's going to be all hogs. I'll make the Government let me do that, somehow...." Now he looked over Dad's shoulder. "You mean they're just going to make us sell a lot at one time, right? But we can build the herd back up—"

"Nope," Dad said. "Those people in them fancy new houses won't be able to stand pig smell. So we can't raise hogs no more." He threw the letter out into the center of the table for all to see. "What'd they expect, building next to a farm?"

From his seat on the stairs, Luke had to hold himself back from going to fish the edge of the letter out of the chicken gravy and looking at it himself.

"They can't do that, can they?" he asked.

Nobody answered. Nobody needed to. Luke felt like a fool for asking as soon as the words were out of his mouth. For once, he was glad of his hiding place.

Mother twisted a dishrag in her hand.

"Those hogs are our bread and butter," she said. "With

grain prices the way they are...what are we going to live on?"

Dad just looked at her. After a moment, so did Matthew and Mark. Luke didn't know why.

CHAPTER SIX

The tax bill arrived two weeks later, the day that Dad, Matthew, and Mark loaded the hogs onto the livestock trailer and took them all away. Most were going to the slaughterhouse. The ones too young and too small to bring a decent price were going to an auction for feeder pigs. Luke watched through the vent at the front of the house as Dad drove by in the battered pickup with each load. Matthew and Mark sat in the back of the pickup, making sure the trailer stayed hitched right. Even three stories up, Luke could see Matthew's hangdog expression.

Then when the three of them came into the house for dinner, after washing the last of the hog smell off their hands in the mudroom, Dad handed Mother the tax bill without comment. She put down the wooden spoon she'd been using to stir the stew and unfolded the letter. Then she dropped it.

"Why, that's—" she seemed to be doing the math in her head as she bent to retrieve it. "That's three times what it usually is. There must be a mistake."

Dad shook his head grimly. "No mistake. I talked to Williker at the auction."

The Willikers were their nearest neighbors, with a house three miles down the road. Luke always pictured them with monster scales and fierce claws because of the number of times he'd been cautioned, "You don't want the Willikers to see you."

Dad went on. "Williker says they raised everyone's taxes because of them fancy houses. Makes our land worth more."

"Isn't that good?" Luke asked eagerly. It was strange— he should hate the new houses for replacing his woods and forcing him to stay indoors. But he'd half-fallen in love with them, having watched every foundation poured, every wooden skeleton of walls and roofs raised to the sky. They were his main entertainment, aside from talking to Mother when she came upstairs for what she called "my Luke breaks." Sometimes she pretended his room needed cleaning as badly as the bread needed baking or the garden needed weeding. Sometimes she just sat and talked.

Dad was shaking his head in disgust over Luke's question.

"No. It's only good if we're selling. And we ain't. All it means for us is that the Government thinks they can get more money out of us."

Matthew was slumped in his chair at the table. "How are we going to pay?" he asked. "That's more than we got for all the hogs, and that was supposed to carry us through for a long time—"

Dad didn't answer. Even Mark, who normally had a smart-alecky comeback for everything, was stupefied.

Mother had turned back to her stew.

"I got my work permit today," she said softly. "The factory's hiring. If I get on there, I can maybe get an advance on my paycheck."

Luke's jaw dropped.

"You can't go to work," he said. "Who will—" He wanted to say, *Who will stay with me? Who will I talk to all day when everyone else is outside?* But that seemed too selfish. Luke looked around. No one else looked surprised by Mother's news. He shut his mouth.

CHAPTER **SEVEN**

By mid-September, Luke's days had fallen into a familiar pattern. He got up at dawn just for the chance to sit on the stairs and watch the rest of his family eat breakfast. They all rushed now. Mother had to be at the factory by seven. Dad was trying to get all the machinery in working order before harvest. And Matthew and Mark were back in school. Only Luke had time to linger over his undercooked bacon and dry toast. He didn't bother asking for butter because that meant someone would have to stand up and bring it over to him, all the while pretending for the sake of the open window that they'd just forgotten something upstairs.

As soon as the rest of his family had stomped out the door, Luke went back to his room and watched out the vents—first out the front, to see Matthew and Mark climb onto the school bus, then out the back, where the new houses were practically finished. They were mansions, as large as the Garners' house and barn put together. They gleamed in the morning sunlight as though their walls were studded with precious jewels. For all Luke knew, maybe they were.

Hordes of workmen still arrived every morning, but almost all of them worked indoors now. They headed into the houses first thing, carrying rolls of carpet, stacks of drywall, cans of paint. Luke couldn't see much of them after that. He spent more time now watching a new kind of traffic: expensive-looking cars driving slowly down the newly paved streets. Sometimes they pulled into a driveway and went into one of the houses, usually trailing a woman who appeared to be talking nonstop. It had taken Luke a while to figure it out—he certainly hadn't dared ask anyone else in his family—but he thought maybe the people were thinking about buying the houses. Once he realized that, he studied each potential neighbor carefully. He'd overheard Mother and Dad marveling that the people moving into the new houses were not just going to be city people, but Barons. Barons were unbelievably rich, Luke knew. They had things ordinary people hadn't had in years. Luke wasn't sure how the Barons had gotten rich, when everybody else was poor. But Dad never said the word "Baron" without a curse word or two in front of it.

The people streaming through the houses did look different from anyone in Luke's family. They were mostly thin, beautiful women in formfitting dresses, and heavyset men in what Luke's dad and brothers called sissy clothes— shiny shoes and clean, dressy pants and jackets. Luke always felt a little embarrassed for them, showing up like that. Or maybe he was embarrassed for his family, that they never looked like any of the Barons. Luke preferred it when the adults had children with them and he could concentrate on them. The smallest ones were always as dressed up as their parents, with hair bows and suspenders and other geegaws Luke knew his parents would never buy. The older kids usually seemed to be wearing whatever they'd grabbed first out of their closet that morning.

Though he knew no one would dare show up with three kids, he always counted: "One, two..." "One..." "One, two..."

What if a family with just one kid moved in behind them, and he sneaked into their house and pretended to be their second child? He could go to school, go to town, act like Matthew and Mark....

What a joke—Luke living with Barons. More likely he'd be shot for trespassing. Or turned in.

When he began thinking things like that, he always jumped down from his perch by the vent and grabbed a book from one of the dusty stacks by the eaves. Mother had taught him to read and do math, as much as she knew herself. "At least we have a few books for you...," she often mumbled sadly when she left in the morning. He'd read all their books dozens of times, even the ones with titles like *Diseases of the Porcine Species* and *Common Grasses of Our Countryside.* His favorites were the handful of adventure books, the ones that let him pretend he was a knight fighting a dragon to rescue a kidnapped princess, or an explorer sailing on the high seas, holding tight to a mast while a hurricane raged about him.

He liked to forget he was Luke Garner, third child hidden in the attic.

Sometime around noon he'd hear the door from the mudroom to the kitchen swing open and he'd go down and eat at the same time as his dad. Without Mother there were no homemade pies now, no mashed potatoes, no roasts that sent good smells throughout the house. Dad always made four sandwiches, checked to make sure no one could see him, then handed two of them to Luke in the stairwell.

Dad never talked—he'd explained that he didn't want anyone overhearing him, and wondering. But he did turn the radio on for the noon farm report, and there was usually a song or two after that before Dad silenced the radio and went outside to work again.

When Dad left, Luke went back to his room to read or watch the houses again.

At six-thirty Mother came home, and she always stopped in and said hi to Luke before rushing out to do a whole day's work in the few hours before bedtime. Usually Matthew or Mark came up to visit him, too, but they could never stay long, either. They had to help Dad before supper, then do homework afterwards. And they always had been nicest to Luke outdoors. Before the woods came

down, the three of them often had played kickball or football or spud in the backyard, after school and chores.
Matthew and Mark always fought about who got to have
Luke on his team, because, even if Luke wasn't very good,
two boys together could always beat the third.

Now they played halfhearted games of cards or checkers
with Luke, but Luke could tell they'd rather be outside.

So would he.

He tried not to think about it.

The best part of the day came at the end, when Mother
tucked him in. She'd be relaxed then. She'd stay for an
hour sometimes, asking him what he'd read that day, or
telling him stories about the factory.

Then one night, when she was telling how her plastic
glove had gotten stuck in a chicken she'd de-gutted that
day, Mother suddenly stopped in the middle of a sentence.

"Mother?" Luke said.

She answered with a snore. She'd fallen asleep sitting
up.

Luke studied her face, seeing lines of fatigue that hadn't
been there before, noticing that the hair around her face
now held as much gray as brown.

"Mother?" he said again, gently shaking her arm.

She jerked. "—but I cleaned that chicken al— oh. Sorry,
Luke. You need tucking in, don't you?"

She fluffed his pillow, smoothed his sheet.

Luke sat up. "That's okay, Mother. I'm getting too old for
this any"—he swallowed a lump in his throat— "anyway. I

bet you weren't still tucking Matthew or Mark in when they were twelve."

"No," she said quietly.

"Then I don't need it, either."

"Okay," she said.

She kissed his forehead, anyhow, then turned out the light. Luke turned his face to the wall until she left.

CHAPTER *EIGHT*

O ne cool, rainy morning a few weeks later, Luke's family left in such a rush, they barely had time to say
good-bye. They dashed out the door after breakfast,
Matthew and Mark complaining about their packed
lunches, Dad calling back, "I'm going to that auction up at
Chytlesville. Won't be home until supper." Mother hurried
back and handed Luke a bag of cracklings and three pears
and some biscuits from the night before. She muttered, "So
you won't get hungry," and gave him a quick kiss on the
head. Then she was gone, too.

Luke peeked around the stairway door, surveying the
chaos of dirty pans and crumb-covered plates left in the
kitchen. He knew not to look out as far as the window, but
he did, anyway. His heart gave a strange jump when he saw
the window was covered. Someone must have pulled the
shade the night before, to try to keep the kitchen warm,
and then forgotten to raise it in the morning. Luke dared
to lean out a little further—yes, the shade was down on
the other window, too. For the first time in almost six
months, he could step out into the kitchen and not worry

about being seen. He could run, skip, jump—dance, even—on the vast linoleum without fear. He could clean up the kitchen and surprise Mother. He could do anything.

He put his right foot out, tentatively, not quite daring to put his full weight on it. The floor squeaked. He froze. Nothing happened, but he retreated, anyway. He went back up the stairs, crawled along the second-floor hallway to avoid the windows, then climbed the stairs to the attic. He was so disgusted with himself, he could taste it.

I am a coward. I am a chicken. I deserve to be locked away in the attic forever, ran through his head. *No, no*, he countered himself, *I'm cautious. I'm making a plan.*

He climbed up onto the stool on top of a trunk that served as his perch for watching out the back vents. The neighborhood behind his house was fully occupied now. He knew all the families and had come up with names for most of them. The Big Car Family had four expensive cars sitting in their driveway. The Gold Family all had hair the color of sunshine. The Birdbrain Family had set a row of thirty birdhouses along their backyard fence, even though Luke could have told them it was pointless to do that until spring. The house he could see best, right behind the Garners' backyard, was occupied by the Sports Family. Two teenaged boys lived there, and their deck overflowed with soccer balls, baseball bats, tennis rackets, basketballs, hockey sticks, and apparatus from games Luke could only guess at.

Today, he wasn't interested in games. He was interested in seeing the families leave.

He had noticed before that all of the houses were empty by nine in the morning, with kids off to school and grown-ups off to work. Three or four of the women didn't seem to have jobs, but they left, too, returning late in the afternoon with shopping bags. Today, he just had to make sure no one was staying home sick.

The Gold Family left first, two blond heads in one car, two blond heads in another. The Sports Family was next, the boys carrying football pads and helmets, their mother teetering on high heels. Then there was a flurry of cars streaming from every driveway onto the still-sparkling new streets. Luke counted each person, keeping track so carefully that he made scratches on the wall, and counted the scratches twice again at the end. Yes—twenty-eight people gone. He was safe.

Luke scrambled down from his chair, his head spinning with plans. First, he'd clean up the kitchen; then he'd start some bread for supper. He'd never made bread before, but he'd watched Mother a million times. Then maybe he could pull the shades in the rest of the house and clean it thoroughly. He couldn't vacuum—that'd be too loud—but he could dust and scrub and polish. Mother would be so pleased. Then, in the afternoon, before Matthew or Mark or the kids in the neighborhood got back, he could put something on for supper. Maybe potato soup. Why, he could do this every day. He'd never considered housework or cooking particularly thrilling before—Matthew and Mark always scoffed at it as women's work—but it was better than nothing. And maybe, just maybe, if this worked, he could convince Dad to let him sneak out to the barn and help there, too.

Luke was so excited, he stepped into the kitchen without a second thought this time. Who cared if the floor creaked? No one was there to hear it. He gathered up dishes from the table and piled them into the sink, scrubbing everything with extraordinary zeal. He measured out flour and lard and milk and yeast and was putting it all in a bowl when it occurred to him it might be okay to turn on the radio, very softly. Nobody'd hear. And if they did, they'd just figure the family had forgotten to turn it off, just as they'd forgotten to raise the shades.

The bread was in the oven and Luke was picking up lint by hand from the living room rug when he heard tires on the gravel driveway. It was two o'clock in the afternoon, too early for the school bus or Mother or Dad. Luke sprinted for the stairs, hoping whoever it was would just go away.

No luck. He heard the side door creaking open, then Dad exclaiming, "What the—"

He was back early. That shouldn't matter. But hiding on the staircase, Luke suddenly felt like the radio was as loud as an entire orchestra, like the smell of baking bread could fill three counties.

"Luke!" Dad yelled.

Luke heard his father's hand on the doorknob. He opened the door.

"I was just trying to help," Luke blubbered. "I was safe. You left the shades down, so I thought it was okay, and I made sure everyone was gone from the neighborhood, and—"

Dad glared. "You can't be sure," he snapped. "People like that—they get deliveries all the time, they get sick and come home from work, they have maids come during the day—"

Luke could have protested, no, the maids never come before the kids get home from school. But he didn't want to give himself away any more than he already had.

"The shades were down," he said. "I didn't turn on a single light. Even if there were a thousand people back there, nobody would know I was here! Please—I've just got to do something. Look, I made bread, and cleaned up, and—"

"What if a Government inspector or someone had stopped by here?"

"I would have hidden. Like always."

Dad was shaking his head. "And leave them smelling bread baking in an empty house? You don't seem to understand," he said. "You can't take any chances. You can't. Because—"

At that precise moment, the buzzer on the oven went off, sounding as loud as a siren. Dad gave Luke a dirty look and stalked over to the oven. He pulled out the two bread pans and tossed them on the stove top. He flipped off the radio.

"I don't want you in the kitchen again," he said. "You stay hidden. That's an order."

He went out the door without looking back.

Luke fled up the stairs. He wanted to stomp, angrily, but he couldn't. No noise allowed. In his room, he hesitated, too upset to read, too restless to do anything else. He kept hearing *You stay hidden. That's an order,* echoing in his ears. But he'd been hidden. He'd been careful. To prove his point—to himself, at least—he climbed back up on his perch by the back vents and looked out on the quiet neighborhood.

All the driveways were empty. Nothing moved, not even the flag on the Gold Family's flagpole or the spokes on the Birdbrain Family's fake windmill. And then, out of the corner of his eye, Luke caught a glimpse of something behind one window of the Sports Family's house.

A face. A child's face. In a house where two boys already lived.

CHAPTER NINE

uke was so surprised, he lost his balance and almost fell backwards off the trunk. By the time he recovered and righted himself, the face was gone. Had he imagined it? Was it just one of the Sports Family brothers home early from school? Kids got sick, like Dad said, or they decided to play hooky. Luke tried to remember every detail of the face he'd seen, or thought he'd seen. It had been younger than either of the Sports Family brothers'. Softer. Hadn't it?

Maybe it was a thief. Or a maid, come early.

No. It had been a child. A—

He didn't even let himself think what another child in that house would be.

He stared for hours at the Sports Family's house, but no face reappeared. Nothing happened until six, when the two Sports Family boys drove in in their jeep, unloaded their football gear, and carried it into the house. They didn't run out screaming about being robbed.

And he'd seen no thief leave. He'd seen no maid leave.

At six-thirty, Luke reluctantly climbed down from his

perch when he heard his mother's knock on the door. He sat down on his bed and muttered a distracted, "Come in."

She rushed to hug him.

"Luke—I'm sorry. I know you were just trying to help. And everything is amazingly clean. I'd love it if you could do this every day. But your father thinks—I mean, you can't—"

Luke was so busy thinking about the face in the window that at first he couldn't figure out what she was talking about. Oh. The bread. The housecleaning. The radio.

"That's okay," Luke mumbled.

But it wasn't, and it never would be. His anger came back. Why did his parents have to be so careful? Why didn't they just lock him in one of the trunks in the attic and be done with it?

"Can't you talk to him?" Luke asked. "Can't you convince him—"

Mother pushed Luke's hair back from his face. "I'll try," she said. "But you know he's just trying to protect you. We can't take any chances."

Even if the face in the window of the Sports Family house was another third child, so what? Luke and the other kid could live right next door all their lives and never meet. Luke might never see the other kid again. And he'd certainly never see Luke.

Luke lowered his head.

"What am I supposed to do?" he asked. "There's nothing

for me to do. Am I supposed to just sit in this room the rest of my life?"

Mother was stroking his hair now. It made him feel itchy and irritable.

"Oh, Lukie," she said. "You can do so much. Read and play and sleep whenever you want…. Believe me, I'd like to live a day of your life right about now."

"No you wouldn't," Luke muttered, but he said it so softly, he was sure Mother couldn't hear. He knew she wouldn't understand.

If there was a third child in the Sports Family, would he understand? Did he feel the way Luke did?

CHAPTER *TEN*

When Luke went down to supper, he saw that Mother had set his two loaves of bread out on the china plate she used for holidays and special occasions. She was showing off the bread the way she used to tape up the crooked drawings Matthew and Mark brought home from school when they were little. But something had gone wrong—maybe Luke hadn't used enough yeast, or he'd kneaded the dough too much or too little—and the loaves had turned out flat. They looked lopsided and pathetic in the center of the table.

Luke wished Mother had just thrown them away.

"It's cold out now. Nobody'd notice if you pulled the shades. Why can't I sit at the table with all of you?" he asked when he reached the bottom of the stairs.

"Oh, Luke—" Mother started.

"Someone might see your shadow through the shade," Dad said.

"They wouldn't know it was mine," Luke said.

"But there'd be five. Someone might get suspicious," Mother said patiently. "Luke, we're just trying to protect you. How about a big slice of your bread? There's cold beef and canned beans, too."

Resignedly, Luke sat down on the stairs.

Matthew asked about the auction Dad had gone to.

"I drove all that way for nothing," Dad said disgustedly. "I waited four hours for the tractors to come up, and then I couldn't even afford the first bid."

"At least you got home in time to fix that back fence before dark," Mother said, cutting the bread.

And yell at me, Luke thought bitterly. What was wrong with him? Nothing had changed. Except he'd maybe seen a face that maybe belonged to someone like him—

Matthew and Mark suddenly noticed the bread Mother was doling out.

"What's wrong with that?" Mark asked.

"I'm sure it will taste fine," Mother said. "It's Luke's first try."

Luke muttered, "And my last," too softly for anyone to hear. There were advantages to sitting on the other side of the room from everyone else.

"Luke made bread?" Mark said incredulously. "Yuck."

"Yeah. And I put special poison in one of the loaves, that only affects fourteen-year-olds," Luke said. He pantomimed death, clutching his hands around his own neck, letting his tongue hang out of his mouth, and lolling his head to the side. "If you're nice to me, I'll tell you which loaf is safe."

That shut Mark up but earned Luke a frown from

Mother. Luke felt strange about the joke, anyway. Of course he'd never poison anyone, but—if something happened to Matthew or Mark, would Luke have to hide anymore? Would he become the public second son, free to go to town and to school and everywhere else that Matthew and Mark went? Could his parents find some way to explain a "new" child already twelve years old?

It wasn't something Luke could ask. He felt guilty just thinking about it.

Mark was making a big ceremony out of bringing the bread to his mouth.

"I'm not scared of you," he taunted, and took a big bite. He swallowed with great difficulty and pretended to gag. "Water, water—quick!" He gulped down half his glass and glared at Luke. "Tastes like poison, all right."

Luke bit into his bread. It was dry and crumbly and tasteless, not like Mother's at all. And everybody knew it. Even Dad and Mother had pained expressions on their faces as they chewed. Dad finally pushed his slice away.

"That's okay, Luke," he said. "I'm not sure I'd want any son of mine getting too good at baking, anyhow. That's what a man gets married for."

Matthew and Mark guffawed.

"Getting married soon, Luke?" Mark teased.

"Sure," Luke said, struggling to sound as devil-may-care as Mark. "But don't think I'd invite *you* to the wedding."

He felt a cold, hard lump in his stomach that wasn't the

bread. Of course he'd never get married. Or do anything. He'd never leave the house.

Mark switched to teasing Matthew, who evidently did have a girlfriend. Luke watched the rest of his family laughing.

"May I be excused?" Luke asked.

Everyone turned to him in surprise. Usually he was the last one to make that request. Mother often begged Matthew and Mark, "Can't you wait, and talk to Luke a little bit longer?"

"Done already?" Mother asked.

"I'm not very hungry," Luke said.

Mother gave him a worried look but nodded, anyway.

Luke went to his room and climbed onto the stool by the back vents. In the dark, it was easier than ever to see into the houses of the new neighborhood. Their windows were lit up against the night. Some families were eating, like his. He could see one set of four people around a dining room table, and one set of three. Some families had their curtains or shades drawn, but sometimes the material was thin and he could still see shadows of the people inside.

Only the Sports Family had all their windows totally blocked, covered by heavy blinds.

CHAPTER *ELEVEN*

L uke watched the Sports Family house constantly after that. Before, he had just looked out the back vents in the early morning and late afternoon, when he knew people were about. But he'd seen the face at two o'clock. Maybe the other kid knew the rhythms of the neighborhood, too, and let his guard down only during times he considered safe.

For three long days, Luke saw nothing.

Then on the fourth day, he was rewarded: One panel of one of the blinds on an upstairs window flipped quickly up and down at eleven o'clock.

The seventh day the blinds in a downstairs window were left up in the morning. Luke saw a light go on and off at 9:07, two full hours after the last of the Sports Family had left. A half hour later, the Sports Family mother drove in in her red car and stomped into the house. Two minutes later, the blind in the downstairs window went down. The mother left immediately.

The thirteenth day was unseasonably warm, and Luke sweated in his attic. Some of the Sports Family's windows were left open, though still covered by the blinds. The wind blew the blinds back a couple times. Luke saw lights on in some of the rooms some of the time, in other rooms as the day wore on. Once he even thought he saw a glow of a TV screen.

He had no doubts anymore. Someone was hiding in the Sports Family house.

The question was, what could he do about it?

CHAPTER TWELVE

Harvest came. Matthew and Mark stayed out of school to help Dad bring the crops in, the three of them working some days from dawn until midnight. Mother's factory got busier, too, and she began working two or three hours of overtime every day. She brought up a store of food to Luke's room so he wouldn't get hungry while they were all away.

"There!" she said cheerfully, lining up boxes of crackers and bags of fruit. "This way, you won't even miss us."

Her eyes begged him not to complain.

"Uh-huh," he said, trying to sound game. "I'll be fine."

He watched the Sports Family house only sporadically now. What other proof did he need? What good did it do him to know about the other third child? What did he expect—that the other kid would run out in his backyard and yell, "Hey, Luke, come out and play!"?

He munched his solitary apples. He ate his crackers alone.

And in spite of himself, a crazy idea grew in his mind, sprouting new details daily.

What if he sneaked into the Sports Family house and met the other third child?

He could do it. It was possible. Theoretically.

He spent entire days plotting his route. He'd be hidden by bushes and the barn through much of his yard. It was only about six feet from there to the nearest tree in the Sports Family's backyard. He could crawl on his stomach. Then he'd be hidden by the fence the Sports Family shared with the Birdbrain Family—all those birdhouses might actually help. After that, it was only three steps to the Sports Family house. They had a sliding-glass door at the back, and on warm days they'd been leaving it open, with just a screen. He could go in there.

Would he dare?

Of course he wouldn't, but still, still—

The first time he looked out the vents and saw maple leaves shot through with shades of red and yellow, he panicked. He needed those leaves to hide him on his way to the Sports Family house. If he waited too long, the leaves would be gone.

He began waking up every morning in a cold sweat, thinking, *Maybe today. Do I dare?*

Just thinking about it made his stomach feel funny.

It rained three days in a row in early October, and he was almost relieved because that meant he couldn't go on those days, didn't even have to think about going. He couldn't risk leaving footprints in the mud. And Dad and Matthew and Mark were in the way, hanging around the house and the barn, grumbling because they couldn't get into the fields.

Finally the rain stopped and the fields dried up and Dad and Matthew and Mark went back to their combine and tractors, acres away from the house.

The backyard and the Sports Family's backyard were dry, too.

And it was warm again. The Sports Family left their sliding-glass door open.

The rain hadn't knocked all the leaves off the backyard trees, but the next rain probably would.

On the third morning after the rain, Luke's stomach churned as he sat on his perch watching the neighborhood empty out. He knew without question that today was the day he'd have to go, if he ever intended to. He couldn't wait until spring. He wouldn't be able to stand it.

He watched twenty-eight people leave in eight cars and one school bus. Hands trembling, he made scratches on the wall again and recounted, once, twice, three times. Twenty-eight. Yes. Twenty-eight. Yes. Twenty-eight. The magic number.

He could hear the blood pounding in his ears. He moved in a daze. Off his perch. Down the stairs. Into the kitchen. And then—out the back door.

CHAPTER *THIRTEEN*

He had forgotten what fresh air felt like, filling his nostrils and lungs. It felt good. With his back pressed against the house, he stood still for a moment, just breathing. All the months he'd spent inside suddenly seemed like a dream. He'd been like some confused animal hibernating during nice weather. The last real thing that had happened to him was being called inside when the woods were coming down. Real life was outdoors.

But so was danger. And the longer he stayed out, the greater the danger.

He forced himself down into a crouch and half-crawled, half-ran alongside the house and the hedges and the barn. At the back edge of the barn he hesitated, staring into the seemingly endless gulf between the barn and the trees at the boundary between his backyard and the Sports Family's.

Everybody's gone, he told himself. *There's not a soul around to see you.*

Still, he waited, staring at the blades of grass just beyond his feet. He'd been taught all his life to fear open spaces like the one in front of him. It faced dozens of windows. He'd never stepped foot in any place that public, even if it was deserted.

Still hidden by the barn, he made himself inch his foot forward. Then he drew it back.

He turned around and looked at his family's house, so safe and secure. His sanctuary. He heard his mother's voice in his head: *Luke! Inside. Now.* It seemed so real, he remembered something he'd read in one of the old books in the attic about telepathy—supposedly if people really loved you, they could call out to you from miles away if you were in danger.

He should go back. He'd be safe there.

He took a deep breath, looking forward toward the Sports Family's house, then back again toward his own. He thought about returning home—trudging up the worn stairs, going back to his familiar room and the walls he stared at every day. Suddenly he hated his house. It wasn't a sanctuary. It was a prison.

Before he had time to think again, he pushed himself off into a sprint, recklessly streaking across the grass. He didn't even stop to hide at any trees. He ran right to the Sports Family's door and tugged at the screen.

It was locked.

CHAPTER *FOURTEEN*

In all his plottings, Luke had never thought of the screen door being locked. Though he knew his own parents locked up at night—when they didn't forget—the doors at his house had always been open for him. And he'd never been near anyone else's door.

"Idiot," he muttered to himself.

He tugged harder on the door, but he couldn't concentrate enough to make his hands work together. Each second that passed made the hair on the back of his neck stand up more. He'd never been so exposed in his entire life.

Hurry, hurry, hurry. Get out of sight....

The door didn't budge. He'd have to turn around. Now.

That was what his brain said. What his hand did was plunge through the screen. He pulled the wire away from the frame and reached through. The screen scraped the back of his hand and his arm, but he didn't stop. He fiddled with the lock inside until he heard it click.

He silently slid the screen door back and stepped past the hanging blinds into the Sports Family's house.

Even with the blinds blocking every window, the room he entered was airy and bright. From the freshly painted walls to the sparkling glass tables to the polished wood floor, everything looked new. Luke stared. Almost all the furniture in his own house had been around as long as he could remember, and whatever patterns and designs it originally carried had long ago been worn away. At his house, even the once-orangish couch and the once-greenish chairs were now all a matching sort of brownish gray. This room was different. It reminded him of a word he'd never heard, only read: "pristine." Nobody had ever stepped on these white rugs with manure-covered boots. Nobody had ever sat on those pale blue couches with corn-dust-covered jeans.

Luke might have stood by the door forever, in awe, but someone coughed in another room. Then he heard a strange *be-be-be-beep*. He tiptoed forward. Better to discover than to be discovered.

He went down a long hallway. The beeps had turned into a drawn-out "buzzzzz," coming from a room at the end.

Holding his breath, Luke stopped outside the door to that room and gathered the nerve to peek in. His heart pounded. There was still time to escape unseen, to go back to his house and attic and normal, safe life. But he'd always wonder—

Luke leaned forward slowly, moving a fraction of an inch at a time, until he could just barely see around the door.

Inside the room was a chair and a desk and a big apparatus that Luke vaguely recognized as a computer. And at the computer, typing away furiously, sat a girl.

Luke blinked, thrown off. Somehow he'd never thought about the Sports Family's third child being a girl. She was mostly facing away from Luke, and she wore jeans and a gray sweatshirt not much different from what the Sports Family brothers always wore. Her dark hair was almost as short as Luke's. But there was something about the curve of her cheek, the tilt of her head, the way her sweatshirt clung or didn't cling to her body—all of that made Luke certain she wasn't like him.

He blushed. Then he gulped.

The girl turned her head.

"I—" Luke croaked.

Before he had a chance to think of another word, the girl was across the room and had knocked him down. Then she pinned him to the floor, his arms twisted behind his back, his face buried in the carpet. Luke struggled to turn his head to breathe.

"So," the girl hissed in his ear. "You think you can sneak up on a poor, innocent, unsuspecting girl, who's home all alone? Guess nobody told you about our alarm system. A call went out to our security guards the minute you stepped on our property. They'll be here any second."

Luke panicked. So this was how he'd die. He had to explain. He had to escape.

"No," he said. "They can't come. I—"

"Oh, yeah?" the girl said. "Who are you to stop them?"

Luke raised his head as much as he could. He said the first words that came into his mind.

"Population Police."

The girl let go.

CHAPTER FIFTEEN

Luke sat up, checking his arms to make sure she hadn't broken anything.

"You're lying," the girl said.

But she made no effort to tackle him again. She crouched, looking puzzled for a few moments. Then she grinned.

"I got it! You're another one. Great code word. I'll have to think about using that for the rally."

Now it was Luke's turn to squint in confusion.

The girl giggled.

"I mean, you're another shadow child. Right?"

"Shadow—?" Luke wondered why his brain seemed to be slowing down. Was it just because she seemed several miles ahead of him?

"That's not the term you use?" she asked. "I thought 'shadow child' was universal. But, you know, an illegal, someone whose parents broke Population Law 3903. A third."

"I—" Luke couldn't bring himself to confess. He'd broken so many taboos today, leaving the house, standing in the open yard, talking to a stranger. Why did one more violation matter?

"You can say it," the girl coaxed. " 'I'm a third child.' Why should there be anything wrong with that?"

Luke was spared having to answer her, because she suddenly sprang to her feet, exclaiming, "Oh, no! The alarm!"

She raced down the hall and around the corner. Luke followed to find her jerking open a closet door, then punching buttons on a panel of colored lights.

"Too late. Drat!"

She ran to a phone, Luke following breathlessly. She dialed. Luke watched in amazement. He'd never talked on a phone. His parents had told him the Government could trace calls, could tell if a voice on a phone was from a person who was allowed to exist or not.

"Dad—" She made a face. "I know, I know. Call the security company and get them to cancel the alarm, okay?" Pause. "And might I remind you that the penalty for harboring a shadow child is five million dollars or execution, depending on the mood of the judge?"

She rolled her eyes at Luke while she listened to what seemed to be a long answer.

"Oh, you know. These things happen." Another pause. "Yeah, yeah. Love you, too. Thanks, Dad."

She hung up. Luke wondered if he should run back to his house immediately, before the Population Police really did show up.

"They can find you now," Luke said. "Just from the phone—"

The girl laughed.

"They *say*. But everybody knows the Government's not that competent."

Luke started inching toward the back door, just in case.

"But there really was an alarm?" he asked. "And you have security guards?"

"Sure. Doesn't everyone?" the girl took another look at Luke. "Oh. Maybe not."

She winced apologetically as soon as she'd said that. Luke decided to ignore the insult.

"Do the security guards know you're here?" he asked.

"Of course not," the girl said. "If they came, I'd have to hide. Personally, I think my family just has the alarm system to make sure I stay in the house. They don't know I can disable it. But"—she gave him an evil grin—"I set it off sometimes just for fun."

"That's fun?" Luke asked. He'd thought another third child would understand him, be just like him. This girl sure wasn't. "Aren't you scared the guards might find you?"

"Not really." The girl shrugged. "And see, doing it on purpose every now and then helped us today—my dad didn't really even ask why the system needed to be stopped. He just thought it was me making trouble again."

In a twisted way, she kind of made sense. But trying to figure everything out made Luke's head hurt. He glanced toward the door. If he could just get safely home, he'd never complain about being bored again. Here, he felt as baffled as Alice in Wonderland from one of the old books in the attic. Or—he remembered something he'd read in a nature book—maybe he was like the prey of a snake that hypnotized its victims before it ate them. He didn't think the girl would hurt him, but she might keep him confused and fascinated until the Population Police or the security guards or someone else arrived.

The girl saw where he was looking.

"Am I scaring you?" she asked. "Shadow kids can be so jumpy. You're safe, you know. How about if we start over? Would you care for a seat, uh—what's your name, anyway?"

Luke told her.

"Nice to meet you," the girl said, shaking his hand in a way that made him feel like she was kind of making fun of him. Then she led him to sit down on a couch in the room he'd first entered. She perched beside him. "I'm Jen. Really, it's Jennifer Rose Talbot. But do I look like a Jennifer?"

She shook her head and spread out her arms as if Luke should understand something from her rumpled sweatshirt and messy hair.

Luke frowned.

"I don't know," he said. "I don't know any Jennifers. Just Matthew and Mark and Mother and Dad." He knew his parents' real names were Edna and Harlan, but he wondered if he shouldn't keep that secret. Just in case. Probably he shouldn't have even mentioned Matthew and

Mark, but he was surprised into it, thinking suddenly about how there was a world full of people outside his house, with a world full of different names he'd never heard of.

"Hmm," the girl said. "Then I have to explain—a Jennifer's supposed to be, like, really girly and prissy. So the joke's on Mom. She wanted some frilly little girl she could put in lacy dresses and sit in the corner. Like a doll." She paused. "Are Matthew and Mark your older brothers?"

Luke nodded.

"So you've never met anyone outside your immediate family?"

Luke shook his head no. Jen looked so amazed, he felt he had to defend himself.

"And you have?" he asked, with almost the same taunting voice he sometimes used with Mark.

"Well, yeah," she said.

"But you're a third child, too," Luke protested. "A shadow child. Right?"

He suddenly felt like it might be easy to cry, if he let himself. All his life, he'd been told he couldn't do everything Matthew and Mark did because he was the third child. But if Jen could go about freely, it didn't make sense. Had his parents lied?

"Don't you have to hide?" he asked.

"Sure," Jen said. "Mostly. But my parents are very good at bribery. And so am I." She grinned wickedly. Then she squinted at Luke. "How *did* you know I was a third child? How did you know I was here?"

Luke told her. Somehow it seemed important to start with the woods coming down, so it turned into a very long story. Jen interrupted frequently with questions and comments—"So you've never been away from your house except to go to your backyard or barn?"; "You've stayed inside for six months?"; and "Gosh, you must really hate these houses, huh?" And then, when he got to the part about seeing her face in the window, she bit her lip.

"My dad would kill me if he knew I'd done that. But the mirrors were messed up, and Carlos bet me I didn't even know what the weather was outside, and—"

"Huh?" Luke said. "Mirrors? Carlos?"

Jen waved away his questions.

"Luke Garner," she announced solemnly, "you have come to the right place. Forget that hiding-like-a-mole stuff. I'm your ticket out."

CHAPTER SIXTEEN

Want any more potatoes, Luke?" Mother offered that night at supper. "Luke?" Her voice got more insistent. "LUKE?"

Luke jerked his attention back to his family. Mother was holding the bowl of mashed potatoes out to him.

"Er—no," Luke said. "No thanks. I've still got some."

"More for me!" Mark crowed.

Luke tuned them out again. He'd barely eaten his first serving of potatoes, he'd been so busy thinking about his secret visit to the Sports Family house. He couldn't believe he'd dared to go. Just the thought of his run through their yard made his heart beat fast, remembering fear and pride. He'd really done it.

And then meeting Jen was—amazing. There was no other word for it. He was so overwhelmed with wonder at everything he'd seen at her house, everything she'd told him, that he started to say, "Did you know that Jen—"

At the last minute, he clamped his teeth shut, holding the words in. He thought he'd burst. He could feel his face flush red with the effort of keeping still. He bent his head low over his plate so nobody would see. How could he ever manage to keep Jen secret? But he had to, because if he told, they'd forbid him to go back.

And he had to go back.

"We'll set up a signal," Jen had said. "Something I can see—"

"But you don't have vents to look out like I do," Luke protested. "You can't look out the windows."

"Oh, when the mirrors work, it's not a problem. Look." She took him over to a window near the sliding-glass door and showed him a mirror that reflected a wide view of the Talbots' backyard and the landscape beyond. It showed just the corner of the Garners' barn, but when Jen turned it a bit, the entire Garner house came into view. Luke wondered if his parents could set up the same kind of system. Then he looked at the mirror again and decided it might be expensive. And, anyway, how would he explain where he'd gotten the idea?

"So, let's see," Jen said. "A signal. I've got it—how about if I look out every morning at nine, and if you can come over, you shine a flashlight at me. I'll shine one back if everything's safe."

"We don't have any flashlights," Luke said. "Not that work, I mean."

Jen frowned.

"Why not?"

"We haven't had any batteries in, I don't know, four or five years," Luke explained. In fact, he felt proud even to remember what a flashlight was.

"Okay, okay," Jen said. "No flashlight, no computer—"

"Oh, we have a computer," Luke said. "My parents do. And I think it still works. But it's in Dad's office in the front of the house, and I'm not allowed in there. And, anyhow, I'd never be allowed to touch the computer." He remembered once when he was very young, maybe three or four, and he'd followed Mother into Dad's office while she was cleaning. The rows of letters on the computer keyboard had looked like a toy to him, and he'd reached one finger up and tapped the space bar, over and over again. Mother had turned around and freaked out.

"They can find you now!" she'd screamed. "If they were watching—"

And for weeks after that, she'd hidden him even more carefully than ever, locking him in his room when she had to go outside.

Jen rolled her eyes.

"Don't tell me your family believes that Government propaganda stuff," she said. "They've spent so much money trying to convince people they can monitor all the TVs and computers, you know they couldn't have afforded to actually do it. I've been using our computer since I was three—and watching TV, too—and they've never caught me. How about a candle?"

"What?" It took Luke a minute to realize she was talking about the signal again. "The candles—they're all in the kitchen, and I'm not allowed—"

Jen mimicked the words as he said them: "—to go in there."

"They've got you on an awfully short leash, don't they?" she asked.

"No. I mean, yes. But they're just trying to protect me—"

Jen shook her head. "Yeah, I've heard that one. Ever hear of disobeying?"

"I—" Luke started defensively. "I'm here, aren't I?"

Jen laughed. "Got me. But, listen, if you can't do candles or a flashlight, how about just turning on a light that I can see?"

Luke was quicker this time figuring out that she was still talking about the signal.

"The one by the back door," Luke said. "You can't miss it."

He wasn't allowed to turn that on, either, but he didn't dare say "not allowed" again.

Now Luke toyed with his mashed potatoes. His entire conversation with Jen had been like that—she mocked, he defended, but she always got her way.

Of course—he defended her to himself—she knew and had seen so much more than him. After he'd finished his story on the couch, she'd told him hers.

"First," she'd said defiantly, "my parents had me on purpose. Thirteen years ago. Mom already had Bull and Brawn from her first marriage—"

"Your brothers?" Luke asked.

"Yeah. Buellton and Brownley, really, but what kind of names are those for knuckleheads like them? Mom was going through some snobbish upper-class phase with husband number one."

"She's had more than one husband?" Luke asked. He didn't know that was possible.

"Sure," Jen said. "Dad—who's really my stepdad—is number three."

Luke found that so confusing, he just kept his mouth shut.

"Anyhow," Jen said. "Mom was dying to have a little girl, so when she and husband number two got together, she went and paid some doctor lots of money so she could get pregnant."

"What if you'd been a boy?" Luke asked.

"Oh, they got in on the beginning of the gender selection experiments." Luke must have given Jen a particularly blank look, because she explained it. "That means they made sure I was a girl. Doctors can do that, you know, but the Government outlawed the procedure because they were afraid it'd throw the population even more out of whack. I'm sure my parents paid a lot for it. Were your mom and dad trying for a girl?"

Luke thought about it. He remembered Mother saying she'd wanted four boys, but would she have wanted a girl even more? Someone like Mother? He couldn't really picture a girl in his house.

"They weren't trying for anything," he said. "I was a surprise. Luck."

Jen nodded. "I didn't think they paid for you," she said. Then she put her hand over her mouth. "That sounded really terrible, didn't it? I didn't mean anything by it. It's just—you're the first person I've met who wasn't a Baron."

"How do you know I'm not?" Luke asked stiffly.

"Well—" Jen waved her hand in a way that made Luke even more aware of the contrast between his ragged flannel shirt and patched jeans, and Jen's perfect house. "Look, don't be mad. It doesn't matter. Or maybe it does, but I think it's cool that you're not a Baron. You can help me even more."

"Help?" Luke asked.

"With the rally," Jen said. She bit her lip. "Should I—there's no way you could be an infiltrator, is there? Can I trust you?"

"Of course you can," Luke said. He felt insulted again.

Jen leaned her head back and stared at the ceiling, as if an answer were written there. Then she looked back at Luke.

"I'm sorry. I'm botching this. I'm not used to really talking, just on the Net. Look, I trust you, but I'm not the only one involved. So let's wait, okay?"

"Okay," Luke said. But he couldn't help sounding injured.

Jen leaned over and gave his shoulders a quick shake.

"Oh, don't say it like that. Say, 'Okay, Jen, I respect your judgment.' Or, 'Okay, Jen, whatever you think is best.'" She giggled. "That's what Dad tells me I should say when I disagree with him. Can you believe it? Lawyers!"

Luke was glad the subject had changed. "Your dad's a lawyer?" he asked.

Jen rolled her eyes. "Yeah, all Mom's husbands have been. Strange taste, huh? Number one was an environmental lawyer, of all things; number two was corporate—that's how they had enough money to get me. And number three, Dad, is with the Government. High up, I might add."

"But—if you're an illegal—" Luke hadn't thought he could get any more confused.

Jen laughed.

"Haven't you learned? Government leaders are the worst ones for breaking laws. How do you think we got this house? How do you think I got Internet access? How do you think we live?"

"I don't know," Luke said, fully honest. "I don't think I know much of anything."

Jen patted his head, as if he were a little kid or a dog.

"That's okay," she said. "You'll learn."

It wasn't long after that that Luke said he had to leave, because he was afraid Dad or Matthew or Mark might come in for lunch a little early. He dreaded the trip back. Jen walked him to the door, chattering the whole way.

"I'll fix the screen and deal with the security system, so

no one will ever know you were here," she said. "And—oh, no!"

Luke followed her gaze. She was staring at three pinpoints of blood on the carpet.

"I'm sorry," Luke said. "That must be from when I scraped my hand. I'll clean it up. There's still time—"

Secretly, he was glad of the delay.

"No, no," Jen said impatiently. "I don't care about the carpet. It's just that Mom and Dad will know, and when they see I don't have any cuts—"

And then, before Luke even knew what she was doing, she thrust her hand toward the torn part of the screen. The jagged edge didn't cut immediately, so she held the screen with her right hand and raked it across her left. When Jen pulled her hand back, Luke saw a gash even deeper than his. Jen squeezed out a few drops of blood and let them fall to the carpet.

"There," she said.

Stunned, Luke backed out the door.

"Come back soon, farmer boy," Jen said.

Luke turned and ran, blindly, not even slowing down to creep alongside the barn. He went straight to the back door of his house, yanked it open, and let it bang shut behind him.

Now, sitting at supper, he felt his heart pounding again as he thought of how dangerous that had been. Why hadn't he looked first? Why hadn't he crawled? He poked his fork into his potatoes, now gone cold and congealed. He watched Mother gathering up dirty dishes while Dad, Matthew, and Mark leaned back in their chairs, talking of grain yields. Jen had scared him—that was why. Seeing her cut her hand had terrified him. How could she do something like that for him, when they'd just met?

CHAPTER SEVENTEEN

Luke spent practically every second of the next three days either reliving his secret visit to Jen or planning another one. The first day, a Government inspector came out to examine the Garners' crop, so Luke stayed in his room the entire day. The second day it rained, and Dad spent the morning doing book work in the house. The third day, Dad was back in the fields, but when Luke crept over to the back door promptly at 9 A.M. and daringly flipped the light switch, he got no answering flash from Jen's house. Maybe the clocks in her house were slow. He left the light on for fifteen whole minutes, terrified the whole time that someone besides Jen might see it. Finally, heartsick, he switched it off and climbed with shaky legs back to his room.

What if something had happened to Jen? What if she were sick—dying, even—alone in her house? What if she'd been caught or turned in? Just from the little time Luke had spent with her, he could tell: She took a lot of risks.

It never had occurred to him that knowing another

person would give him someone else to worry about.

He steadied himself by leaning against the wall at the top of the stairs and reminded himself of less frightening possibilities: Maybe one of her parents was just out running errands, not working, so they were going to be home soon. Maybe...he tried to think of another safe reason Jen hadn't signaled for him to come. But he had so much trouble picturing her ordinary life that his imagination failed him.

He found out the next day, when he risked a dash to Jen's house as soon as Jen answered his signal.

"Where were you?" he asked instantly.

"When? Yesterday?" She yawned, sliding the door shut behind him. "Did you try to come over? I'm sorry. Mom had a free day and made me go shopping."

Luke gaped at her. "Shopping? You went out?"

Jen nodded nonchalantly.

"But I didn't see you leave—" Luke protested.

Jen looked at him as if she seriously wondered if he had a brain. "Of course not. I was hiding. The backseat of our car is hollowed out—Dad had it custom-built."

"You went out—" Luke repeated in awe.

"Well, it's not like I saw anything until we got to the mall. Two hours of riding in the dark is not my idea of fun. I hate it."

"But at the mall—you got out? You didn't have to hide?"

Jen laughed at his amazement.

"Mom got me a forged shopping pass a long time ago.

Supposedly, I'm her niece. It's good enough to convince store clerks, but if the Population Police ever found me in a roadside stop, I'd be dead. There you have it, my mother's priorities. Shopping is more important than my life."

Luke shook his head and sat down on the couch because his knees were feeling a little shaky.

"I didn't know," he said. "I didn't know thirds could do that."

What if Mother and Dad got him a forged pass? For a minute he could almost picture it—they could hide him under burlap bags in the pickup truck bed until they got into town.

Everybody in town knew Mother and Dad. Everybody knew Mother and Dad had only two sons. Matthew and Mark.

"You went to the city," he said.

"Well, yeah," Jen said. "You don't see any malls around here, do you?"

"What was it like?" Luke almost whispered.

"Boring," Jen said. "Really, really boring. Mom wanted to buy me a dress—who knows why—so we went to one store after another, and I had to try on all these dresses that scratched and pricked and poked me. And then she made me get a bunch of bras—oh, sorry," she said when Luke blushed a deep red. "I guess you don't talk much about bras at your house."

"Matthew and Mark do, sometimes, when they're being...dirty," Luke said.

"Well, bras aren't *dirty*," Jen said. "They're just torture devices invented by men or mothers or something."

"Oh," Luke said, looking down.

"But, anyway," Jen said, with a bounce that propelled her off the couch. "I checked you out on the computer and you're all right, you don't exist. Not officially, anyway. So you're safe. And—"

Hearing Jen say that so flippantly—*you don't exist*—made Luke feel funny.

"How do you know I'm safe?" he interrupted.

"Fingerprints," Jen said. When Luke gave her a blank look, she explained. "My brother Brawn went through this phase where he wanted to be a detective—not that he ever would have been smart enough for it—and I remembered he still has a fingerprinting kit. So I dusted for your fingerprints on things you touched, just like on TV. I got a really good print off the wall. Then I scanned that into the computer, linked into the national file of fingerprints and, *voilà*, I discovered your fingerprints don't exist, so neither do you. Officially."

She made a mocking face for emphasis. Luke wanted to ask, *The Population Police can't find me because of what you did, can they?* But he understood so little of what she'd explained that he didn't think it would help to ask anything. And Jen was already onto the next thought.

"And, anyhow, you seem trustworthy. So-oo, now that I know you're safe, I can tell you about the rally and show you our secret chat rooms and everything—"

Jen was already leaving the room, so he had to follow just to hear the rest of her sentence.

"Want something to eat or drink?" she asked, hesitating at the doorway to the grand kitchen. "I was so surprised, I forgot to be a good hostess the last time. What'll it be? Soda? Potato chips?"

"But those are illegal," Luke protested. He remembered reading something about junk food in one of the books in the attic and asking his mother about it. She'd explained that it was something people used to eat all the time, until the Government shut down the factories that made it. She wouldn't tell him why. But, as a special treat, she'd brought out a bag of potato chips she'd been saving for years and shared them, just with him. They were salty, but hard to chew. Luke had pretended to like them only because Mother seemed to want him to.

"Yeah, well, we're illegal, too, so why shouldn't we enjoy ourselves?" Jen asked, thrusting a bowl of chips at him. To be polite, Luke took one chip. And then another. And another. These potato chips were so good, he had to hold himself back from grabbing them by the handful. Jen stared at him.

"Do you go hungry sometimes?" she asked in a low voice.

"No," Luke said in surprise.

"Some shadow children do because they don't have food ration cards, and the rest of their family doesn't share," she said, opening a refrigerator that was bigger than every appliance in the Garners' kitchen put together. "My family can get all the food we want, of course, but"—she looked at him in a way that once again made him conscious of his ragged clothes—"How does your family get food for you?"

The question puzzled Luke.

"The same way they get it for themselves," he said. "We grow it. We have a garden—I used to work in it a lot, before, you know. And then, we have the hogs, or used to, and I guess sometimes we'd trade a butchered hog for someone else's butchered steer, so we'd have beef—"

Those were all shadowy transactions in Luke's mind. He had to strain his brain to remember overhearing Dad or Matthew reporting to Mother, "Ready to cook some steak? Johnston up near Libertyville wants some ham..."

Jen dropped a plastic bottle full of brown liquid. "You eat *meat*?" she exclaimed.

"Sure. Don't you?" Luke asked.

"When Dad can get it," Jen said, bending to pick up the bottle. She poured a glassful for Luke and one for herself. Both drinks fizzed and bubbled. "Even his clout isn't *that* great. The Government's been trying to force everyone, even the Barons, to become vegetarians."

"Why?" Luke asked.

Jen handed him his glass.

"Something about vegetables being more efficient," she said. "Farmers have to use a lot more land to produce one pound of meat than to produce a pound of—what's it called?—soybeans."

Luke wrinkled his nose at the thought of eating soybeans.

"I don't know," he said slowly. "We always fed our hogs the grain we couldn't sell because it didn't meet Government standards. But since the Government made us get rid of our hogs, Dad just lets that grain rot in the field."

"Really?" Jen grinned as if he'd just announced the overthrow of the Government. She thumped him on the back just as he took his first sip of soda. Between the bubbly drink and her enthusiastic pounding, Luke started coughing. Jen didn't seem to notice. "See, I told you you'd be a big help. I'm going to go post that on a bulletin board right now!"

"Wait—" Luke sputtered between coughs. He didn't know what she was talking about. But he couldn't let her get his family in trouble. He chased her down the hall, catching up just as she was sliding into the chair in front of the computer. She switched it on, and it made the *be-be-be-be-beeep* sounds Luke had heard the last time. Luke stood to the side, carefully out of sight of the screen.

"It's not going to bite you," Jen said. "Grab a chair. Sit down."

Luke inched back.

"But the Government—" he said.

"The Government's incompetent and stupid," Jen said. "Get it? Believe me, if they were watching through my computer screen, I'd know by now."

Meekly, Luke pulled over a padded chair and sat down.

He watched as Jen typed in, "If the Government let farmers feed their animals the grain they can't sell, there'd be more meat."

Luke was relieved that she hadn't mentioned his family. But, unless the Government was spying on them, he couldn't understand what difference it made for her to write that.

"Where'd that go?" he asked as the words disappeared. "Who's going to see it?"

"I put it on a Department of Agriculture bulletin board. Anyone with a computer can find it now. Maybe a Government worker with half a brain will see it and actually think for the first time this decade."

"But—" Luke squinted in confusion. "Why does it matter?"

Jen fixed her gaze on Luke.

"You don't even know, do you?" she asked. "You don't know why they passed the Population Law."

"N-no," Luke admitted.

"It's all about food," Jen said. "The Government was scared we'd all run out of food if the population kept growing. That's why they made you and me illegal, to keep people from starving."

Luke suddenly felt doubly guilty for the potato chips he was still cramming into his mouth. He swallowed hard and lowered his hands to his lap, instead of back into the chip bowl.

"So if I didn't eat, my food would go to someone who

was legal," Luke said. But in his family, that would just be Matthew or Mark, and they were hardly starving. Matthew was even starting to sport the same roll of fat around his waist that Dad had. Then Luke remembered the tramp from long ago, saying, "I ain't et in three days...." Was that Luke's fault?

Jen laughed.

"Stop looking so worried," she said. "That *is* what the Government thinks, but they're wrong. My dad says there's plenty of food, it's just not distributed right. That's why they've got to stop the Population Law. That's why they've got to recognize you and me and all the other shadow kids. That's why we're going to have the rally."

As ignorant as he was, Luke could tell from the way she said it that the rally was important.

"Can you tell me about the rally now?" he asked humbly.

"Yes," Jen said. She pushed away from the computer and twirled on her chair. "Hundreds of us—all the shadow children I could track down—are going to march on the Government in protest. We'll go right to the president's house. We won't leave them alone until they give us the same rights everybody else has."

Just my luck, Luke thought. I finally meet another third child, and she's absolutely crazy.

"And"—Jen said, as bubbly as the shaken soda—"You can come, too. Won't it be great?"

CHAPTER EIGHTEEN

—" Luke said. He couldn't look at Jen's triumphant grin. "I don't think I—"

He thought about how terrifying it was just running back and forth between his house and Jen's. Even this morning, on his third run through their yards, his heart had pounded so hard, he'd wondered if it could burst from fear. And in the yard at least, he was sure—or as sure as he could be—that no one was watching. How could Jen think he would dare go out in public, where he knew people could see him—people in Government, no less—and say, "I am a third child! I want to be treated like everyone else!"

"Scared?" Jen said softly.

Luke could only nod.

Jen turned back to the computer.

"Well, I am, too," she said matter-of-factly. She typed something, then looked back at Luke. "Some. But don't you think it'll be a relief? No more hiding, no more pretending, just—being free!"

Luke wondered if he'd always misunderstood the meaning of the word "relief." Jen's rally sounded like his worst nightmare.

"You can think about it," she said. "You don't have to decide anything today. Now, ready to chat?"

Luke looked back at the computer screen, where rows of words were unfurling:

Carlos: It's 105 here, and my parents think it's a waste to run the a.c. during the day. Can you say heartless?

Sean: Why don't you just crank it up, then turn it off again right before they get home? That's what Pat and I do. They'll never know.

Carlos: Yeah, but my parents probably read their electric bill.

Yolanda: So what are they going to do? Ground you?

Carlos: Good point. I'm searching for the temp control right now.

Yolanda: Where's Jen?

Sean: You know she never gets up this early.

Carlos: Curses—my parents have the temp control locked somehow. Told you they were evil. Where is Jen? I can't wait for her sarcarstic comment.

Luke read the words Jen was typing: "I'm right here, and, Sean, I do so get up early. I just don't always choose to see *you* first thing. And Carlos—what's wrong? Is there sweat in your eyes? There's only one 'r' in 'sarcastic.'"

She hit another key, and the words appeared right up

with everyone else's. They were followed quickly by another line:

Sean: Good morning to you, too, Jen. Glad to see you're still among the living.

Jen typed quickly: "No, just among the hidden. Not the same thing at all!!!!" Then she sent it, too.

"What is this?" Luke asked. "Some sort of game?"

He remembered Jen mentioning a Carlos before, and never explaining who he was. Were these some sort of computerized imaginary friends?

"Carlos, Sean, Yolanda—they're all other third children. Sean's even got a brother, Pat, who's a fourth child. This is how I talk to them."

Luke watched the next line of type appear: "Carlos: Thanks for the sympathy, Jen."

"But how—?" Luke asked, still doubtful.

"Oh, you know. It's the Net," Jen said. "If you've got a spare hour or two sometime, I'll give you the technical gobbledygook to explain it. All I care about is that it works. I'd die without someone to talk to."

She was typing even as she talked. Luke craned his head to see what she wrote: "Guess what? The kid I told you about, Luke, is here with me."

Quickly, three "Hi, Luke"s appeared on the screen.

Luke fought down panic.

"But the Government—" he said. "They'll find me—"

Jen playfully slugged his arm. "Chill, okay? Nobody from the Government can get in this chat room. We all use a password. Just third children know it. And, anyhow, even if someone else read this, what would they know? Just that somewhere in the world, there's a kid named Luke. Big deal."

"But they can trace you through the computer, and then they'd find me, too." Luke's heart was still pounding.

"Look, if they could trace people through the computer, or through this chat room, wouldn't they have found me a long time ago?" Jen asked.

Luke tried to think clearly. "Your parents," he said. "You said they bribe people. So you're safe. But mine—"

Jen was shaking her head.

"No, I'm not safe," she said grimly. "Even my parents couldn't bribe the Population Police if they found me. Maybe to keep them from looking—but maybe not even that. The Population Police get some ridiculously big reward for every illegal they find. Why do you think I hide at all? Why do you think we have to have the rally? *Everybody* ought to be safe. And nobody should have to use bribes just to walk down the street or go to a mall or take a ride in a car...."

Luke glanced back at the computer screen, where the conversation continued.

"How did all those people find out the password?" he asked. "How did you?"

"Well, I created the chat room, so I made it up," Jen said.

"And I knew a couple other shadow kids, and I got my parents and their parents to get the password to them. And then some of those kids spread the password to other kids they knew. Last time I counted, I had contact with eight hundred kids."

Luke shook his head. He didn't think even his parents knew that many people.

"So what is the password?" he asked.

" 'Free,' " Jen said. "It's 'free.' "

CHAPTER *NINETEEN*

Luke left Jen's that day with a pile of books and computer printouts clutched to his chest.

"Some reading material for you," she'd said. "So you'll understand."

Back in his own room, Luke sat down on his bed and opened the first book. It was thick and carried its title in ominous black letters: THE POPULATION DISASTER. The type inside was small and closely spaced. Luke read a sentence at random: "While debate continues over the carrying capacity of the earth—" He skipped ahead. "If the Total Fertility Rate in industrialized countries had remained at or below 2.1—" Luke saw that reading this book would be like puzzling out the letters Dad got from the Government. He glanced at the other two books: *The Famine Years Revisited* and *The Population Reversal*. They looked no easier. The computer printouts were at least brief, but both "The Problem of the Shadows" and "The Population Law: Our Country's Biggest Mistake," were full of big words.

Luke sighed. He was tempted to put the books aside and just ask Jen to explain them to him. And he might have, except for what she'd said as she'd begun handing them to him. "Oh, my gosh! I didn't think—you can read, can't you?"

"Of course," Luke had answered stiffly. "I was reading in the chat room, wasn't I?"

"Yes, but you could have been—oh, never mind. I've offended you again, haven't I? Me and my big mouth. It wouldn't have been anything to be ashamed of, even if you couldn't. Oh, I'm making things worse. I'll shut up. Here."

And it had seemed to Luke that she'd pulled even bigger books off the bookshelves after that.

Now he resolutely turned to the beginning of *The Population Disaster* and began reading: "Since some elements of the overpopulation crisis were foreseen in the 1800s, an uninformed observer could only wonder why humankind came so near to total annihilation. But—"

Luke reached for the dictionary and settled in for the long haul.

It rained for the next several days, so Luke read constantly, not even tempted to race over to Jen's instead. He could hear Dad banging around downstairs, stomping in and out from the barn or the machine shed. Now that the harvest was in, Luke thought Dad might be bored without the pigs to take care of. So Luke read cautiously, always ready to shove his population book under his pillow and replace it with one of his adventure books. The preparation paid off on the fourth day, when he heard Dad's footsteps on the stairs.

"Hey, Luke, what're you up to?"

"Nothing," Luke said, turning *Treasure Island* right side up at the very last moment. Dad didn't notice.

"Want to play cards?"

They played rummy on Luke's bed. Luke could feel the corner of *The Population Disaster* poking his back throughout the entire game. And he kept wanting to ask Dad about what he was learning. He spent most of the first game biting his tongue. Dad won.

"Again?" Dad asked, shuffling the cards.

"If you don't have any work you've got to do."

"In November? With no livestock? Only work I've got now is figuring out how we're going to pay our bills once the hog money runs out."

"Isn't there some way to grow stuff inside during the winter? Like down in the basement, with special lights, lots of water and extra minerals. And then you could sell it?" Luke asked without thinking. He'd just finished reading a chapter in the population book about hydroponics.

Dad squinted.

"Seems I did hear tell of that once."

Luke won the next hand. Dad didn't seem to be concentrating. At the end, Dad said, "Mind if we quit now?"

Luke was terrified Dad would ask where he'd heard of hydroponics. So he just said, "No problem."

Dad left muttering, "Growing food inside...hmmm..."

Luke wished he'd had the nerve to ask about the Population Law, or the famines, or even some family history.

Once he got past the dense language, the books Jen had loaned him were full of revelations. As best he could understand it, the world had simply gotten too full of people about twenty years earlier. Poor countries had it particularly bad, and people there often starved or were malnourished. But then something worse happened: Terrible droughts struck the parts of the world that always grew the most food. For three years, they grew almost nothing. People everywhere starved. In Luke's country, the Government began rationing food, only allowing people to have 1,500 calories a day. And, to make sure there was food, they seized control of all food production. They forced factories that had made junk food to crank out healthy food instead. They forced farmers to move to land that would be more likely to produce. *(Is that why we don't live near our grandparents?* Luke wanted to ask his parents.) But the Government didn't think that was enough. They wanted to make sure there would never again be more people than the farmers could feed. So they passed the Population Law, too.

In the evenings, spooning in his stew or cutting up his meat, Luke felt pangs of guilt now. Perhaps someone was starving someplace because of him. But the food wasn't *there*—wherever the starving people were—it was *here*, on his plate. He ate it all.

"Luke, you're so quiet lately. Is everything all right?" Mother asked one night when he waved away second helpings of cabbage.

"I'm fine," he said, and went back to eating silently.

But he was worrying. Worrying that maybe the Government was right and that he shouldn't exist.

Only when he got to the two computer printouts did he begin to feel better. One of the articles began, "The Population Law is evil." The other said, "Hundreds of children are hidden, mistreated, starved, neglected, abused—even murdered—for no reason. Forcing children into the shadows can be counted as genocide."

"How can this be?" he asked Jen a week later when he finally got a chance to go back to her house. "How can the books and the articles be so different?"

She handed him a glass of soda.

"What do you mean?" she asked.

Luke pointed to *The Population Disaster*. "This book says the human race would have gone extinct if we hadn't had the Population Law. And this"—he held up and shook "The Problem of the Shadows" article—"this says the Population Law was totally unnecessary and cruel. It says there was plenty of food, even during the famines, except that the Barons were hoarding it." Belatedly, he remembered that Jen was a Baron. "Sorry."

Jen shrugged, not the least bit offended.

"So what's the truth?" Luke asked.

Jen shook potato chips into a bowl.

"Well, think about it. The Government allowed those books to be published—they probably even paid for them. So of course they're going to say what the Government wants people to believe. They're just propaganda. Lies. But the articles, the authors of those probably put themselves at risk getting the information out. So they're right."

Luke pondered that. "Then why'd you make me read the books?" he asked.

"So you'd understand how stupid the Government is," Jen said. "So you'd understand why we have to make them see the truth."

Luke looked at the stack of thick books on the Talbots' kitchen counter. They looked so official, so important— who was he to say they weren't true?

CHAPTER *TWENTY*

Luke feared he'd have to wait months between visits to Jen once the snow started. But the weather proved kind that winter—most days were dry and clear. He didn't have leafy trees to hide behind, but he began to feel safe, anyway, crawling through his and Jen's backyards. By mid-January he could make the entire journey without his heart beating abnormally at all. The odds against someone watching from one of the other Baron houses seemed too astronomical to worry about. His only concern was Dad.

Dad usually hung around the house a lot during the winter. Without the hogs to tend to, he could easily have been there even more than usual, preventing Luke from ever sneaking out. But suddenly Dad had taken to heading to town many mornings, yelling up to Luke, "I'm going to the library. You've got something up there to eat for lunch, don't you?" or, "There's some plastic tubing over to Slyton I want to check out. Tell the boys when they get in from school, you hear?"

"It's that hydroponics notion," Luke bragged to Jen one day in late January while they were sitting at the computer together. "I got Dad all excited about it, and now he's too busy with that to notice what I do."

"What's hydroponics?" Jen asked.

"It was in one of your books—you know, growing plants indoors, without soil, just using water and special minerals."

"Oh," Jen said. "Does he think the Government would actually let him do that?"

"I guess so," Luke said. "Why wouldn't they?"

Jen shrugged. "Why does the Government do anything?"

Luke didn't have an answer to that. Jen turned back to the computer chat room, where everyone was debating fake I.D.'s.

Carlos: Mom says they won't buy me one until I'm 18, because she thinks the Gov. wouldn't challenge an adult's as much. And maybe they'll be cheaper then.

Pat: Maybe Sean and I will get ours by the time we're ninety. Dad and Mom have been saving for them as long as we can remember.

Yolanda: My dad sez he's waiting to find one that's foolproof. He sez there are too many bad ones out there.

Jen began typing furiously. "Who needs a fake I.D.? Carlos, they'd probably get one for you that says 'John Smith,' and you'd have to spend the rest of your life trying to pass for an Anglo. My parents have been begging me to get a fake I.D. for years, but I won't until I can have one that says 'Jen Talbot' and is really *mine*.

"Have you all forgotten the rally? We're all gonna get real I.D.'s that say who we really are!!!! WE AREN'T FAKES! WE SHOULDN'T HAVE TO HIDE!"

She jabbed the Enter button so hard, the computer shook.

"But, Jen," Luke said timidly, "I thought you used a fake I.D. to go shopping with your mom. It said you were her niece."

Jen turned her fierce gaze to Luke.

"No, that was just a shopping pass," she said. "I don't like using that, either, but I figured I can't fight my parents about everything. What they're talking about"—she pointed at the computer screen—"is taking on a fake identity permanently. Most shadow kids do that eventually—they go live with another family and pretend to be someone they aren't for the rest of their lives."

"So you'd rather hide?" Luke asked. He thought about using a different name, living in a different family, being a different person. He couldn't imagine it.

"No, of course I wouldn't rather hide," Jen said irritably. "But getting one of those I.D.'s—that's just a different way of hiding. I want to be me and go about like anybody else. There's no compromise. Which is why I've got to convince these idiots that the rally's their only chance."

There was a shocked blankness on the computer screen after Jen's entry. Then Carlos ventured, "Um, Jen, got any of your parents' blood pressure medicine handy? Sounds like you need it."

Jen stabbed the power button on the computer. The screen instantly went dark. She spun around in her chair and clenched her fists.

"Argh!" she screamed, with a grimace of frustration.

"Jen?" Luke asked. He leaned away from her in case she decided to use those clenched fists.

Jen turned to Luke in surprise, as though she'd forgotten he was there.

"Don't you ever feel like saying, 'I can't take this anymore'?" she asked. She leaped up and began pacing the floor. "Don't you ever want to just walk out into the sunshine and say, 'Forget hiding! I don't care!'? Am I the only one who feels this way?"

"No," Luke whispered.

She whirled around and pointed at the computer.

"Then what's wrong with them? Why don't they understand? Why aren't they taking this seriously?"

Luke bit his lip.

"I think," he said, "people just have different ways of expressing what they feel. Those kids make jokes and complain. You run around screaming your head off and tackling people."

He was proud of himself for figuring that out, considering he really only knew five people in the whole world. But for the first time, he wondered how the rest of his family would cope if any of them had to hide. Dad would get grumpy. Mother would try to make the best of it, but you'd be able to tell that she was really unhappy. Matthew would be quiet, but would look sad all the time, the way he looked every time anyone mentioned the pigs they couldn't keep anymore. Mark would gripe so much that he'd make everyone miserable. For the first time, Luke felt a glimmer of pride, that he dealt with hiding better than anyone else in his family would. He thought.

Jen snorted at his explanation. "Whatever," she said. She slid back into her chair by the computer. "But the rally's in April. I've got three months to make sure everyone's ready."

She switched on the computer and began typing furiously again.

Luke slipped away a few hours later. He wasn't sure Jen noticed him leaving.

CHAPTER *TWENTY-ONE*

I n February, Dad got the letter from the Government forbidding him from trying to grow anything indoors.

"It has come to our attention that you have been purchasing excess amounts of plastic pipe, such as is used in the germination, cultivation, and development of vegetative matter in an interior structure," the letter began. "Due to the preponderance of such agricultural methods in the cultivation of illegal substances, we order you to cease and desist immediately...."

Luke read the letter at supper, after everyone else in the family had had a stab at trying to figure out what it meant. Somehow, after reading all the big books that Jen had loaned him, he didn't find the fancy words so daunting.

"They want you to stop," Luke said. "They're scared you're going to grow something illegal. And this part"— he pointed at the letter, although everyone else was at the table, several feet away, and he was in his usual spot on the stairs—"this part, where they say, 'render all such materials for our adjudication,' that means you have to turn over all the stuff you bought and they'll decide if they're going to fine you or not."

The rest of the family looked at Luke in amazement. Then Mark started giggling.

"Drugs," he said. "They think you're going to grow drugs."

Dad flashed him a look of pure disgust.

"Think it's funny? We'll see what you think next year when your feet grow and we don't have money for new shoes."

Mark stopped laughing.

"We'll get by," Luke's mother said quietly. "We always have."

Dad shoved back from the table.

"Why didn't I get a permit?" he asked no one in particular. "Maybe if I just get a permit—"

By then, Luke had read the rest of the letter.

"They don't give out permits for hydroponics," he said. "This says it's always illegal."

This time he only got a glare from Dad.

Luke felt his father's disappointment, and seeing his parents so worried about money made a small voice whisper in the back of his head, *Maybe if they didn't have you, they could afford everything they want.* But he didn't eat that much, and all of his clothes were hand-me-downs from Matthew and Mark. And how much could it cost to heat his attic room? Sometimes he found ice crystals on the chair he sat in to watch the neighborhood. He tried to ignore the voice.

What bothered him more was that, without the hydroponics idea to keep him busy, Dad barely left the farm for the rest of the winter. Luke made it over to Jen's only once in all of February, and twice in March, when Dad began driving around looking for the best seed corn prices.

But each time, Jen greeted him with big hugs and acted genuinely thrilled to see him. Her tantrum in January seemed forgotten. One day, the two of them made a huge mess of the Talbots' kitchen baking cookies.

"Won't your parents mind?" Luke asked when Jen scolded him for attempting to clean the flour handprints off the cabinets and refrigerator and stove.

"Are you kidding? I want this preserved. They'll be thrilled to see any sign of domesticity on my part," Jen said.

Another time, they played board games all morning, sprawled out on the floor of the Talbots' family room.

The third day, they just spent the whole time talking. Jen kept Luke enthralled with stories of places she'd been, people she'd met, things she'd seen.

"When I was little, Mom used to take me to a play group that was all third children," Jen said. She giggled. "The thing was, it was all Government officials' kids. I think some of the parents didn't even like kids—they just thought it was a status symbol to break the Population Law and get away with it."

"What'd you do at the play group?" Luke asked.

"Played, of course. Everybody had a lot of toys. And one

of the kids had a dog he brought with him sometimes, and we all took turns feeding it dog biscuits."

"These people had pets, too?" Luke asked incredulously.

"Well, you know, they were Barons," Jen said.

Luke frowned. He slid down in the soft couch, so different from anything in his own house.

"My dad says that when he was little, just about everyone he knew had pets. He had a dog named Bootsy and a cat named Stripe. He talks about them all the time. Why'd the Government make pets illegal?"

"Oh, you know, the food thing," Jen said. She took a chocolate chip cookie from a pack they were sharing and waved it for emphasis. "Without dogs and cats, there's more food for humans. My dad says if it weren't for the Barons breaking the law, lots of species would have gone extinct."

Luke looked at the cookie in his own hand. So now was he supposed to feel guilty about eating food that should have gone to animals, as well as to other people?

Jen saw his expression. "Hey, don't go dopey on me," she said. "It's all a scam, remember? There's more than enough food in the world, especially now that there aren't enough babies being born."

"What?" Luke asked.

"Well, besides passing the Population Law, the Government went on this big campaign to make women think it was something evil to get pregnant and have kids. They put posters up in all the cities, with things like, 'Who's the worst criminal?' under a picture of a pregnant lady and, I don't know, some tough-looking crooks. And then if you read the whole sign it'd tell you the woman was the worst of all. Another one"—Jen giggled—"it had a picture of a huge pregnant belly, with the label, 'Ladies, do you want to look like this?' And women aren't allowed to go anywhere once they get pregnant. So now, my dad told me, there are so few babies being born that the population's going to be cut in half."

Luke shook his head, confused as usual. "So why doesn't the Government take down the signs and let people have as many babies as they want?"

Jen rolled her eyes. "Luke, you've got to quit thinking this makes any sense," Jen said. "It's the Government, remember? That's why we've got to have the rally—"

Luke changed the subject as quickly as he could. "What do women do if they can't go anywhere the whole time they're pregnant? I don't know about humans, but pigs take almost four months to have a baby. Do the women stay home all that time?"

"Hiding like us, you mean?" Jen asked. But she took the distraction. "Lots of them pretend they're just getting fat. My mom said she went shopping the day before I was born, and nobody noticed. But that's my mom and shopping."

And then she was off on a tale about her mother taking Jen shopping in a city ten hours away, just because she'd heard a store sold good purses there.

"That's probably the only reason my brothers don't turn me in," Jen said. "If she didn't have me, my mother would drag them around shopping. Can you see those two gorillas with shopping bags?"

Jen did an impression, walking around with her arms dragging from imaginary loaded-down bags. Even though Luke had only seen her brothers from a distance, he caught the resemblance and laughed.

"Your brothers would never turn you in," he protested. "Would they?"

"Of course not," Jen agreed. "They lo-ove me." She hugged herself mockingly and flopped back onto the couch beside Luke. "Anyhow, they wouldn't be smart enough to figure out how to turn me in without getting the rest of the family in trouble. What about your brothers?"

"They're not stupid," Luke said defensively. "Or—do you mean—"

"Would they ever betray you?" Jen narrowed her eyes, truly curious. "Not now, necessarily, but, say, years from now, if your parents were dead and it wouldn't hurt anybody but you, and they'd get lots of money for it—"

It was a question Luke had never considered. But he knew the answer.

"Never," he said, his voice cracking with earnestness. "I can trust them. I mean, we grew up together."

It was strange how he could be so sure, because they barely took time even to tease him anymore. Matthew was getting very serious with his girlfriend, and spent every spare moment at her house. Mark had suddenly gone basketball-crazy, and talked Dad into nailing an old tire rim to the front of the barn for a hoop. Luke could hear him outside, throwing balls late into the night. No matter how certain he was of their loyalty, Luke sometimes felt like his brothers had outgrown him. He missed them.

But it didn't matter. He had Jen now.

Luke kept Jen from talking about the rally the rest of that day, and they didn't even go near the computer. They just had fun. He crawled back to his house a few hours later, thinking that he didn't mind at all anymore, having to hide. He could go on this way forever, as long as he got to visit Jen. The leaves would come back to the trees soon, and he'd feel even safer on his trips to her house. And when planting season started, Dad would be out in the fields all day, and Luke could see Jen all the time.

But April came before planting season.

MARGARET PETERSON HADDIX

CHAPTER *TWENTY-TWO*

It rained the first two weeks of April, and Luke was in a tizzy wondering when he would ever get to see Jen again. Finally the ground dried out, and Dad headed out to the fields to plow. Luke raced to Jen's house.

"Oh, good!" she greeted him. "You can get the advance battle plans. I was afraid we were just going to have to pick you up Thursday night and fill you in then."

Luke carefully slid the door shut behind him and straightened the blinds so he and Jen would be totally hidden. Then he turned to face her.

"What are you talking about?" he asked. But he knew. His heart began to thump harder than it had in his rush through the backyards.

"The rally, of course," Jen said impatiently. "Everything's set. I'm taking one of my parents' cars, and I'm picking up three other kids on my way. But I made sure there'd be room for you. You should feel lucky—lots of kids are just going to walk. We're all meeting at the president's house at 6 A.M."

Luke clutched the cord to the blinds.

"Do you know how to drive?" he asked.

"Well enough." She flashed him a wicked grin. "My brothers told me how. Come on."

She waved him over to the couch. He sank into it while Jen perched on the edge.

"What if the Population Police stop you before you get to the capital?" he asked.

"Us, you mean. We. You're going, too, remember? Don't worry—nobody'll stop us." She giggled. "I checked the national employee staffing schedules through the computer. Let's just say several of the Population Police got some unexpected days off."

"You mean you changed their schedules? You can do that?"

Jen nodded, a wicked gleam in her eye.

"It took me a whole month to figure out how, but you are now looking at an accomplished hacker."

Dimly, Luke realized why Jen had seemed so relaxed and happy on his last several visits. They'd been vacations for her, breaks from intense work on plans for the rally. He looked closer and saw the fatigue in her eyes. She looked like a younger version of Mom after a twelve-hour shift in the chicken factory, or Dad after a long day of baling hay. But there was something more in her expression—his parents had never looked so feverishly giddy.

"What if someone finds out what you did? And changes it back?"

Jen shook her head. "They won't. I was very selective—

I coordinated everyone's travel plans and only eliminated the police who had to be eliminated. Aren't you excited? We're going to be free after all these years." She leaned down and pulled a sheaf of papers out from under the couch. "Best hiding place in the world. The maid's too lazy to clean under there. Now, let's see, I'll pick you up at 10 P.M., and—"

Luke was glad she was looking at the papers instead of him. He wouldn't have been able to meet her eyes.

"Okay, okay, so nobody's going to be caught on the way to the capital. But once you're there, at the president's house, someone will call the Population Police, and then—" Luke felt panicky just thinking about it.

Jen wasn't fazed. "So what?" she asked. "I don't care who gets called once we're there. Heck, I may call the Population Police myself. They're not going to do anything to a crowd of a thousand, especially not when lots of us are related to Government officials. We'll make them listen to us. We're a revolution!"

Luke looked away. "But your friends—you were mad at them because they weren't into it—what if they don't show up?"

"What do you mean?" Jen's voice was fierce.

Luke could barely speak for the panic welling inside him. "In the chat room, they were making jokes. Carlos and Sean and the others. You said they weren't taking it seriously."

"Oh, *that*. That was—a long time ago. They're all on

board. They're psyched. Why, Carlos is my lieutenant in all of this. You wouldn't believe how much he's helped. So, okay, ten o'clock, and then it's eight hours to the capital, and—" she consulted her papers again. "What kind of sign do you want to carry? 'I deserve a life' or 'End the Population Law now!' or—this is one I found in an old book—'Give me liberty or give me death'?"

Luke tried to imagine what Jen seemed to be taking for granted. He could get in a car. He'd sat in the pickup in the barn—a car wasn't much different. And for eight hours, that would be all he had to do—sit. Not that difficult. Except that panic would be coursing through him for the entire eight hours because of where the car was going. And then to get out, in public, at the president's house? And carry a sign? His imagination failed. He broke out in a cold sweat.

"Jen, I—" he started.

"Yes?"

Jen waited. The silence between them seemed to be growing, like a balloon. Luke struggled to speak.

"I can't go."

Jen gaped at him.

"I can't," he said again, weakly.

Jen shook her head briskly. "Yes, you can," she said. "I know you're scared—who isn't? But this is important. Do you want to hide all your life, or do you want to change history?"

Luke made a stab at humor.

"Isn't there another choice?"

Jen didn't laugh. She sprang from the couch.

"Another choice. Another choice." She paced, then jerked back to face Luke. "Sure. You can be a coward and hope someone else changes the world for you. You can hide up in that attic of yours until someone knocks at your door and says, 'Oh, yeah, they freed the hidden. Want to come out?' Is that what you want?"

Luke didn't answer.

"You've got to come, Luke, or you'll hate yourself the rest of your life. When you don't have to hide anymore, even years from now, there'll always be some small part of you whispering, 'I don't deserve this. I didn't fight for it. I'm not worth it.' And you are, Luke, you are. You're smart and funny and nice, and you should be living life, instead of being buried alive in that old house of yours—"

"Maybe I just don't mind hiding as much as you do," Luke whispered.

Jen faced him squarely, her gaze unwavering.

"Yes, you do. You hate walls as much as I do. Maybe more. Have you ever listened to yourself? Every time you talk about how you used to go outdoors and work in the garden or something, you glow. You're alive. Even if you don't want anything else, don't you want to get the outdoors back?"

What Luke wanted was to get away from Jen. Because she was right. Everything she said was right. But that couldn't mean he had to go. He huddled deeper in the couch.

"I'm not brave like you," he said.

Jen grabbed his shoulders and peered into his eyes.

"Oh, yeah?" she said. "You dared to come over here, didn't you? And here's something—why are you always the one who makes the trip? Ever think of that? If I'm so much braver, how come I'm not risking my life to see you?"

There were a thousand answers to that. *Because I found you first. Because your house is safer than mine. Because I need you more than you need me. You've got your computer and all your chat room friends. And you go places.* Luke squirmed away.

"My dad hangs around my house too much," he said. "It's safer this way. I'm—I'm just protecting you."

Jen backed up. "Thanks for the chivalry," she said bitterly. "I've got enough people protecting me. If you care so much, why don't you help me get free? You say you won't come to the rally for yourself—so do it for me. That's all I'll ever ask of you."

Luke winced. When she put things that way, how could he not go? Except—he couldn't.

"You're crazy," he said. "I can't go, and neither should you. It's too dangerous."

Jen flashed him a look of pure disgust.

"You can leave now," she said coldly. "I don't have time for you."

Luke could feel the ice in her words. He stood up.

"But—"

"Go," Jen said.

Luke stumbled toward the door. He stopped by the blinds and turned around.

"Jen, can't you understand? I do want it to work. I hope—"

"Hope doesn't mean anything," Jen snapped. "Action's the only thing that counts."

Luke backed out the door. He stood on the Talbots' patio, blinking in the sunlight, breathing in the smell of fresh air and danger. Then he turned and ran home.

CHAPTER *TWENTY-THREE*

Luke let the kitchen door slam behind him and didn't care. He was so mad, his eyes blurred. The nerve of her, saying *I don't have time for you.* Who did she think she was? He tramped up the stairs. She'd always thought she was better than him, just because she was a Baron, showing off with her soda and her potato chips and her fancy computer. So what? It didn't mean she was special, just because her parents had lots of money. It wasn't like she'd earned it or anything. Who was she, anyway? Just some dumb old girl. He wished he'd never gone over there. All she did was brag, brag, brag and show off. That's all the rally was, anyhow, showing off: *Hey, look, I'm a third child and I can go to the president's house and nobody will hurt me.* He hoped someone shot her. That would show her.

Luke stopped in the middle of pulling the attic door shut behind him. No, no, he took it back. He didn't want anyone to shoot her. His knees went weak, and he had to sit down on the stairs, all his anger suddenly turned to fear. What if someone did shoot her? He remembered the sign she'd asked if he wanted to carry: "Give me liberty or give me death." Was she serious? Did she expect to—? He stopped himself from thinking the rest. What if she never came back? He should go, if only to protect Jen. But he couldn't—

Luke buried his face in his hands, trying to hide from his own thoughts.

Mother found him there, hours later, still crouched on the stairs.

"Luke! Were you getting impatient waiting for me to get home? Did you have a nice day?"

Luke stared at her as though she were a vision from another life.

"I—" he started, ready to spill everything. He couldn't hold it all in.

Mother felt his forehead.

"Are you sick? You're so pale—I worry about you, Luke, all day long. But then I remind myself, you're safe here at home, out of harm's way." She gave him a weary smile and ruffled his hair.

Luke swallowed hard and recovered himself. What was he thinking? He couldn't tell anyone about Jen. He couldn't betray her.

"I'm fine," he lied. "I just haven't been out in the sun for a while, remember. Not that I'm complaining, of course," he added hastily.

Hiding again.

CHAPTER *TWENTY-FOUR*

For three days, Luke agonized. Sometimes he decided he had to stop Jen, to persuade her not to go. Sometimes he decided he ought to go with her. Sometimes he was mad again, and thought he should just stalk over there and demand an apology.

But anything he might do required seeing Jen, and that wasn't possible. It poured every day, the rain coming down in long, dreary sheets that made Luke feel worse as he watched from the attic vents. Downstairs he could hear Dad stomping around, muttering every now and then about the time and topsoil being lost with every raindrop. Luke felt like a prisoner.

Thursday night he went to bed convinced he'd never be able to sleep for imagining Jen and the others in her car, getting farther and farther from him and closer and closer to danger. But he must have dozed off, because he woke to total darkness. His heart pounded. He was sweaty. Had he dreamed something? Had he heard something? A floorboard creaked. His ears roared as he tried to listen. Was that someone else's breath or just his own, loud and scared? A beam of light swept across his face.

"Luke?" A whisper.

Luke bolted up in bed.

"Jen? Is that you?"

She switched off her flashlight.

"Yes. I thought I'd kill myself coming up your stairs. Why didn't you tell me they were so narrow?" She sounded like the same old Jen, not mad. Not crazy.

"I didn't know you'd ever be climbing them," Luke said.

It was insane to be talking about stairs now, in the middle of the night, in his room. Every word either of them spoke was dangerous. Mother was a light sleeper. But Luke was delighted not to be moving on, not to be talking about what Jen had really come to talk about.

"Your parents didn't lock your doors," Jen said. She seemed to be stalling, too. "Guess I'm lucky the Government outlawed pets. Didn't farmers always used to keep big guard dogs that would chomp people's heads off in one bite?"

Luke shrugged, then remembered Jen couldn't see him in the dark. "Jen, I—" He wasn't sure what he was going to say until he said it. "I still can't go. I'm sorry. It's something about having parents who are farmers, not lawyers. And not being a Baron. It's people like you who change history. People like me—we just let things happen to us."

"No. You're wrong. You can make things happen—"

Luke sensed, rather than saw, Jen shaking her head. Even in the dark, he could visualize each precisely cut strand of hair bouncing and falling back into place.

"I'm sorry," she continued. "I didn't come here to harp at you. This is dangerous, and no one should go unwillingly. I was too hard on you the other day. I just wanted to say—you've been a good friend. I'll miss you."

"But you'll be back," Luke said. "Tomorrow—or the next day—after the rally. I'll be over to visit. If your rally works, I'll be walking in the front door."

"We can hope," Jen said softly. Her voice faded away. "Good-bye, Luke."

CHAPTER *TWENTY-FIVE*

L uke lay awake the rest of the night. At first light, he got up and quietly scrubbed away the mud Jen had tracked in and up the stairs. Trust her not to think about mud. He fervently hoped she'd thought of all the details about the rally.

Luke was just finishing the last of the kitchen floor when he heard the toilet flushing upstairs. He hid the muddy rags in the trash and scrambled back to his place on the stairs just in time to meet Mother coming down.

"'Morning, early bird." She yawned. "Were you up during the night? I thought I heard something."

"I had trouble sleeping," Luke said truthfully.

Mother yawned again.

"And you're up early...feeling okay?"

"Just hungry," Luke said.

But he picked at his food. Everything he ate stuck in his throat.

After the rest of his family left, he risked sneaking over and turning the radio on low. There were weather reports and commercials for soybean seed and lots of music.

"Come on, come on," he muttered, keeping one eye on the side window, watching for Dad.

Finally the radio voice announced the news. Someone's cattle had gotten out and caused a minor car wreck. Nobody hurt. A Government spokesman predicted a poor planting season because of all the rain.

Nothing about the rally.

Dad came back toward the house. Luke snapped off the radio and bolted for the stairs.

At lunch, Dad forgot to turn the radio on, and Luke had to remind him. The announcer promised a big story after the commercials. His sandwich gone, Dad reached over to turn the radio off.

"No, no—wait!" Luke said. "This might be interesting—"

Dad harrumphed, but waited.

The announcer came back. He cleared his throat and declared that new Government statistics proved last year's alfalfa harvest had set a record for the decade.

It was like that for days. Luke kept waiting, desperate to hear anything. But the few times he could get to the radio, it said nothing.

Every time Dad left the house for any length of time, Luke switched on the light by the back door, his old signal to Jen. He stared so hard, willing her answering light to go on, that he thought he would go blind. But there was nothing.

He took to watching her house as obsessively as he had when he had first discovered her existence. There was no sign of her. The rest of her family came and went as usual. Did they look sadder? Happy? Worried? At peace? From a distance, he couldn't tell.

He got so desperate, he asked Mother if she'd thought about going over to visit the new neighbors, to welcome them to the area. She looked at him as if he were deranged.

"They've been there for months. They're hardly new anymore. And they're *Barons*," she said. She laughed in a way that didn't hide her bitterness. "Believe me, they don't want us visiting."

And what was she supposed to do, say, "Nice to meet you. Now, tell me everything about the child you never talk about"?

After a week, Luke did feel deranged. Every time anyone spoke to him, he jumped. Mother asked him, "Are you all right?" so many times, he took to avoiding her. But he couldn't just sit in the attic, waiting. He paced. He fidgeted. He chewed his fingernails.

He came up with a plan.

CHAPTER TWENTY-SIX

Finally, finally, a week and a half after the rally, a day dawned that was so clear and dry, Luke knew Dad would be in the fields all day. Without hope, Luke turned on the light by the back door. After five minutes without a response, he turned it off and quietly slipped out the door.

The cool air was a jolt, and for the briefest time, he paused. This was more dangerous than ever.

"But I have to *know*," he muttered fiercely, and crept alongside the barn before making his dash for Jen's house.

He had to rip the screen and break the pane of one of the Talbot's windows, which he felt bad about. But it didn't matter. If Jen was there, she could think of an excuse. And if she wasn't...if she wasn't, he'd never be back at the Talbots' again.

Once inside, he knew he had to do something about the alarm quickly. Jen had explained it to him once, told him the exact sequence of buttons to hit to disable it. He ran to the hall closet, yanked open the door, and punched buttons quickly, afraid he'd forget the sequence if he hesitated even a second. Green-blue-yellow-green-blue-orange-red.

The lights blinked out before he hit the last button, and that spooked him. Was that how it worked before?

"Hurry, hurry," he urged himself. The words kept replaying in his brain.

"Jen?" he called. "Jen?"

He went up and down stairs, looking in every room.

"Jen? You don't have to hide. It's me. Luke."

The house was enormous, three floors and a basement. He couldn't search everywhere, but if Jen was there, why would she hide? Against reason, he kept hoping she was.

"Jen? Come on. This isn't funny."

He found the bedrooms—huge, elegant rooms with beautifully carved beds and long, mirrored closets. He couldn't even tell which one was Jen's.

Finally, he admitted defeat and rushed down to the computer room.

He hurried over to the keyboard and typed in the same sequence of letters he'd watched Jen type so many times. His fingers were clumsy, and he kept messing up. Finally, he got to the chat room password. F-E-R-E. No. Erase. F-E-E-R. No. At last he got it. F-R-E-E.

The screen went blank, with none of the friendly banter that had magically appeared every time he'd watched Jen. Had he done something wrong? Frantically, he exited and entered the chat room again, his hands shaking. Still nothing. Timidly, using only his right index finger, he typed, "Where's Jen?" He had to hold one hand with the other to steady his finger enough to hit the Enter button.

Almost instantaneously, his words vanished and reappeared at the top of the screen. He waited. Nothing. The screen stayed blank below his question.

Because nothing was worse than doing nothing, he typed again, "Hello? Is anybody there?"

Still nothing. He slammed his fist down on the computer desk so hard, it hurt.

"I have to know!" he shouted. "Tell me! I can't go home until I know!"

He heard the door too late to react. And suddenly a voice boomed behind him: "Turn around slowly. I have a gun. Who are you and why are you here?"

CHAPTER *TWENTY-SEVEN*

L uke stifled his instinct to run. He turned around as slowly as he could. Guns had been outlawed for everyone but Government officials long before he was born. But he recognized the object pointed at him from books and Dad's descriptions. Dad had always talked about hunting rifles and shotguns, big guns to bring down deer or wolves. This gun was smaller. Meant to kill humans.

All that flashed through Luke's mind before he looked beyond the gun, to the man holding it. He was tall and fleshy, his expensive clothes only partially hiding his bulk. Luke had seen him only from a distance before.

"You're Jen's dad," he said.

"I didn't ask who I was," the man snapped. "Who are you?"

Luke exhaled slowly.

"A friend of Jen's," he said cautiously.

Only because he was watching very, very closely did he see the man lower the gun by a fraction of an inch.

"Please," Luke said. "I just want to know where she is."

This time the man clearly relaxed his gun hand. He circled around behind Luke and snapped off the computer.

"Jen says you have to park the hard drive before you do that," Luke said.

"How do you know about Jen?" the man asked. He narrowed his eyes.

Luke blinked. The man was bargaining, he realized, offering to negotiate. He wanted something from Luke before he would tell Luke anything about Jen. But what?

"I'm a third child, too," Luke said finally. The man's expression didn't change, but Luke thought he saw a flicker of interest in his eyes. "I'm a neighbor. I found out about her, and I started coming over, when I could."

"How did you know she was here?" the man said.

"I saw—" Luke didn't want to get her in trouble. "I saw lights when I knew everyone was gone. I guessed. I—I really wanted there to be another third child for me to meet."

"So Jen was careless," the man said, with an edge to his voice that Luke didn't understand.

"No," Luke said uncertainly. "I was observant."

The man nodded, only to accept Luke's answer. Then he sat down in the chair by the computer desk, and rested the gun on his leg. Luke took that as a sign that the conversation might last long enough for him to find out something.

"Did Jen teach you how to disable our alarm system?" the man asked.

Luke saw no point in lying. "Yes. But I must have screwed up, since you came—"

"No," the man said. "If you'd screwed up, the security

guards would have come. But I have it set so I'm automatically notified if the system's shut down while I'm away.... Given the circumstances, I decided to investigate myself."

Luke longed to ask what "circumstances" he meant, but the man was already asking another question. "So what else did you and Jen do together?" the man said. Luke couldn't understand why he sounded so accusatory.

"Nothing," Luke said. "I mean, we talked a lot. She showed me the computer. She—she wanted me to go to the rally, but I was too scared."

Too late, Luke thought to wonder if the man knew about the rally. Was Luke betraying Jen's confidence? But the man didn't seem surprised. He was studying Luke as intently as Luke had been studying him.

"Why didn't you stop her?" the man asked.

"Stop Jen? That's like trying to stop the sun," Luke said.

The man gave Luke the faintest of smiles, one that contained no happiness. "Just remember that," he said.

"So where is she?" Luke asked.

The man looked away.

"Jen's—" His voice broke. "Jen is no longer with us."

"She—?"

"She's dead," the man said harshly.

Somehow Luke had known without wanting to know. He still stumbled backwards, in shock. He bumped into the couch and sagged into it.

"No," he said. "Not Jen. No. You're lying."

His ears roared. He thought crazy things. *This is a dream.*

A nightmare. I will make myself wake up. He remembered Jen talking a mile a minute, gesturing wildly. How could she be dead? He tried to picture her lying still, not moving. Dead. It was impossible.

The man was shaking his head helplessly.

"I'd give anything to have her back," he whispered. "But it's true. I saw. They gave us...they gave us the body. Special privilege for a Government official." His voice was so bitter, Luke could barely listen. "And we couldn't even bury her in the family plot. Couldn't take a bereavement day off work. Couldn't tell anyone why we're going around with red eyes and aching hearts. No—we just had to pretend to be the same old family of four we'd always been."

"How?" Luke asked. "How did she...die?"

He was thinking, if the car had wrecked, it wouldn't be so bad. Or maybe it had nothing to do with the rally. Maybe she just got really sick.

"They shot her," Jen's father said. "They shot all of them. All forty kids at the rally, gunned down right in front of the president's house. The blood flowed into his rose-bushes. But they had the sidewalks scrubbed before the tourists came, so nobody would know."

Luke started shaking his head no, and couldn't stop.

"But Jen said there'd be too many people to shoot. She said there'd be a thousand," Luke protested, as if Jen's words could change what he was hearing.

"Our Jen had too much faith in the bravery of her fellow hidden," Jen's father said.

Luke flinched. "I told her I couldn't go," he said. "I told her! It's not my fault!"

"No," Jen's dad said quietly. "And you couldn't have stopped her. It's not your fault. There are plenty of other people who deserve the blame. They probably would have shot a thousand. Or fifteen thousand. They don't care."

His face twisted. Luke thought he had never seen such pain, not even the time Matthew dropped a sledgehammer on his foot. Tears began to spill down Jen's father's face.

"What I don't understand is—why did she do this, this Children's Crusade? She wasn't stupid. We'd been warning her about the Population Police all her life. Did she really think the rally would work?" he said.

"Yes," Luke assured him. Then, unbidden, the last words she'd spoken to him came back to him: *We can hope*—after she'd told him hope was worthless. Maybe she knew the rally would fail. Maybe she even knew she would probably die. He remembered the first day he'd met her, when she'd cut her hand to cover the drops of his blood on the carpet. There was something strange in Jen he couldn't quite understand, that made her willing to sacrifice herself to help others. Or to try to.

"I think at first she thought the rally would work," Luke told Jen's dad. "And then, even when she wasn't sure…she still had to go. She wouldn't call it off."

"Why?" Jen's dad asked. He was sobbing. "Did she want to die?"

"No," Luke said. "She wanted to live. Not die. Not hide. Live."

The words played over and over again in his brain: "Not hide. Live. Not hide. Live." As long as he held on to them, he felt like Jen was there. She'd just left the room for a minute, to get more potato chips, maybe, and soon she'd be back to lecture him again about how they both deserved a better life than hiding. He could believe it was her voice echoing in his ears.

But if he let go, let the words stop for a minute, he was lost. He felt like the whole world was spinning away from him, and he was all alone. He wanted to cry out, "Jen! Come back!"—as if she could hear him, and stop the spinning, and come to him.

As if from a great distance, Luke heard Jen's father heave a sigh and blow his nose in a businesslike way.

"You may not be ready to hear this," he said. "But—"

Dizzily, Luke raised his head and listened halfheartedly.

"When you logged into that chat room," Jen's father said, "a buzzer went off in a room in Population Police headquarters. They're monitoring the chat room very closely—they found it after the rally. I've managed to...uh, cover up things about Jen, but they'll trace your message back to our computer. The Population Police are backlogged right now, following leads from the rally, so I should have a day or two to come up with a plausible-sounding explanation. But if they investigate too carefully, you may be in danger."

"More than usual?" Luke said sarcastically.

Jen's dad took the question seriously.

"Yes. They will begin actively looking for you. They'll search every house around this one. It wouldn't take them long to find you."

A chill ran down Luke's spine. So he would die, just like Jen. Or not like her—she had gone bravely. He would be caught like a mouse in its hole.

"But if you'll let me," Jen's dad continued, "I can get you a fake I.D. You can be miles away before they come looking."

"You would do that for me?" Luke asked. "Why?"

"Because of Jen."

"But—how?"

"I have connections. You see"—Jen's dad hesitated—"I work for the Population Police."

CHAPTER *TWENTY-EIGHT*

Luke began screaming and couldn't stop. Suddenly his brain didn't seem to have any control whatsoever over what his body did. He felt his legs spring up and propel him toward Jen's dad. He saw his own hand grab for the gun and wrestle it away. He heard a voice he barely recognized as his own scream, again and again, "No! No! No!"

"Stop!" Jen's dad yelled. "Stop, you little fool, before you get us both killed—"

Somehow, the gun was in Luke's hand. Jen's dad lunged at him, and Luke could picture Jen's dad tackling him, just as Jen had tackled him all those months ago. But this time Luke stepped to the side at the last moment, and Jen's dad crashed uselessly into the far wall. Luke pointed the gun at him and struggled to hold it steady.

Jen's dad turned around slowly.

"You can shoot me," he said, holding his hands helplessly up in the air. "I might even welcome the chance to stop missing Jen. But it would be a mistake. I swear to you, in the name of everything that's sacred—in Jen's name— I'm on your side."

Jen's dad stared into Luke's eyes, waiting. Luke felt a surge of pride that he'd gotten the upper hand, that he had earned the right to decide what happened next. But how could he know what was right? Surely Jen's own father wouldn't lie in her name. Would he?

Luke squeezed his eyes shut. Then he lowered the gun to his side.

"Good," Jen's dad said, audibly releasing his breath.

Luke let Jen's dad walk toward him, gently take the gun, and lay it on the desk.

"I was going to explain," Jen's dad said, panting a little. He sat down. "I only work at Population Police headquarters. I don't agree with what they do. I try to sabotage them as much as I can. Jen never understood, either— sometimes you have to work from inside enemy lines."

Jen's dad talked and talked and talked. Luke thought he was repeating everything he said two or three times, but that was okay, because Luke's brain was functioning so slowly, he needed the extra help.

"Do you know much history?" Jen's dad asked.

Luke tried to remember if there were any history books among his family's collection in the attic. Did adventure stories of long ago count?

"Just—" He cleared his throat. "Just from the books Jen loaned me."

"Which ones?"

Luke pointed to the ones on the shelves above the computer.

"And she gave me some articles, printouts from the computer."

Jen's dad nodded. "So you got the propaganda from both sides," he said. "No truth."

"What do you mean?" Luke asked.

"The Government publications are trying to convince people of one thing, so they stretch the facts. And the underground is just as extreme in its own way, making statistics match their cause. So you know nothing."

"Jen said the stuff from the computer was true," Luke said defensively. Just saying her name made him wince. And now she was dead. How could she be dead?

Jen's dad waved that away impatiently.

"She believed what she wanted to. But I'm afraid—" He stopped, and Luke was afraid Jen's dad might start crying again. Then he swallowed hard and went on. "I'm afraid I encouraged her. I passed along some slanted information. I wanted to give her hope that someday the Population Law would be repealed. I didn't know she'd...she'd..."

Luke knew he wouldn't be able to bear seeing Jen's dad break down again.

"So what should I know?" Luke asked. "What is the truth?"

"The truth," Jen's dad muttered, catching onto those two words as though Luke had thrown him a lifeline. He recovered himself quickly. "Nobody really knows. There have been too many lies for too long. Our Government is totalitarian, and totalitarian governments never like truth."

That made no sense to Luke, but he let Jen's dad go on talking.

"You know about the famines?"

Luke nodded.

"Before that, our country believed in freedom and democracy and equality for all. Then the famines came, and the government was overthrown. There were riots in every city, over food, and many, many people were killed. When General Sherwood came to power, he promised law and order and food for all. By then, that was all the people wanted. And all they got."

Luke squinted, trying to understand. This was grown-up talk, pure and simple. No, it was worse than the grown-up talk he was used to, because all his parents ever talked about was the corn harvest and bills and the likelihood of frost at the end of May. Those Luke understood. Governments being overthrown, cities rioting—they were beyond his comprehension.

"Barons got more," he blurted, then blushed because it sounded so rude.

Jen's dad laughed. "True. You noticed. I know it's not fair, and I'm not proud of it, but...Government officials made a conscious decision to allow one class of people to have special privileges—Jen probably introduced you to junk food, didn't she?"

Luke nodded.

"That's a good example. Officially, it's illegal, but no one ever got arrested for supplying Barons with junk food. Which is mighty convenient, considering that all the powerful Government officials are Barons." The cynicism in his voice sounded so much like Jen that Luke almost gave in to grief again. But he forced himself to focus on what Jen's dad was saying.

"The Government justifies keeping everyone else in poverty because people seem to work the hardest when they're right on the edge of survival," he continued. "The Government does try to make sure that most people—the ones who cooperate—do survive. If you've heard your parents talking about other farmers, you'll know that nobody loses their farms anymore. But, also, nobody ever makes enough to live comfortably."

Luke thought about his parents' constant worries about money. Was it all unnecessary? Were they just being manipulated? He felt a spark of anger, but buried that, too, because he had other questions.

"But even Barons have to follow the Population Law," he said. "Is that because"—he gulped—"because it's necessary? Were there too many people? Are there?"

"Probably not," Jen's dad said. "If food had been distributed fairly...if people hadn't panicked...if we'd had good leaders being honest about the need for everyone's cooperation...we could have survived the crisis without curtailing anyone's rights. And now—it shouldn't be a problem if some people choose to have three or four kids, as long as some other people choose to have none. But the Population Law became General Sherwood's proudest accomplishment. That's why even Barons aren't exempt. He points to that and says, 'See how much control I have over my people's lives.'"

"So it is wrong," Luke said, trying to grasp the point.

"I believe so. Yes," Jen's dad said.

Luke felt a strange sense of relief, that it wasn't truly wrong for him to exist, just illegal. For the first time since he'd read the Government books, he could see the two things being separate. Maybe that was why he'd been too scared to go to the rally. If he'd truly believed, the way Jen had, then he might have gone.

And would he have been killed, as she was?

It was all too confusing and scary to think about.

Jen's father looked at his watch.

"I need to get back to work. I can only hide so much. If you want it, I can have the fake I.D. for you by tomorrow night. In the meantime, I'd advise you to—"

He broke off. Luke knew why: a sound from his worst nightmares—pounding on the door, and then the command, "Open up! Population Police!"

CHAPTER TWENTY-NINE

Before Luke had a chance to move, Jen's dad had picked him up and thrust him into the closet.

"There's a secret door at the back," he hissed. "Use it."

Luke groped blindly, fighting through what felt like piles of hair. Behind him, he could hear Jen's dad yelling, "I'm coming! I'm coming! That's a twelve-thousand-dollar door. If you break it down, you're going to pay!" Then Luke heard the computer making its *be-be-be-beeep!* and Jen's dad muttering, "Fine time for them to discover efficiency. Come on, come on, connect—"

The pounding at the door grew louder, and a gruff voice yelled out, "You have three seconds, George!"

Luke dug deeper into the closet. He couldn't even find the back wall, let alone any secret door. And then he heard a splintering sound from the front of the house. Seconds later, there were stomping footsteps in the computer room.

"What is the meaning of this?"

It was Jen's dad's voice coming from the hall, full of outrage. If he hadn't witnessed it himself, Luke never would have guessed that Jen's dad had been crying only moments before. He sounded too forceful, too assured, too confident that he was right and anyone who opposed him was wrong. The stomping stopped. From deep inside the closet, Luke heard someone snicker.

"Caught you with your pants down, eh, George?"

"Yes, yes, very funny," Jen's father replied, not sounding the least bit amused. There was a sound that could have been a zipper being zipped. "Has it come to this? A man can't even go to the bathroom without his door being broken down by a bunch of morons with power complexes? And you will pay for that door, I assure you."

If Luke had been one of the Population Police, Jen's dad would have scared him to pieces. Luke would have backed out, muttering, "I'm sorry. I'm sorry." He never would have believed that Jen's dad was hiding a third child. Hopefully, Luke paused in his burrowing into the Talbots' closet.

But the voice that answered Jen's father carried only the slightest edge of doubt.

"Come off it, George. You know we're entitled to search and seizure. We have reports of that computer being used for illegal purposes. Just a half an hour ago."

"You're even bigger fools than I thought," Jen's dad answered. "Don't any of you read your memos? I reported to Central Command this morning that I was going to continue my sting operation in the illegal chat rooms. See, I wrote, 'Where's Jen?' and, 'Hello? Is anybody there?', which is what some lost, confused, third child who missed the rally might write. Are you so low-ranking that you don't know I was pretending to be the guerrilla leader Jen all along? Did you miss the commendation ceremony where I was rewarded for the disposal of forty illegals?"

Luke wondered that Jen's dad could say her name without his voice giving him away. If Luke didn't know Jen—hadn't known her, he corrected himself with a wince—and if he didn't know how much she'd trusted her father, he would have been certain that Jen's father had double-crossed her. As it was, his head swam with the fear that Jen's father still might betray him. How could he trust anyone who spoke so coldly of the "disposal" of third children? Luke struggled on through the closet, reaching a stack of blankets at the back. Finally he touched the wall, but everything he felt was smooth. Jen's father said there was a door. There had to be a door.

The voices from outside the closet were muffled now.

"—see the memo—"

"I'm sure it's on your desk back at the office, with all the paperwork you never read." Jen's dad raised his voice, so Luke could hear him clearly. "Or can you even read?"

The Population Police officer ignored the insult.

"Show us on the computer."

"Very well."

Luke prayed that Jen's dad had something to show them. He could not find the door, though he ran his fingers along the wall, again and again. His heart was beating so loudly, he was sure the Population Police could hear him.

All he could hear of the Population Police and Jen's father were mutterings. Then the one officer's voice rang out, "You're lying, George. We're going to search."

"Just because of a computer malfunction? Fine. It's not my problem." Luke was stunned by the indifference in Jen's father's voice. "But when you don't find anything— and you won't—you know that I'm entitled to the Illegal Search and Seizure Benefits granted to Barons, and I will press charges. Should I use the extra money on caviar or champagne?"

"Aw, George, you wouldn't really sue."

"You don't think so? Then go ahead. Start here."

Suddenly the closet was flooded with light. Luke stifled a gasp. How could Jen's father have flung open the door of the very place Luke was hiding? Desperately, Luke yanked a blanket over his head.

None of the Population Police answered Jen's father, but the pattern of shadows that fell on Luke's blanket made him think the Population Police were standing right in the doorway of the closet. He heard hangers scraping against a metal bar. And then the Population Police walked away.

Confused and terrified, Luke remained huddled under the blanket. He could hear muffled footfalls elsewhere in the house, and was certain they'd be returning to the computer room any minute. Before they killed him, he hoped they let him go back to his parents and tell them how much he loved them. He could apologize to Matthew and Mark, too, for not appreciating the checkers and card games they played with him when he knew they'd rather be outside. And probably he should apologize to his parents for disobeying, and coming to Jen's house in the first place. Except, even scared to death of being found, he couldn't scrape up full regret for that.

Anyhow, it wasn't likely that they'd let him see his parents before they killed him. He'd have to protect his parents, and refuse to even reveal who they were....

Luke's mind was still racing with frantic plans when he heard someone coming back to the computer room. There was only one set of footsteps, so he dared to hope—

"You could have swept up the glass on your way out!"

It was Jen's dad. Luke strained to hear an answer, but none came. Were the Population Police gone?

Luke kept his head down. He heard Jen's dad wading into the closet. Then he pulled the blanket off Luke and clamped his hand over Luke's mouth. Luke started to struggle until he read the words on the paper Jen's dad held in front of his face:

They're gone.

You're safe,

but

DON'T TALK!!!

Luke relaxed and nodded to show he would obey. Jen's dad released him, flipped the paper over, and began writing furiously.

House bugged now.

Luke gave Jen's dad a puzzled look.

"B—" he started to say, then remembered and stopped. He took the pen from Jen's dad and wrote, *Bugged? Ants? Roaches?*

Jen's dad shook his head frantically. *Bugs = little listening devices—Population Police hear everything. That's why can't talk. They do that when a bust's unsuccessful. Even left one bug on me.*

Jen's dad turned around and pointed, and Luke saw a small disc sticking to the back of his collar.

Luke frowned and wrote on the paper, *Why not take off?*

Jen's dad shook his head. *Safer this way. Long as they think they hear everything, they won't come back.*

Jen's dad pointed to the hairy lumps on the hangers behind him.

Bribed them with fur coats. Very rare, very valuable.

Luke looked at the coats. There did seem to be a lot fewer of them now. Were they animal skins? Why would anyone want such a thing? He couldn't ask, though, because Jen's dad was already scribbling more.

Just bought time. My goose probably cooked now—I didn't file that memo. They'll find out.

Luke reached for the pen. *What will they do to you?*

Jen's dad shook his head. *Don't know,* he wrote. *I've survived this kind of thing before. But everything's chancy now. The fact they got here so fast = they have it in for me.*

Weakly, Luke leaned his head back against the closet wall. That reminded him of his frantic search along its surface. He reached for the paper and wrote, *Where's the door?*

Jen's dad pulled out a new sheet of paper. Shaking his head, he wrote, *Isn't one. Just wanted to get you to back of closet.*

Luke buried his face in his hands. Jen's dad was a good liar, there was no doubt about that. How could Luke trust him? Luke raised his head and watched as Jen's dad scribbled something else on the paper. His expression was full of concern, and Luke knew, somehow, that he was trustworthy. He easily could have turned Luke in, and gotten praise and another commendation ceremony. But how confusing, to never know when someone was lying.

Jen's dad turned the paper to face Luke. It said, *So. Want fake I.D. or not?*

Luke gulped. After a minute, he wrote back, *Am I safe if I don't?*

Jen's dad seemed to be weighing the question. He narrowed his eyes and wrote, *Probably. They're after me now, not you. If they really thought there was an illegal here, they wouldn't take bribe. Or would take it and you, too. But I'd advise—get I.D.*

Luke wrote back, *Can't I wait? Think about it for a while?*

That was what Luke wanted. Or not even to think, but to hide from thinking for a while. He wanted to remember Jen, and grieve for her by himself. He didn't want to have to think about what parts of the Population Law were good, and what parts were bad, or why his family didn't have more money. He didn't want to have to figure out Jen's dad, and other people like him, who could pretend to be so many different things. He didn't want to have to decide something now that could change the rest of his life.

But Jen's dad had written back, *Don't know. May be case of 'now or never.'*

Luke scrawled, *Why?*

Jen's dad wrote for a long time. Then he turned the paper to Luke. It said: *I have power now. Tomorrow, probably. Next week????? Next year????? Can't tell with our Gov't. Favored lackey one day,* persona non grata *the next. Never know. No guarantees.*

Luke stared at the paper until the words blurred together. He had to decide. Now.

He thought about reading and daydreaming in the attic the rest of his life. His parents were kind to him, even if they weren't around much. And as much as Matthew and Mark had always teased him, he was pretty sure they would take care of him if his parents couldn't someday. His life was very limited—he understood that now more than ever. But he was used to it. It was safe. He could make himself be happy.

Except...

Luke remembered how bored he'd felt before meeting Jen, how desperate he'd been to do something—anything!—besides read and daydream. He'd been so desperate that he'd risked his life for the chance of meeting another third child. Did he want to spend the rest of his life feeling that desperate? Did he want to just...waste it?

But even if he got a fake I.D., what would he do?

The answer was there instantly, as if he'd known it all

along and his brain was just waiting for him to come looking.

He could do something to help other third children come out of hiding. Not with another big dramatic rally, like Jen had tried, or by finding fake I.D.'s the way Jen's dad did. Maybe there was something smaller and slower he could do. Studying ways to grow more food, so no one would go hungry, no matter how many kids people had. Or changing the Government so that farmers were allowed to raise pigs or use hydroponics, and ordinary people, not just Barons, could have better lives. Or figuring out ways for people to live in outer space, so they wouldn't be too crowded on Earth and chop down beautiful woods just for houses. He didn't know exactly how he could do those things, or even what the right thing to do was. But he wanted to do something.

He remembered what he'd told Jen, the last time he'd seen her: *It's people like you who change history. People like me— we just let things happen to us.* And he'd believed it. That was how his family had always lived. But maybe that was wrong. Maybe he could succeed where Jen had failed precisely because he wasn't a Baron—because he didn't have her sense that the world owed him everything. He could be more patient, more cautious, more practical.

But he'd never be able to do anything staying in hiding.

He bit his lip. His hand shook as he wrote his answer.

I want a fake I.D. Please.

CHAPTER *THIRTY*

L ee Grant settled into the car that would take him away from the farm where he'd found refuge, after running away from home. He'd gotten lost—he'd certainly never intended to end up *here*. He surveyed the dusty barnyard in front of him, the ugly ruts of dried mud where tractors and trucks had left their tracks. He stared at the ramshackle barn and the peeling paint on the weathered house, sights that should have been entirely foreign to him, but weren't. He—

Luke gulped, unable to keep thinking in his new identity quite yet. It was too soon, too hard, when his shoulders still felt the warmth of Mother's last hug. He looked down at his hands, clenched together in his lap, and they already seemed like someone else's against the background of his crisp new trousers. No more ragged blue jeans and hand-me-down flannel shirts for him—he had a whole suitcase in the trunk full of the same kind of fancy Baron clothes he'd laughed at all those months ago. He didn't care about the clothes, but he wished they'd let him keep his name, at least. Yet Jen's father had been proud that he'd gotten to keep the same initials.

"A rush job like this, it's a wonder you're not stuck with Alphonse Xerxes," he'd bragged in the letter he'd dropped off the night before, pretending he was just coming to ask Luke's parents to cut back the willow tree that draped over onto the Talbots' land.

The real Lee Grant was a Baron. He had died in a skiing accident just the night before. His parents wanted nothing to do with Luke—"too painful," Jen's father had explained—but they had agreed to donate their son's name and identity card the way people had once donated hearts and kidneys. Some secret group that helped third children had arranged it. The group also had agreed to pay for Luke to go to a private school as a boarder, year-round. Supposedly he was transferring in during the middle of a term as punishment for running away. He'd read about such places in the old books in the attic. It seemed a strange way to live, without family, but he was just as glad not to have to pretend to love another set of parents.

Now Luke looked back at his family's porch, where Mother and Dad and Matthew and Mark were standing and already waving. Dad and Matthew looked gruff, and Mark merely looked serious—strange enough for him—but tears were streaming down Mother's face.

She'd cried, too, the night Luke had told his parents everything.

He'd started with his first visit to Jen's house, and Mother had immediately scolded, "Oh, Luke, how could you? The danger...I know you're lonely, but honey, promise us, never again..."

"That's not all," Luke said.

He told the rest of the story without looking at her, until he reached the end and his decision to get a fake I.D. Then the sound of her sobbing made it impossible to avoid looking. She was red-eyed, devastated.

"Luke, no. You can't," she'd gasped. "Don't you know how we'd miss you?"

"But, Mother, I don't want to go," Luke said. "It's just that...I have to. I can't spend the rest of my life hiding in the attic. What will happen when you and Dad can't take care of me anymore?"

"Matthew or Mark will," she replied.

"But I don't want to be a burden on them. I want to do something with my life. Figure out ways to help other third kids. Make—" All the things he'd thought of sounded too childish to explain, in the face of Mother's sobbing. So he finished weakly, "Make a difference in the world."

"I'm not saying you can never do that," she answered. "But that's years away. We'll figure out some way to get a fake I.D. for you when you're grown up. Somehow." She turned to Luke's father. "Tell him, Harlan."

Dad sighed heavily.

"The boy's right. He needs to go now, if he can."

Luke could tell his father's words came out painfully, but they still stabbed at him. Maybe part of him had been secretly hoping his parents would forbid him to go, would lock him in the attic and keep him as their little boy forever.

"I've checked around some, quietlike, to see if anyone's heard of a third child getting to live a normal life. Around here, they can't," Dad said. "Far as I can tell, he's not going to get another chance."

Luke turned back to his mother, because it was too hard to look at Dad while he was saying that. But the pain twisting Mother's face was worse.

"Then I guess we don't have a choice," she'd murmured.

That had been two days ago, and ever since then she'd called in sick to work and stayed home, spending every second with Luke. They'd played board games and cards, but she'd interrupted every move with, "Do you remember..." or, "I remember..."

The coos he'd made as a baby. His first steps. His delight in discovering dirt the spring he was two. The first time he'd hoed a straight row. The zucchini he'd grown as long as his arm. The bedtime stories and tucking-ins.

She was filling him up with memories, he knew, for the times when he'd have no one to talk to about his childhood. But it was hard to listen to. He wished they could just move their Monopoly pieces and pretend the time wasn't ticking away.

But all too soon this morning had come. Jen's dad had pulled up in his fancy car, and sprang out to shake hands with Luke's parents.

"Mr. Garner, Mrs. Garner, thank you very much for reporting this boy's arrival immediately. From what I hear, the Grants were worried sick." He turned to Luke. "Young man, what you did was irresponsible and reckless. The only smart thing you did was remember to take your I.D. card. I guess you must have heard that the Population Police shoot first and ask questions later."

He clapped Luke on the back and slid his hand down to slip something into Luke's pocket. Luke reached down to touch the stiff edge of an I.D. card. His I.D. card.

"Do we have to start pretending already?" Luke's mother whispered, the tears beginning in her eyes.

Jen's dad was shaking his head sternly and patting his chest, as if looking for something in a hidden pocket.

"Bugged," he mouthed.

When Luke's parents nodded to show they understood, he stopped patting and pulled out an official-looking paper.

"Ah, here they are. Your travel papers. Your parents are sending you to Hendricks School for Boys. And if you don't shape up—" Jen's dad gave him a stern look that somehow also conveyed his sympathy.

"Would"—Mother cleared her throat—"Would it be all right if we gave him a good-bye hug? We've gotten kind of fond of him in…in the time he's been here."

Jen's father nodded, and then both Luke's parents held him tight and released him.

"Be a good boy, now, you hear?" Mother said. Luke could tell she was trying to make it jokey, the way she might talk to some other mother's runaway son. But for the life of him, he couldn't come back with a joking response. He only nodded, blinking hard.

And then he stumbled to the car and tried to be Lee.

Jen's dad circled the car and slid in on the driver's side. He started the car and pulled out.

"You're just lucky you're getting such a highly paid chauffeur," he said. "If I weren't a personal friend of your father's cousin—"

Luke wasn't sure if there was a hidden message in the words, or if Jen's dad was just talking for the sake of the bug. He decided he couldn't analyze it yet. He peered back at his frantically waving family until they were out of sight. Soon the car was passing the other side of the barn and the field beyond, views Luke had never seen, though he'd lived his entire life within a hundred yards of them. In spite of the fear gnawing in his stomach and the anguish of missing his family—already—he felt a thrill of excitement. There was so much to see. He'd have to tell Jen—

Jen. The grief he'd been avoiding for days welled over him again. But, "I'm doing this for you, too, Jen," he whispered, too softly for Jen's dad or the bug to hear over the car's hum. "Someday when we're all free, all the third children, I'll tell everyone about you. They'll erect statues to you, and name holidays after you...." It wasn't much, but it made him feel better. A little.

Luke stared back at his family's farm as long as he could. He could see just the roof of Jen's house beyond the sparse line of trees. And then, in no time at all, it seemed, everything familiar disappeared over the horizon.

Lee Grant turned around to see what lay ahead.

For Doug

Among
the Impostors

CHAPTER *ONE*

S ometimes he whispered his real name in the dark, in the middle of the night.

"Luke. My name is Luke."

He was sure no one could hear. His roommates were all asleep, and even if they weren't, there was no way the sound of his name could travel even the short distance to the bed above or beside him. He was fairly certain there were no bugs on him or in his room. He'd looked. But even if he'd missed seeing a microphone hidden in a mattress button or carved into the headboard, how could a microphone pick up a whisper he could barely hear himself?

He was safe now. Lying in bed, wide awake while everyone else slept, he reassured himself of that fact constantly. But his heart pounded and his face went clammy with fear every time he rounded his lips for that "u" sound—instead of the fake smile of the double "e" in Lee, the name he had to force himself to answer to now.

It was better to forget, to never speak his real name again.

But he'd lost everything else. Even just mouthing his

name was a comfort. It seemed like his only link now to his past, to his parents, his brothers.

To Jen.

By day, he kept his mouth shut.

He couldn't help it.

That first day, walking up the stairs of the Hendricks School for Boys with Jen's father, Luke had felt his jaw clench tighter and tighter the closer he got to the front door.

"Oh, don't look like that," Mr. Talbot had said, pretending to be jolly. "It's not reform school or anything."

The word stuck in Luke's brain. Reform. Re-form. Yes, they were going to re-form him. They were going to take a Luke and make him a Lee.

It was safe to be Lee. It wasn't safe to be Luke.

Jen's father stood with his hand on the ornate doorknob, waiting for a reply. But Luke couldn't have said a word if his life depended on it.

Jen's father hesitated, then pulled on the heavy door. They walked down a long hallway. The ceiling was so far away, Luke thought he could have stood his entire family on his shoulders—one on top of the other, Dad and Mother and Matthew and Mark—and the highest one still would barely touch. The walls were lined, floor to ceiling, with old paintings of people in costumes Luke had never seen outside of books.

Of course, there was very little he'd ever seen outside of books.

He tried not to stare, because if he really were Lee, surely everything would look familiar and ordinary. But that was hard to remember. They passed a classroom where dozens of boys sat in orderly rows, everyone facing away from the door. Luke gawked for so long that he practically began walking backwards. He'd known there were a lot of people in the world, but he'd never been able to imagine so many all in one place at the same time. Were any of them shadow children with fake identities, like Luke?

Jen's father clapped a hand on his shoulder, turning him around.

"Ah, here's the headmaster's office," Mr. Talbot said heartily. "Just what we were looking for."

Luke nodded, still mute, and followed him through a tall doorway.

A woman sitting behind a mammoth wood desk turned their way. She took one look at Luke and asked, "New boy?"

"Lee Grant," Jen's father said. "I spoke with the master about him last night."

"It's the middle of the semester, you know," she said warningly. "Unless he's very well prepared, he shan't catch up, and might have to repeat—"

"That won't be a problem," Mr. Talbot assured her. Luke was glad he didn't have to speak for himself. He knew he wasn't well prepared. He wasn't prepared for anything.

The woman was already reaching for files and papers.

"His parents faxed in his medical information and his

insurance standing and his academic records last night," she said. "But someone needs to sign these—"

Jen's father took the stack of papers as if he autographed other people's documents all the time.

Probably he did.

Luke watched Mr. Talbot flip through the papers, scrawling his name here, crossing out a word or a phrase or a whole paragraph there. Luke was sure Jen's father was going too fast to actually read any of it.

And that was when the homesickness hit Luke for the first time. He could just picture his own father peering cautiously at important papers, reading them over and over before he even picked up a pen. Luke could see his father's rheumy eyes squinted in concentration, his brow furrowed with anxiety.

He was always so afraid of being tricked.

Maybe Jen's father didn't care.

Luke had to swallow hard then. He made a gulping noise, and the woman looked at him. Luke couldn't read her expression. Curiosity? Contempt? Indifference?

He didn't think it was sympathy.

Jen's father finished then, handing the papers back to the woman with a flourish.

"I'll call a boy to show you your room," the woman said to Luke.

Luke nodded. The woman leaned over a box on her desk and said, "Mr. Dirk, could you send Rolly Sturgeon to the office?"

Luke heard a roar along with the man's reply, "Yes, Ms. Hawkins," as if all the boys in the school were laughing and cheering and hissing at once. Luke felt his legs go weak with fear. When this Rolly Sturgeon showed up, Luke wasn't sure he'd be able to walk.

"Well, I'll be off," Jen's father said. "Duty calls."

He stuck out his hand and after a moment Luke realized he was supposed to shake it. But he'd never shaken hands with anyone before, so he put out the wrong hand first. Jen's father frowned, moving his head violently side to side, and glaring pointedly at the woman behind the desk. Fortunately, she wasn't watching. Luke recovered. He clumsily touched his hand to Jen's father's.

"Good luck," Jen's father said, bringing his other hand up to Luke's, too.

Only when Mr. Talbot had pulled both hands away did Luke realize he'd placed a tiny scrap of paper between Luke's fingers. Luke held it there until the woman turned her back. Then he slid it into his pocket.

Jen's father smiled.

"Keep those grades up," he said. "And no running away this time, you hear?"

Luke gulped again, and nodded. And then Jen's father left without a backward glance.

CHAPTER *TWO*

uke wanted to read the note from Mr. Talbot right away. He was sure it would tell him everything—everything he needed to know to survive Hendricks School for Boys. No—to survive anything that might come his way in this new life, outside hiding.

It was just one thin scrap of paper. Now that it was in his pocket, Luke couldn't even feel it there. But he had faith. Jen's father had hidden Luke from the Population Police, double-crossing his own employer. He'd gotten Luke his fake I.D., so he could move about as freely as any-one else, anyone who wasn't an illegal third child. Jen's father had risked his career helping Luke. No, it was more than that—he'd risked his life. Surely Mr. Talbot would have written something incredibly wise.

Luke slid his hand into his pocket, his fingertips touching the top of the note. Ms. Hawkins was looking away. Maybe—

The door opened behind Luke. Luke jerked his hand out of his pocket.

"Scared you, didn't I?" a boy jeered. "Made you jump."

Luke was used to being teased. He had older brothers,

MARGARET PETERSON HADDIX

after all. But Matthew and Mark's teasing never sounded quite so mean. Still, Luke knew he had to answer.

"Sure. I'm jumpy like a cat," Luke started to say. It was an expression of his mother's. Being cat-jumpy was good. Like being quick on his feet.

Just in time, Luke remembered he couldn't mention cats. Cats were illegal, too, outlawed because they might take food that was supposed to go to starving humans. Back home, Luke had seen wild cats a few times, stalking the countryside. Dad had liked having them around because they ate rats and mice that might eat his grain. But if Luke were really Lee Grant, filthy-rich city boy, he wouldn't know a thing about cats, jumpy or otherwise.

He clamped his mouth shut, closing off his "Sure—" in a wimpy hiss. He kept his head down, too scared to look the other boy right in the eye.

The boy laughed, cruelly. He looked past Luke, to Ms. Hawkins.

"What's wrong with him?" the boy asked, as if Luke weren't even there. "Can't talk or something?"

Luke wanted Ms. Hawkins to stick up for him, to say, "He's just new. Don't you remember what that's like?" But she wasn't even paying attention. She frowned at the boy.

"Rolly, take him to room one fifty-six. There's an empty bed in there. Just put his suitcase down. Don't waste time unpacking. Then take him back to Mr. Dirk's history class with you. He's already behind. Lord knows what his parents were thinking."

Rolly shrugged and turned around.

"I did not dismiss you!" Ms. Hawkins shrieked.

"May I be dismissed?" Rolly asked mockingly.

"That's better," Ms. Hawkins said. "Now, get. Go on with you."

Luke picked up his suitcase and followed, hoping Rolly's request for dismissal would work for both of them. Either it did, or Ms. Hawkins didn't care.

In the hallway, Rolly took big steps. He was a good head taller than Luke, and had longer legs. It was all Luke could do to keep up, what with the suitcase banging against his ankles.

Rolly looked back over his shoulder, and started walking faster. He raced up a long stairway. By the time Luke reached the top, Rolly was nowhere in sight.

"Boo!"

Rolly leaped out from behind the newel post. Luke jumped so high, he lost his balance and teetered on the edge of the stairs. Rolly reached out, and Luke thought, *See, he's not so bad. He's going to catch me.* But Rolly pushed instead. Luke fell backwards. He might have tumbled down all the stairs, except that Rolly's push was crooked, and Luke landed on the railing. Pain shot through his back.

Rolly laughed.

"Got you good, didn't I?" he said.

Then, strangely, he grabbed Luke's bag and took off down the hall.

Luke was afraid he was stealing it. He galloped after Rolly.

Rolly screamed with laughter, maniacally.

This was not what Luke had expected.

Rolly dodged around a corner and Luke followed him. Rolly discovered a secret about Luke's bag that Luke had missed—it was on wheels. So Rolly could run at full-speed with the bag rolling behind him. He careened this way and that, the bag zigzagging from side to side. Luke got close enough to tackle it if he wanted, but he hesitated. If the bag had been full of his own clothes, all the hand-me-down jeans and flannel shirts he'd gotten after Matthew and Mark outgrew them, he would have leaped. But the bag held Baron clothes, stiff shirts and shiny pants that were supposed to make him look like Lee Grant, instead of Luke Garner. He couldn't risk ruining them. He focused on Rolly instead. Instinctively, Luke dove over the bag to catch Rolly's legs. It was like playing football. Rolly fell to the ground with a crash.

"Just what is the meaning of this?" a man's voice boomed above them.

Rolly was instantly on his feet.

"He attacked me, sir," Rolly said. "I was showing the new boy his room and he attacked me."

Luke opened his mouth to protest, but nothing came out. He'd learned that from Matthew and Mark: Don't tattle.

The man looked dismissively from Rolly to Luke.

"What is your name, young man?"

Luke froze. He had to stop himself from saying his real name automatically. Then he had a split second of fearing he wouldn't be able to remember the name he was supposed to use. Was he taking too long? The man's glare intensified.

"L-L-Lee. Lee Grant," Luke finally stammered.

"Well, Mr. Grant," the man snapped. "This is a fine way to begin your academic career at Hendricks. You and Mr. Sturgeon each have two demerits for this disgraceful display. You may report to my room after the final bell to do your time."

"But, sir, I told you," Rolly protested. "He attacked me."

"Very well, Mr. Sturgeon. Make that three demerits for each of you."

"But—" Rolly was undeterred.

"Four."

Rolly was going to complain again. Luke could tell by the way he was standing. But the man turned away and began walking down the hall, as if Rolly and Luke were both too unimportant to bother with, and he'd wasted enough time already.

Luke's head swam with questions. What were demerits? When was final bell? Where was this man's room? Who was he, anyway? Luke tried to muster up the nerve to call after the man—or to ask Rolly, which seemed even more dangerous. But then he was blindsided with a shove that sent him crashing into the wall.

"Fonrol!" Rolly exploded.

Luke slumped against the wall. His shoulder throbbed. Why did Rolly seem to hate him so much?

"Well, come on, you little exnay," Rolly taunted. "Want to get demerits from Mr. Dirk, too?"

He stepped backwards, tugging on Luke's suitcase. Then he shoved it through a nearby doorway. Luke looked up and saw 156 etched on a copper plaque on the door. Relief overwhelmed him. Finally something made sense. This was his room. The rest of the day would be horrible—he'd already resigned himself to that. But eventually it would be night, and he'd be sent to bed, and he could come to this room and shut the door. And then he could read the note from Jen's dad, if he didn't get a chance to read it before bedtime. Come nightfall, he'd know everything and be safe, alone in his own room.

Imagining the haven that awaited him in only a matter of hours, he got brave enough to peek around the corner.

The room held eight beds.

Seven of them were made up, with rich blue spreads stretched tautly from top to bottom. Only one, a lower bunk, was covered just by sheets.

Luke felt as desolate as that bed looked. He knew it was his. And he knew he wouldn't get to be alone in this room.

He probably wouldn't be safe, either, not if any of his seven roommates were anything like Rolly.

He edged his hand into his pocket, his fingers brushing the note from Jen's dad. What if he just pulled it out and read it now, right in front of Rolly?

He didn't dare. The way the last ten minutes had gone, Rolly would probably rip the note to shreds before Luke even had it completely out of his pocket.

And Jen's dad had acted like it was secret. If Ms. Hawkins wasn't supposed to see it, there was no way Rolly could be trusted.

Rolly hit Luke on the shoulder.

"Tag! You're it!" he hollered, and took off running. Panicked, Luke chased after him.

CHAPTER *THREE*

Luke managed to keep up with Rolly only because Rolly slowed to a dignified walk when he began passing classrooms instead of sleeping quarters. But it was a fast dignified walk, and Luke was terrified that Rolly might dart around a corner unexpectedly and disappear. Then Luke would be totally lost. So Luke dared to jog a little, hoping to keep pace.

A tall, thin man with a skimpy mustache came out of one of the rooms as Luke passed by.

"Two demerits, young man," he said to Luke. "No running allowed. You know the rules."

Luke didn't, and didn't have the nerve to say so.

Rolly smirked.

The thin man went back into his classroom. Luke knew he'd have to risk asking Rolly a question.

"Wha—" he began. But just then Rolly opened a tall, wooden door to one side of the hall and slipped through. Luke's reflexes weren't fast enough. The door shut behind Rolly and then Luke had to fumble with the knob. It was ornate and gold, and had to be turned further to the right than all the doorknobs at home.

Home . . .

For the second time in less than an hour, Luke was overcome with an almost unbearable wave of homesickness.

Stupid, Luke chided himself. *How can you be homesick for doorknobs?*

Blinking quickly, he shoved on the door and it gave way. Blindly, he stepped in.

He was at the back of a huge classroom. Boys sat in row upon row upon row, dozens of them, it seemed to Luke, all the way to the front of the room. There, the tall, thin man who'd just given Luke demerits was writing on the wall.

Or was it the same man? Luke squinted, confused. Oh. There was a door at the front of the room, too. That was the door the man had used. But had Luke and Rolly really walked so far between the doors? Suddenly, Luke wasn't sure of anything.

Luke scanned the row of boys in front of him, looking for Rolly. He was supposed to stay close to Rolly, so that's what he'd do. But now he couldn't even remember if Rolly had brown hair or black, short or long, curly or straight. He'd really never looked that closely at Rolly, just followed him and gotten beat up by him. Any of the heads in front of him might belong to Rolly.

The man at the front of the class turned around.

"And the Greeks were—sit down—" he interrupted himself impatiently.

He was looking at Luke.

"M-Me?" Luke squeaked. "W-Where should I sit?"

His voice wasn't much more than a whisper. There was no way the man could have heard him, all the way at the front of the room. Probably the boy sitting a foot away hadn't even heard him. But suddenly every boy in the room turned around and stared at Luke.

It was awful. All those eyes, all looking at him. It was straight out of Luke's worst nightmares. Panic rooted him to the spot, but every muscle in his body was screaming for him to run, to hide anywhere he could. For twelve years—his entire life—he'd had to hide. To be seen was death. "Don't!" he wanted to scream. "Don't look at me! Don't report me! Please!"

But the muscles that controlled his mouth were as frozen as the rest of him. The tiny part of his mind that wasn't flooded with panic knew that that was good—now that he had a fake I.D., the last thing he should do was act like a boy who's had to hide. But to act normal, he needed to move, to obey the man at the front and sit down. And he couldn't make his body do that, either.

Then someone kicked him.

"Ow!" Luke crumbled.

Rough hands jerked him backwards. Miraculously, he landed on the corner of a chair, barely regained his balance, and managed not to fall completely. He slid to his right and was solidly in the seat.

"*Thank* you," the man at the front said with exaggerated,

mocking gratitude. "See me after class. As I was saying before I was so rudely interrupted, the Greeks were quite technologically advanced for their time. . . ."

Then Luke could no longer hear the man's words over the buzzing in his ears. His heart kept thumping hard, as if it, at least, still thought Luke would be wise to run. But Luke resolutely gripped the edge of the chair. He was acting normal now. Wasn't he? The boys who had been staring at him slowly began turning back to face the teacher again. Luke wiped sweat from his forehead and looked around for whoever had kicked and pulled and shoved him. Had they been trying to help him? Luke desperately wanted to believe that. But all the boys near him were looking at the teacher, nonchalantly, as though Luke weren't even there. And if they'd been trying to help, wouldn't they be trying to catch Luke's eye, to get him to say thanks?

Luke really didn't know. He knew how his family would act—Mother and Dad, Matthew and Mark. Mother and Dad would never kick him, and his older brothers would be poking him now, taunting him, "Want us to kick you again?"

The only other people Luke had ever met before today were Jen's dad—who was practically as big a mystery as the boys sitting beside him now—and Jen. And Jen would . . .

Luke couldn't bear to think about Jen.

A bell rang suddenly, and it was such an alarming sound that Luke's heart set to pounding again.

"Remember! Chapter twelve!" the teacher called as all the boys scrambled up.

Luke meant to go see the teacher, as he'd been instructed. This had to be the end of the class. But the tide of boys swept him out the back door of the classroom before he quite knew what was happening. By the time he got his feet firmly on the ground, and felt like he might be able to break away, he was around a corner and down another hall. He fought his way back to what he thought was the original hallway. But then he couldn't figure out which way to turn. He looked all around, frantically searching for either the teacher or Rolly—as nasty as he'd been, Rolly was at least sort of familiar. But all the faces that flowed past him were strangers'.

Of course, the way Luke's mind was working, both Rolly and the teacher could have paraded past Luke five times and he might not have even recognized them.

The crowd in the hall was thinning out. Luke began to panic again.

"Get to class," an older boy standing nearby ordered him.

"Where?" Luke said. "Where's my class?"

The boy didn't hear him. Luke thought about asking again, louder, but the boy seemed to be some sort of guard, someone in charge, like a policeman.

Like the Population Police.

Luke put his hand over his mouth and veered away, down another hall. Another bell rang and boys started running, desperate to get into their classrooms. Hopelessly, Luke followed a group of three or four through a doorway, into another classroom. At least, he thought it was another classroom. For all he knew, he might have circled around and gone into the same one all over again. Maybe that was good. Maybe after class this time, he could make it up to talk to the teacher—

It was a short, fat man who stood up to talk this time. As confused and panicky as Luke felt, even he could tell it wasn't the same teacher.

Luke hastily sat down, terrified of drawing attention to himself again. He resolved to listen carefully this time, to pay attention and learn. He owed it to everyone—to Mother and Dad, to Jen's father, even to Jen herself.

It was ten minutes before he realized that the man at the front was speaking some other language, one Luke had never heard before and didn't have a prayer of understanding.

CHAPTER *FOUR*

W hen the bell rang after this class, Luke didn't even try to go against the crowd. This time the flow of traffic carried him to a huge room with tables instead of desks, and bookshelves instead of portraits on the wall. All the other boys sat down and pulled out books and paper and pens or pencils.

Homework. They were doing homework.

Luke felt brilliant for figuring that out. How many times had he watched his older brothers groan over math problems, stumble over reading assignments, scratch out answers in history workbooks? Matthew and Mark did not like school. Once, years ago, Luke had been peering over Mark's shoulder at his homework, and noticed an easy mistake.

"Isn't eight times four thirty-two?" he'd innocently asked. "You wrote down thirty-four."

Mark stuck out his tongue and pushed so hard on his pencil that the lead broke.

"See what you made me do?" he complained. "If you're so smart, why don't you go to school for me?"

Mother was hovering over them.

"Hush," she said to Mark, and that had been the end of it.

Luke's family didn't dwell on what they all knew: Because Luke was the third born, he was illegal, violating the Population Law with every breath he took and every bite of food he ate. Of course he couldn't go to school, or anywhere else.

But here he was, now, at school. And it wasn't Matthew and Mark's little country school, but a grand, fancy place that only the richest people, Barons, could afford. Rich people like the real Lee Grant, who had died in a skiing accident. His family had concealed his death and secretly given his identity card to help a shadow child come out of hiding.

Couldn't everyone tell that Luke was an impostor?

Luke wished the real Lee Grant were still alive. He wished that he, himself, were still at home, hiding.

"Young man," someone said in a warning voice.

Luke glanced around. He was the only one still standing. Quickly he slipped into the nearest vacant chair. He didn't have any books to study or work to do. Maybe this was the time to read the note from Jen's dad.

But as he reached into his pocket he knew it wasn't safe. The boy across the table from him kept looking up, the boy two chairs down kept whispering and pointing. Though Luke kept his head down, he could feel eyes all around him. Even if no one was looking directly at him, Luke felt itchy and anxious just being in the same room with so many other people. He couldn't read the note. He could barely keep himself from bolting out of his chair, running out the door, finding some closet or small space to hide in.

And then everybody would know that he wasn't really Lee Grant. Everybody would know that all he knew was how to hide.

Luke forced himself to sit still for two hours.

When a bell went off again, everyone trouped down a hall to a huge dining area.

Luke hadn't eaten since breakfast at home—his mother's lightest biscuits and, as a miraculous farewell treat, fresh eggs. Luke could remember the pride shining in her eyes as she had slid the plate in front of him.

"From the factory?" he had asked. Eggs usually were not available for ordinary people, but his mother worked at a chicken factory, and if her supervisors were in a good mood, sometimes she got extra food.

Mother had nodded. "I promised them forty hours of overtime in exchange. Unpaid."

Luke had gulped.

"Just for two eggs for me?"

Mother had looked at him.

"It was a good trade," she'd said.

Remembering breakfast gave him a lump in his throat as big as an egg. He wasn't hungry.

But he sat down, because all the other boys were sitting. Instantly another boy turned on him and glared.

"Seniors only," he said.

"Huh?" Luke asked.

"Only seniors are allowed at this table," the boy said, in the same kind of mocking voice that Mark always used with Luke when Luke had said something dumb.

"Oh," Luke said.

"What are you, some kind of a lecker?" another boy asked.

Luke didn't know how to answer that. He was so eager to get up, he tripped and crashed into the next table.

"Juniors only," a boy said there.

Luke tried to swallow the lump in his throat, but it had grown even bigger.

He went from table to table, not even bothering to try to sit down. At each table, someone said in a bored voice, "Sophomores only," or "Freshmen only," or "Eights only" ... Luke didn't know what he was, so he kept moving.

Finally he reached an empty table and sat down.

A bowl of leaves and what looked like germinating soybeans sat in front of him. Was this supposed to be food? The other boys were eating it, so he did, too. The leaves were clammy and bitter and stuck in his throat.

Luke let himself think about potato chips. Nobody was supposed to have junk food, because of the food shortages that led to the Population Law. But Jen had given him potato chips when he'd gone over to her house, secretly, at great risk. He could still taste the salt, could still feel the crisp chips against the roof of his mouth, could still hear

Jen saying, when he protested that potato chips were illegal, "Yeah, well, we're illegal, too, so why don't we enjoy ourselves?"

Jen. If Jen were here now, she wouldn't put up with bitter leaves and tasteless bean sprouts for supper. She'd be standing up, demanding decent food. She'd go to any table she wanted. She'd march up to the person in charge—the headmaster?—and say, "Why won't anyone tell me what classes to go to? What are demerits? What are the rules, anyway? You're not running this school very well!" She'd punch Rolly right in the eye.

But Jen wasn't there. Jen was dead.

Luke bent his head low over his food. He stopped even pretending to chew and swallow.

After supper everyone was herded into another vast room. A man stood at the front talking about how glorious the Government was, about how their leaders' wisdom had kept them all from starving.

Lies, Luke thought, and marveled that he had the will even to think that.

Finally another bell rang and the other boys scattered. Luke walked uncertainly up and down strange halls.

"To your room," a man warned him. "Lights out in ten minutes."

Luke was so eager to get to his room, he actually found his voice.

"I-I'm new. I don't know where my room is."

"Well, then, find out."

"How?" Luke asked.

The man sighed, and rolled his eyes.

"What's your name?" he asked, slowly, as though Luke might be too stupid to understand the question.

"L—" Somehow Luke couldn't bring himself to claim his fake identity. "I know my room number. One fifty-six. I just don't remember where it is."

"Why didn't you say so?" the man growled. "Up those stairs and around the corner."

Even with the man's directions, Luke got turned around and had to search and search. By the time he finally saw the engraved 156, his legs were trembling with exhaustion and his feet were blistered from walking in the stiff, unfamiliar shoes. Luke was used to going barefoot. He was used to sitting in the house all day, not walking up and down stairs and through labyrinth-like halls.

He stepped through the doorway and headed straight for his bed. It had a spread on it and looked like all the others now. All Luke wanted to do was fall into it and go to sleep and forget everything that had happened that day.

"Did you ask permission?" someone barked at him.

Luke looked around. He was so tired, he hadn't even noticed that seven boys were sitting on the floor in a circle, playing some sort of card game.

"Per-Permission?" he asked.

One of the boys—probably the one who'd spoken—threw back his head and laughed. He was tall and thin, and older than Luke. Maybe even as old as Luke's brother

Matthew, who was fifteen. But Matthew was familiar, known. Luke couldn't read this boy's expression. He had a strange cast to his dark eyes, and his face was oddly shaped. Something about him reminded Luke of the pictures he'd seen in books of jackals.

"Hey!" the boy said. "They sent us a voice replicator. Amazingly human-like form. Voice is a little off, though. Let's try another one. Repeat after me: 'I am an exnay. I am a fonrol. I am a lecker. I don't deserve to live.'"

Most of the other boys were laughing now, too, but quietly, as if they didn't want to miss Luke's answer.

Luke hesitated. He'd heard those words before: Rolly had called him an exnay and a fonrol, and someone had called him a lecker at dinner. Maybe they were from that foreign language the short, fat teacher had been speaking. Luke had no idea what the words meant, but he could tell that they were probably bad things. Thanks to Matthew and Mark, he could spot a setup.

Luke shook his head.

The jackal boy sighed in exaggerated disappointment.

"Broken already," he said. He stood up and knocked his fist against Luke's side the way Luke had seen his father tap on the engine of broken tractors or trucks. "You just can't get good junk nowadays."

Luke pulled away. He stepped toward his bed.

Jackal boy laughed again.

"Oh, no, not so fast. Permission, remember? Say, 'I am your servant, O mighty master. I shall do your bidding forever. I will not eat or sleep or breathe unless you say it is to be so.'"

The boy moved between Luke and his bed. The others leaned forward, menacingly. *Like a pack of jackals,* Luke thought.

Jackals were nasty, vicious animals. Luke had read a book about them. They tore their prey limb from limb sometimes.

These were really boys, not jackals, Luke reminded himself. But he was too tired to fight.

"I am your servant," he mumbled. "I—I don't remember the rest."

"Why do they always send us the stupid ones?" the jackal boy asked. He looked down at Luke. "Bet you don't even know your own name."

"L-Lee," Luke whispered, looking down at his shoes.

"Lee, repeat after me. 'I—'"

"I—"

"'Am—'"

"Am—"

The jackal boy fed him each word and Luke, hating himself, repeated it. Then the boy made him touch his elbow to his nose. Cross his eyes. Stand on one foot while reciting, "I am the lowest of the low. Everyone should spit on me," five times. The lights flickered and went out in the middle of this ordeal, and still the jackal boy continued. Finally he yawned. Luke could hear his jaw crack in the dark.

"New boy, you bore me," he said. "Remove yourself from my presence."

"Huh?" Luke said.

"Go to bed!"

Meekly, Luke slipped beneath his covers. He was still wearing his clothes—even his shoes—but he didn't dare get back up to take them off. The unfamiliar pants bunched up around his waist, and he silently smoothed them out. Touching his pocket reminded him: He still hadn't read the note from Jen's dad.

Tomorrow, Luke thought. He felt a little bit of hope return. Tomorrow he would read the note, and then he would know how to find out what classes to go to, how to deal with boys like Rolly and his roommates, how to get by. No—not just to get by. Luke remembered what he'd hoped for, leaving home—was it only that morning? It seemed so long ago. He'd been thinking about making a difference in the world, finding some way to help other third children who had to hide. Luke didn't expect the note from Jen's dad to tell him how to do that, but it would give him a start. It would make that possible.

All he had to do was go to sleep and then it would be tomorrow and he could read the note.

But Luke couldn't sleep. The room was filled with unfamiliar sounds: first the other boys whispering, then breathing deeply, in sleep. The beds creaking when someone turned over. Some vent somewhere blowing air on them all.

Luke ached, missing his room at home, his family, Jen.

And his own name. He felt his lips draw together.

"Luke," he whispered soundlessly, in the dark. "My name is Luke."

He waited silently, his heart pounding, but nothing happened. No alarm bells went off, no Population Police swooped in to carry him away. His feeling of hope surged, even more than the fear. His name was Luke. He was nobody's servant. He was not the lowest of the low. He was Dad and Mother's son. He was Matthew and Mark's brother. He was Jen's friend.

Or—he had been.

CHAPTER *FIVE*

uke didn't get a chance to read the note from Jen's dad the next day. Or the next. Or the next.

In fact, an entire week went by with him resolving every night in bed, "Tomorrow. Surely I'll find a way to read the note tomorrow." But the next nightfall found him still stymied.

At first, he thought there was an easy solution. The bathroom, for example. He could go in, shut the door, read the note.

But none of the bathrooms at Hendricks were like the bathroom at home, closed-in and private. The Hendricks bathrooms were rows of urinals and commodes, right out in front of everyone. Even the shower was communal, just an open, tiled room with dozens of spigots sprouting from each wall.

Luke could barely bring himself to lower his pants with everyone watching, let alone read the note. He always lingered until most of the other boys were gone, but he never found a bathroom that fully emptied out. Finally, after three days had passed and he was getting desperate, he resolved to wait in the bathroom for as long as it took, regardless of bells or classes. The bell rang for breakfast and still he remained, pretending to be very concerned with scrubbing his face.

Finally it was just Luke and another boy, standing by the door.

"Out," the boy said.

The boy was mean-faced and muscular. Luke's legs trembled, but he didn't shut off the water.

"I'm not done," Luke mumbled, trying to sound nonchalant, unconcerned. He failed miserably.

The boy grabbed Luke's arm.

"Didn't you hear me? I said OUT!" The boy jerked so hard on Luke's arm that Luke felt pain shoot through his whole body. Then the boy shoved Luke out the door. Luke landed in a heap on the hallway floor. A hall monitor looked down at him in disgust.

"You're late for breakfast," he said. "Two demerits."

Luke feebly looked from the hall monitor to the other boy, who was now standing menacingly in the bathroom doorway. Then he understood: They were alike. There were guards in all the bathrooms, as well as in all the halls. He couldn't read the note in either place.

He wondered about trying to read the note in his room. He would get there first at bedtime, he decided. The first several days this was impossible because, no matter how hard he tried, he couldn't ever remember which way to go. Left at the top of the stairs, then right, then right, then left? Or was it right, then left, then left, then right? Most nights, it was a miracle if he found the room at all before lights out. Though that was just as well, because it reduced the amount of time that jackal boy could spend tormenting him.

Finally, in the middle of Luke's second week at Hendricks, he sat at the back of the hall during the evening lecture, so he was the first one up the stairs. Holding his breath, he counted off the turns. Right—yes. Right—yes. Left. And there—yes! Room 156.

Luke rushed in past the hall monitor. He slipped behind the door, out of sight, and jammed his hand in his pocket. And heard, "So my servant's reporting for duty early tonight, eh?"

It was jackal boy, lounging on his bed.

Luke had to bite his lip to keep from screaming.

That night jackal boy was crueler than ever.

Luke had to repeat, "I am a fonrol," fifty times. He had to hop up and down on one foot for five minutes. He had to do one hundred push-ups. (He'd never seen anyone do a push-up before. All the other boys howled with laughter when he stammeringly confessed, "I—I don't know how.") He had to push a marble across the floor with his nose.

Lying in bed that night, Luke despaired. His shoulders ached from the push-ups; his side was still bruised from being thrown out of the bathroom.

I'll never get to read the note, he thought. *I'll never be alone.*

It wasn't just that he wanted to read the note. It was maddening to always be around other people, to know that his every action might be observed, to never have a second of privacy.

How could he long to be alone, and feel so lonely, all at once?

CHAPTER **SIX**

L uke got by.

    It wasn't really that hard, as long as he didn't let himself want anything.

As long as he didn't linger in the bathroom or halls, as long as he sat down promptly when he entered a class-room, as long as he didn't try to eat at the wrong table, nobody bothered him except jackal boy. And jackal boy's torture was bearable, even at its worst.

The problem was, Luke couldn't always stop himself from wanting more.

He wanted home and he wanted his family and he wanted Jen alive again. And he wanted all the third chil-dren to be free, so he didn't have to go around pretending to be someone else anymore.

Those were impossible dreams, little fantasies that he played with in his mind in the middle of the night when he couldn't sleep.

The glow of those fantasies always made reality seem even bleaker the next morning.

But everything else he wanted seemed impossible, too.

He wanted to be able to climb into bed each night without even looking at jackal boy—without saying, "I am the dumbest lecker alive," a hundred times, without doing a single push-up, pull-up, sit-up, or toe-touch. Once during a nightly session, he dared to mumble, "Leave me alone," to jackal boy. But when Luke looked up, jackal boy was laughing hysterically.

"Did you—did you say what I thought—you said?" he sputtered between laughs. "'Leave me alone.' Oh, that's a good one, you stupid fonrol. You going to make me? Go ahead. Make me."

Jackal boy had his fists up, a taunting grin smeared across his face. Behind him, their other roommates gathered, eager for a fight. Eager, it seemed, to help jackal boy pound every shred of courage out of Luke.

Luke sized up the height and weight difference just between him and jackal boy. Never mind the rest of the boys. Nobody had to swing a single punch. Luke's courage was already gone.

At least jackal boy tortured Luke only once a day.

Three times a day, in the cavernous dining hall, Luke longed for food that tasted good. Mouthing bitter greens and mealy bread, he dreamed of Mother's stews, her biscuits, her apple pies. He could remember the exact sound of her voice asking him, "Want to lick the bowl?" whenever she made a cake. And then the taste of sweet batter.

He could remember every detail of the one time that he and Jen had made cookies together. They'd used special chips made of chocolate, and when the cookies were done and hot from the oven, the chips were melted and sweet on his tongue. He and Jen sat in the kitchen laughing and talking and eating cookie after cookie after cookie.

That was one of the best visits he'd ever had with Jen.

It was also one of the last.

He tried to forget that, but he couldn't. He knew that if he sat down in the Hendricks dining hall and someone put a whole plateful of the Jen cookies in front of him, they'd taste every bit as bitter as the greens. He wouldn't be able to eat a bite.

And Mother's biscuits, flown in fresh—if that were possible—would crumble in his mouth just like the mealy bread. Nothing could taste good when you ate alone in the midst of hundreds of boys who didn't even know your name. Who didn't care.

For Luke wanted a friend at Hendricks, too. Sometimes he forced himself to stop daydreaming and start paying attention to the other boys. He wasn't brave enough to speak to any of them, but he thought if he listened, then someday . . .

He couldn't tell the boys apart.

Maybe it had something to do with being in hiding all those years. He wasn't blind—he could tell that some of them had different-colored hair, even slightly different-colored skin. Some were taller, some were shorter; some were fatter, some were thinner. Some of them were older even than Luke's brothers; others were a few years younger than Luke himself. But Luke could never fix any of them in his mind. Even jackal boy was unrecognizable outside of their room. Once he came up to Luke and said, "Ah, my servant! Just when I need a pen. Give me yours, kid." And Luke stared, openmouthed, for so long that jackal boy just eased the pen out of Luke's hand and headed off, muttering, "Fine time to turn statue on me."

Another time, during breakfast, he overheard boys joking at a nearby table.

"Oh, come on, Spence," one boy said to another.

Luke stared. *Spence,* he repeated to himself, memorizing the boy's features. *That boy's name is Spence. Now I know who he is.* It gave him a warm glow all morning, to think that he'd be able to recognize somebody now.

At lunch he watched Spence slip into his seat. Luke practically smiled. Then Spence knocked over his water glass, dousing the boy beside him.

"Ted, you lecker!" the other boy exclaimed.

Ted? But—

At dinner, the boy Luke would have sworn was Spence looked up when someone called out, "Hey! E. J.!"

"Not now," Spence/Ted/E. J. said irritably. Or was he simply E. J., and Spence and Ted were totally different boys?

Luke gave up trying to keep track of anybody's names. He thought he noticed other boys responding to multiple names, too, but he could never be sure.

Why was he so easily confused?

It was like the halls of the school, which always seemed to double back on themselves. From one day to the next, Luke could rarely find his way to the same classroom twice. So it didn't matter that he was never sure which class he was supposed to be sitting in—he'd never be able to get to the right place, anyhow. The teachers didn't seem to notice Luke, or anyone else. They'd occasionally point at a boy and declare, "Two demerits," but they almost never called anyone by name.

Luke wondered about sneaking up to his room during classtime, and reading the note from Jen's dad, since nobody cared where he was, anyway. But the hall monitors guarded the stairs, too. They guarded everything.

So, Luke reflected gloomily, the note that could save him was doomed to turn to lint in his pocket. And Luke was doomed to endlessly wander the halls of Hendricks, unnoticed, unknowing, unknown.

In bed at night, Luke took to having imaginary conversations with his family, Jen, Jen's dad. His part was all apologies.

I'm sorry, Mr. Talbot. You risked your life to get me a fake I.D., and I wasn't worth it. . . .

I'm sorry, Jen, I'm not doing anything for the cause. . . .

I'm sorry, Mother. This was the hardest one of all. *You wanted me to stay but I said I had to go. I said I was going to make a difference in the world. But I can't. I wanted to make sure there was enough food for everyone in the world, so third children could be legal again. But I can't* even understand a word my teachers say. Even the ones who are speaking my language. I'll never learn anything. I'll never be able to help anyone.

I'm sorry, Mother. I should have never left you. I wish—

But Luke wished for so much, he couldn't go on.

He was so busy longing for big, impossible changes, he never gave a thought to wanting anything smaller or more practical. Like an open door.

But that was what he got.

CHAPTER *SEVEN*

L uke saw the door one morning on the way to class. He'd barely slept the night before, so he was groggy and stupid. He was shuffling along looking for a familiar classroom to duck into before the hall monitor yelled at him. Between classrooms, he stared down at his feet, too miserable to lift his head. But just as he turned a corner, someone bumped into him. Luke looked up in time to see the other boy barrel past without an apology. Then, as Luke turned his head forward again, he saw it.

The door was on the outside wall. Luke couldn't have said if he'd passed it a hundred times before, or never. It was solid wood with a brass knob, just like dozens of other doors in the school. It was barely even ajar.

But beyond it, Luke could see grass and trees and sky. Outdoors.

He didn't think. He didn't even pause to make sure a hall monitor wasn't watching him. In a flash, Luke was out the door.

Outside, Luke stood still, his back to the wall of the school. He was breathing hard. *Read the note and get back inside!* some tiny, rational part of his brain urged him. *Before someone sees you!*

But he couldn't move. It was May. The lawn ahead of him was a rich green carpet. Redbuds were blooming, and lilacs. He thought he even smelled honeysuckle. His mind played a trick on him, and suddenly he was almost a whole year back in time, standing outside for what he had thought might be the last time in his entire life. The Government workers were just starting to cut down the woods behind his family's house, and his mother was fearfully ordering him, "Luke! Inside. Now."

And when the woods were gone, Jen's house replaced it.

His mind skipped ahead, and he remembered his first trip to Jen's house. He'd stepped outside and felt paralyzed, just like now. And he'd marveled at the feel of fresh air on his face, just like now.

And he'd been in danger.

Just like now.

Luke looked back at the school, hopelessly. Anyone could easily look out a window and see him, and report him. Maybe they'd just give him more of those meaningless demerits. Or maybe this would make them realize that he really wasn't Lee Grant, that his papers were forged, that by the laws of the land, he deserved to die.

Strangely, Luke could see no windows. But the door was opening.

Luke took off running. He raced as blindly as he had that first day, trying to keep up with Rolly Sturgeon. Luke was crashing through the undergrowth of a small woods before his mind fully registered that there was a woods. Brambles tore at his arms and legs and chest, and he kept running. He whipped willow branches out of his way. He was so frenzied, he felt like he could run forever.

Then he tripped over a log and fell.

Silence. Only now that he'd stopped did Luke realize how much noise he'd been making. So stupid. Luke lay facedown in ferns and moss, and waited for someone to grab him and yell and punish him.

Nothing happened. Over the pounding of his pulse, Luke could hear nothing but birdsong. After what seemed like a very long time, he cautiously raised his head.

Trees formed a canopy over his head. A flash of movement caught Luke's eye, but it was only a squirrel jumping from branch to branch. Branches swayed, but only because of the wind.

Slowly, Luke inched back the way he had come. Finally he crouched, hidden by the underbrush, and spied on the school.

Nobody was in sight.

Luke peered at the door. It moved out again, and he stiffened, terrified. But then it moved in.

In, out, in, out—so slow—it was like the school was breathing through the door. Suddenly Luke understood.

Nobody had pushed the door open. It was the wind, or maybe the change in air pressure as the boys walked past.

Luke stuck his head out a little further. He could see one whole side of the school building this way. And he realized for the first time: There were no windows in any part of the wall. It was solid brick, up and down.

How could that be?

Luke thought about all of the rooms he'd been in, since coming to Hendricks, and it was true—he couldn't remember a single window in any of them. Even the room he shared with jackal boy and his minions was window-less. Why hadn't he ever noticed before?

And why would someone build so many windowless rooms?

Suddenly Luke didn't care. There were no windows, nobody was coming out of the door—he was safe.

"I can read the note now!" he said aloud, and chuckled. It was strangely thrilling to hear his own voice—not timid, not stammering—Luke's voice, not the pretend-Lee's.

"I'm going to read it right over there!" he said, speaking just for the pleasure of it. "Finally!"

He strolled deeper into the woods, and sat down on the very log he'd tripped over before. Slowly, ceremoniously, he slipped the note from Jen's dad out of his pocket. Now he would know everything he needed to do.

He unfolded the note, which had grown worn from all the times he'd palmed it, secretly transferring it from the pocket of one pair of pants to another. Then he stared, try-ing to make sense of Mr. Talbot's scrawl.

The note only held two words:

Blend in

CHAPTER EIGHT

"**N**o!" Luke screamed.

That was it? "Blend in"? What kind of advice was that? Luke needed help. He'd been waiting weeks.

"I was counting on you!" Luke screamed again, past caring who might hear.

The "B" on "Blend" blurred before his eyes. Desperately, he turned the note over, hoping there was more on the other side. The real message, maybe. But the other side was blank. What he held was just a small, ragged scrap of paper, not much more than lint. Even Mother—who saved everything, who reused envelopes—even she wouldn't think twice about tossing this useless shred in the trash.

And this tiny piece of nothing was what Luke had pinned all his hopes on.

Too furious to see straight, Luke ripped the note in half. In fourths. In eighths. He kept ripping until the pieces of paper were all but dust. Practically microscopic. Then he threw them as far away as he could.

"I hate you, Mr. Talbot!" Luke yelled.

The words echoed in the trees. Even the woods seemed

to be making fun of him. That was probably all Mr. Talbot had meant to do, too, when he'd handed Luke the note that first day. Luke could just imagine Mr. Talbot chuckling as he drove away from Hendricks after leaving Luke. He probably thought it was funny to drop off a dumb farm boy at a snobby Baron school and tell him, "Blend in." He probably laughed about it all the time. If Jen were still alive, she probably would have laughed at Luke, too.

No. Not Jen . . .

Luke buried his face in his hands and slipped down to the ground, sprawled beside the log. Without the note to count on, he didn't even have enough backbone of his own to sit.

CHAPTER *NINE*

uke wouldn't have thought he could have fallen asleep there in the woods, in danger, boiling mad. But somehow he found himself waking up some time later, stiff and sore and confused. The birds were still singing, a mild breeze ruffled his hair—before he remembered everything, Luke actually smiled. What a pleasant dream. But why did he feel so unhappy?

Then he sat up and opened his eyes and everything came back to him. The note he'd believed in so fervently was worthless dust now—no matter how hard he peered off into the underbrush, he couldn't see a single sign of it. He was out in the woods, violating who knew how many rules of the Hendricks School for Boys. And he had no idea how long he'd been gone—squinting at the sun, Luke guessed that it was at least mid-afternoon. They must have noticed him missing by now. He should be thinking up his excuse now. He should sneak back so at least they wouldn't find him out here. It wouldn't look so bad. Maybe he could convince them that he'd started to run away—the real Lee Grant had done that, supposedly—then repented and turned around. But that story depended on him going back *now*.

Luke didn't move.

He didn't want to go back to school. Not now, not ever. There wasn't anything there for him. He knew that now. No friends, no helpful teachers, no good choices. He was just like some windup toy there, marching mindlessly from class to class, meal to meal, trying not to be watched.

Just the thought of school made his stomach churn.

"You can't make me go back," Luke muttered, though he wasn't sure who he thought he was defying.

That was settled. So where else could he go?

Home . . .

Luke was overcome with a stronger longing than he'd ever felt before. To see Mother again, to see Dad . . . This was how miserable Luke felt: He even missed his brothers. He watched a chipmunk race across the ground. The chipmunk's feet barely seemed to touch. It could be just that easy for Luke, going home. All he had to do was start walking.

But.

He didn't know how to get there. Even if he had a map, he wouldn't be able to find his parents' farm on it.

He didn't have his fake I.D. card with him. He didn't carry it at school. He could picture it clearly, tucked in the pocket at the back of his suitcase. He couldn't go back for it. And getting caught without an I.D. card was as good as admitting, "I'm a third child. Kill me."

Luke tried to pretend those weren't obstacles. He still couldn't picture a perfect homecoming.

Even if he managed to find his family's farm without running into the Population Police first, he'd just be bringing danger with him. The penalties for harboring an illegal child were almost as harsh as the penalty for *being* an illegal child. Every second he'd lived with his parents, he'd put their lives in jeopardy. And now there was a record of his existence. If he disappeared now, someone would have to look for him. And when they found him, cowering in his family's attic, they'd be sure to find out the truth as well.

Luke picked up a pebble and threw it far into the woods. It wasn't fair. His only choices were to be miserable at school or a virtual murderer at home. He threw another pebble, and another. Not fair, not fair, not fair. He ran out of pebbles and switched to bark chips, peeled off the log beside him. Some of the pebbles and bark chips hit tree trunks with a satisfying thud. Luke began aiming.

"Take that!" he yelled, forgetting himself.

Then, terrified, he clapped his hand over his mouth. How could he be so stupid?

He froze, listening so hard, his ears began to buzz. But there was no sound of anyone tramping through the woods looking for him. There was no sound from the school at all. Peering around at the ferns and the trees and the sunlight filtering through the branches, Luke could practically convince himself the school didn't exist at all.

It was a shame he couldn't just stay here.

Luke had a moment of hope—he could live on nuts and berries. He could hide in the trees whenever they came looking for him.

But that was a childish plan. He dismissed it immediately. If he stayed in the woods, he'd be caught or starve.

He glanced around again, this time regretfully. The trees looked friendlier than any of the boys or teachers at schools. He was a farm boy who'd spent most of his life outdoors, until the woods were cut down behind his house. Just being outside was a joy. And no matter how much he'd risked, running out here, it was wonderful to be alone, not packed in and watched at every turn.

Luke dug the toe of his fancy Baron shoe into the dirt and stood up. He'd come to a decision without realizing it. He had to go back to school. He owed it to his family, and Jen's dad, and maybe even Jen herself.

But nothing could stop him from visiting the woods again.

CHAPTER *TEN*

L uke put off returning to school as long as possible. His stomach growled and he ignored it. The angle of the sun's rays grew sharper and sharper, but he consoled himself, "It's still daylight. It just starts looking like twilight sooner, when you're deep in the woods."

Finally he could ignore the truth no longer. It was getting dark. And even if nobody had noticed his absence so far, he'd be missed at bedtime. Jackal boy was sure to complain if Luke wasn't there for him to pick on.

Strangely, that thought almost made him feel good.

Luke didn't stop to figure that one out. He strode to the edge of the woods, looked around carefully, then took off running across the lawn.

Halfway to the school, he was struck by a horrible thought: What if the door was locked?

A few steps later, he was close enough to tell: The door wasn't open anymore. It wasn't even ajar.

Luke dashed even faster across the lawn, as if he could outrun his panic. His heart pounded, and it wasn't just from running. He'd been so stupid, going out the door in the first place. Or, if he'd had to step outside, why hadn't he gone back right away? Why had he risked everything for a day in the woods?

He knew why.

Luke was finally close enough to touch the doorknob. He reached out with a trembling hand, prepared for the worst.

Stay calm, stay calm, he told himself. *If it's locked, maybe you can find another door that works. Maybe you can still slip back in undetected. Maybe . . .* Luke didn't have much faith in "maybes."

Hopelessly, he twisted the knob.

The knob turned easily.

Barely daring to believe his luck, Luke pulled the door open a crack. He couldn't see anyone, so he slid in and let the door close behind him. It was dark at this end of the hall. He appreciated the shadows.

Luke was tiptoeing past vacant classrooms when he heard the shout.

"Hey! What are you doing down here?"

It was one of the hall monitors.

"I—I got lost," Luke said, not stammering any more than he would have under normal circumstances. And the excuse was entirely plausible—hadn't he been lost a million times so far at school? But he didn't know what he was missing. Supper? The evening lecture? Lights out?

The hall monitor peered at him suspiciously.

"Nobody's supposed to be in this wing of the building

right now," he said. "Why did you leave the dining hall?"

Luke got a sudden inspiration.

"I got sick," he said. "I ran out to go to the bathroom. Then I got lost when I was going back."

The hall monitor looked skeptical.

"The bathroom's right across from the dining hall," he said.

"I—I wasn't paying attention. I'm new. I was sick." Luke tried to look dumb enough—and queasy enough—to have made such a stupid mistake.

The hall monitor took a step back, like he didn't want to catch anything.

"Okay," he relented. "Go back immediately."

Relieved, Luke turned to go. Then he stopped. Only the day before, he would have obeyed unthinkingly. But now he had a secret to protect. Now he had to be crafty. He turned back to the monitor.

"I don't know how to get there. Remember?"

"Oh, for crying out loud. Why do I have to baby-sit all the leckers?" He took Luke's arm and jerked him to the right. "Go that way. Turn left at the first hallway, then left and right again. Just get out of here!"

The hall monitor sounded a little panicked himself. The day before, Luke wouldn't have noticed, but now he had to pay attention. *Something about that door,* Luke thought. *Why is the hall monitor so desperate to get me away from it?*

Luke was still pondering that question when he reached the doors to the dining hall. They burst open, and boys streamed out. Luke's timing was perfect: He'd gotten there just as everyone was heading toward the evening lecture. He blended in. *See, Mr. Talbot?* he thought bitterly. *I am following the only bit of advice you saw fit to give me. Aren't you proud? Mighty generous of you, I'm sure.*

But some of Luke's bitterness had eased. The note had been worthless, but he had the woods to think about now. And if the note had led him to the woods—well, he did have reason to be grateful to Jen's dad, didn't he?

Nobody challenged Luke as he walked into the lecture room and sat down. Nobody asked, "Where have you been all day?" Nobody ordered him, "Never leave this building again!"

He'd gotten away with it. He could get away with it again.

CHAPTER *ELEVEN*

L uke longed to race straight to the woods as soon as he woke up the next morning. It was torture to stand patiently beside all the other boys, splashing water on his face. It was torture to sit still and slowly spoon in the lumpy oatmeal, when he longed to gulp it down and get out of there. (Though, since he'd missed two meals the day before, it was amazing how delicious the oatmeal seemed for once.) It was torture waiting for the cafeteria doors to open and release everyone else to classes, and Luke to the woods.

As soon as breakfast was over, he took off, all but run-ning. Surprisingly, given how confused he usually got in the Hendricks halls, he managed to make a beeline straight for the door, without once making a wrong turn and hav-ing to retrace his steps. Approaching the door, he slowed down, waiting for the crowd to clear in the hall. Finally, there was only Luke and a hall monitor, several yards away. The door wasn't open today, but Luke was confident that it wasn't locked. He was confident that he could slip out quickly enough. He glanced back. The monitor was looking the other way. Now! Luke reached for the doorknob—

—and then drew back.

At the last minute, it was like someone or something screamed, *"No!"* in his mind. Mother had talked about God sometimes—maybe that's who it was. Or maybe it was Jen's spirit, come to help Luke when her father's note hadn't. Maybe it was just Luke's own common sense. Luke didn't know what he thought about God or ghosts or even his own intelligence, but he knew: He couldn't risk going to the woods today.

Luke walked on, pretending to be casually dawdling.

"Get to class," the monitor growled.

Luke nodded, and stepped into the next classroom he passed. He felt as disappointed as if he'd discovered bars on the door. What was he—a coward?

Luke remembered all the mind games he'd played with himself trying to get up the nerve to go to Jen's house that first time. He'd waited weeks, always telling himself he was just waiting for the right moment. He had been a coward then.

But he wasn't being a coward now. Sinking into a seat, as anonymous as every other boy in the room, he actually felt brave, clever, crafty.

Probably he'd just gotten lucky the day before. If he wanted to be able to go the woods again and again and again, without getting caught, he'd have to be smart about it. He'd have to pay attention to everything. Maybe he'd even have to figure out why the hall monitor the night before had been so panicky. Before he went back again, he'd have to know it was safe.

Luke looked around the room. Up front, the teacher was drawing complicated-looking mathematical formulas on the chalkboard. Luke couldn't have solved any of them if his life depended on it. But for once, instead of sinking into despair and staring down at the desk in front of him, Luke got the nerve to peer around at the other boys. A few were watching the teacher. A few were taking notes—er, no, they were drawing pictures of naked girls. Some were blatantly sleeping, their mouths slack-jawed. And some were sitting off to the side, their arms clutched around their legs, rocking.

Luke stared. He didn't have much to go on, since he'd only known six people before in his entire life, but that rocking certainly didn't seem like normal behavior.

Eventually the bell rang, and he stumbled into another class. It was the same there: some boys acting normal, some boys rocking endlessly.

Why hadn't he noticed anything like that before?

He knew why. Every other time he'd looked directly at any of the other boys, he'd glanced quickly, then looked away, for fear that they might actually look back.

You could miss a lot, doing that.

Walking through the hall to his next class, Luke tried an experiment: He stared directly into the eyes of every single boy who went past him.

It was terrifying—even worse than running blindly

across a lawn. Luke's stomach seized up, and he thought he might actually throw up his breakfast oatmeal. He thought his legs might crumple under him, in fear.

But it was also interesting.

Most of the other boys he passed looked away as soon as Luke made eye contact. Some of them seemed to have a sort of sixth sense that warned them off from letting Luke look at them in the first place. Only two or three stared boldly back, their eyes locked on Luke's just as Luke's were locked on theirs.

Remember them, Luke ordered himself. But it took all his willpower just to keep himself from looking away.

When he finally arrived in a classroom doorway, Luke was shaking all over.

I gave something away, just then, he thought. *Now they'll know.*

But he didn't know who "they" were.

CHAPTER *TWELVE*

L uke made himself wait an entire week before he went back to the woods. But in that time, no matter how closely he paid attention to everything, the mysteries only seemed to multiply.

For example, by the end of the week, Luke was even more baffled by the lack of windows than ever before. Because he'd discovered: There wasn't a single window in the entire place.

To learn that, Luke had to make himself figure out the floor plan of the entire school. He had to be sure that he peeked into every classroom, every sleeping room, every office. One morning at breakfast, he even pretended to get turned around and plowed straight into the kitchen. Two cooks screamed, and Luke was given a stern lecture and a record ten demerits, but he found out what he wanted to know: Even the kitchen lacked windows.

Why? Why would anyone build a windowless school?

Luke wondered if there'd been something unusual about his family's house, that it had had windows, and he'd just accepted it as the norm. But, no—all the houses and schools and other buildings Luke had seen in books had had windows. And when the Government built Jen's neighborhood, all the houses there had windows. And Jen's family and their neighbors were Barons—if Baron houses had windows, why didn't Baron schools?

Luke couldn't figure out the other boys, either. There were rocking boys in most of his classes, he realized now. Several times, Luke practically hypnotized himself staring at them. But they seemed harmless enough.

The boys who worried Luke were the ones he called "the starers"—the ones who looked back when he looked at them.

All the hall monitors were starers.

So was jackal boy.

Luke tried to tell himself that the starers bothered him only because he'd spent so much time in hiding. Of course he didn't like being stared at. They were probably just acting normal, and he was in danger of giving away his real identity by getting disturbed by it.

Somehow he couldn't believe that.

At night when jackal boy tormented him, Luke kept his eyes trained carefully on the ground. But he could feel jackal boy's gaze on the side of his face as definitely as he would feel a slap or a punch.

"Say, 'I am an exnay of the worst order,'" jackal boy ordered him as usual one evening.

Luke mumbled the words. He wondered what would happen if he looked up and unleashed his questions on jackal boy: Why do you stare? Why aren't there any windows? Why do we never go outside? Why was the door open that one day? And finally: Are there any other shadow children here?

But of course he couldn't ask jackal boy. Jackal boy thought it was funny to make Luke wave his arms for five minutes straight. Jackal boy was only interested in humiliating Luke. He'd probably think it was amusing to tell the Population Police, "I know where you can find a third child. How big's my reward?"

So Luke bit his tongue and gritted his teeth and touched his finger to his nose fifty times, as ordered. He jogged in place until his legs ached. He reached for his toes again and again, until jackal boy said in a bored voice, "Get out of my sight."

Luke crawled into bed unsure whether to be relieved that he hadn't blown his cover, or disappointed that he hadn't found the answers to his questions.

That night in bed, he was too busy puzzling over all his mysteries to even think about whispering his own name. When he had his pretend conversations, he asked advice, instead of offering apologies.

What do you think, Jen? What's wrong with this place? Is there something wrong? You went out into the world on fake passes all the time. Do people everywhere act like the boys at Hendricks?

And, *Mother, Dad, what's your opinion? Is it okay if I go out into the woods again?*

But it was ridiculous to feel like he had to get permission from parents he'd never see again. Or to ask advice from a friend who was dead. It was just too bad that that was all he had.

Luke swallowed a lump in his throat. He couldn't solve the school's mysteries. But he was going back to the woods no matter what.

CHAPTER THIRTEEN

Luke worked out a plan for leaving the school every day after lunch, and coming back right before dinner. It was sort of a compromise—he thought he ought to go to some classes, no matter how little sense they made to him. And this way he wouldn't miss any meals. He was already hungry all the time. He already had trouble keeping his fancy Baron pants hitched up on his scrawny frame.

The first day he left, he slipped out while the hall monitor was looking the other way. He knew now that none of the other boys would even notice.

So easy, Luke thought to himself as he jogged across the lawn to the woods. *Why don't all the boys escape out here?*

He decided it wasn't worth troubling himself with unanswerable questions.

The sun was shining, and he could tell that even the leaves that had been curled up and tiny a week earlier were full grown and spread out now. High overhead, the arc of tree limbs in some parts of the woods blocked out the sky

MARGARET PETERSON HADDIX

completely. *It's like a cave,* Luke thought. But that reminded him of hiding and cowering indoors. He moved out into a clearing, where grass struggled to grow through last fall's dead leaves. It looked like there were raspberry plants, too, mostly buried in tangled brush.

"Raspberries," Luke whispered, his mouth watering. Mother grew raspberries, back home, and every June she kept the whole family stuffed with raspberry pies and cakes and breads. She made raspberry jam, too, and spread it on their toast and spooned it into their cornmeal mush all year long.

Luke eagerly searched the branches in front of him— tasting a raspberry would be like visiting home, just for a minute. But there weren't any berries yet, only an occasional bud. And it was likely the weeds would choke out those buds before they matured.

Unless Luke cleared the brush around them.

It only took Luke ten or fifteen minutes to pull the weeds and give the raspberry plants room, but by the time he was done, he had a full-blown idea in his head.

He could grow a whole garden out here. Surely no one would mind, or even find out. In his imagination he saw neat rows of sweet corn, tomato plants, and peas. He could put strawberries and blueberries over at the side of the clearing, where they'd get some shade. He'd want beans, too. Squash wasn't practical, because it wasn't much good raw. But there was always cucumber and zucchini, cantaloupe and watermelon . . . Luke's stomach growled.

Then he remembered seeds. He didn't have any.

Luke's dream instantly withered. How stupid was he that he thought he could grow a garden without seeds? Luke could imagine how Matthew and Mark would make fun of him if they knew. Even Dad and Mother would have a hard time not laughing. Just a month away from home and he'd already forgotten what you needed for a garden.

Luke stared at the measly raspberry plants in disappointment. Then he could almost hear Mother's voice in his ears: *Make the best of what you've got.* How many times had he heard her say that?

Even one raspberry would be delicious.

And maybe he could find blueberry or strawberry plants somewhere in the woods, and transplant them.

And maybe he could get seeds from some of the food at school. The bean sprouts they were always feeding him, for example—could he plant those? He didn't know what kind of beans they would grow into, but even if they were soybeans, Jen had told him once that the Government thought those were edible. Roasted, maybe. He could build a fire.

And maybe later in the summer, they would serve tomatoes or cantaloupe or watermelon, and he could smuggle the seeds to his room somehow. It would be too late for planting by then, but he could save the seeds for next year. . . .

It made Luke's throat ache to think of staying at Hendricks School a whole year. A whole year without his family, a whole year of grieving for Jen, a whole year of not speaking to anyone but jackal boy. A whole year of having nothing but a fake name and clothes that didn't fit.

Luke stood up and planted his feet firmly on the ground.

"I have the woods," he said aloud. "I'll have the garden. This is mine."

CHAPTER FOURTEEN

By the end of the week, Luke had a nice plot of land cleared. The raspberry plants were at the center, and he had straight lines of bean sprouts planted on either side. It was Dad he pretended to appeal to most now.

"What do these look like to you, Dad?" he'd say aloud, as though Dad were really there to answer. "Am I just wasting my time? Or will I have a good crop come fall?"

Luke truly wasn't sure. But he felt so proud, looking at the neat little garden. He kept meaning to explore more of the woods, but he was always too busy digging and weeding, tending his plot. Anxiously he shooed away squirrels and chipmunks, and wished that he could stay out and guard his garden all the time.

But each afternoon he kept a close eye on the Baron watch he now wore on his wrist, so he could run back to the school promptly at six o'clock. He'd found the watch in his suitcase, and faced quite a chore figuring out how to read it. Those lines and "V's" and "X's" on it were numbers, he knew, but different from what he was used to. Why did Barons always have to make everything so fancy and complicated? Back home Mother and Dad had just a single digital clock, in the kitchen. It blinked off the minutes as clear as could be. This watch was like a foreign language to Luke. But he stared at the angle of the rays of sun, he studied the digital clocks at school and compared them with the watch on his wrist—eventually he understood the Baron watch as well as any other.

That made him feel proud, too.

So did his next accomplishment.

One day at lunch they served baked potatoes in the school dining hall. They were so undercooked, they practically crunched. Luke bit into a raw end that hadn't even had its eye removed. Spitting it out, he complained to himself, *I'd rather plant this than eat it.*

Plant this. Of course. How many springs had Luke spent cutting up potatoes for planting? He and Mother, perched over a three-gallon bucket, knives flashing. When he was little, he'd always tried to rest his feet on the top of the bucket, the same way Mother did, but he was never tall enough. Even when he was tall enough, he never balanced things right. He'd tip the whole bucket over. Mother would look at him sternly and sigh, "Pick it up." But then she'd smile, like she wasn't really mad. She'd talk to him the whole time they worked: "Careful with the knife—don't cut toward your hand. You're making sure there's an eye in every potato, aren't you? Nothing will grow without an eye."

But potatoes would grow without a seed. He just needed a raw potato.

Covertly, Luke used his fork to separate the cooked and raw part of his potato. The raw part he dropped into his hand, and slipped into his pocket. Probably nobody had ever used Baron pants for transporting potato parts before, but Luke didn't care.

As soon as the bell rang for the end of lunch, Luke moved quickly among the tables, grabbing the left-behind potato pieces wherever he could. His pockets were stuffed in a matter of minutes.

He walked stiffly down the hall and out his door, trying not to smash the potatoes.

Nobody noticed.

Out in the woods, Luke dumped out his pockets and examined his treasure. He had eight potato pieces that looked like good candidates for planting. He wished he'd thought to smuggle a knife out of the dining hall, too, but that couldn't be helped. He halved as many of the potatoes as he could using his fingernails and brute force. Then he planted them in a row beside the beans.

When he was done, Luke sat back against a tree trunk and surveyed his work. It looked good. In a few days he'd know if anything was going to grow. He thought the bean sprouts looked bigger. At least they weren't withering yet.

After a few minutes of rest, Luke walked down to a creek that ran through the woods and cupped his hands in it, making trip after trip to bring back water for his garden. If only he had one of those three-gallon buckets now! Even a cup would help. Maybe he could bring one from the dining room.

In the meantime, he really didn't mind using his hands. Walking back and forth between the creek and his garden, Luke felt a strange surge of emotion, one he hadn't felt in so long that he'd practically forgotten what it was.

Happy, he thought in amazement. *I'm happy.*

CHAPTER *FIFTEEN*

The very next day Luke raced out to his garden even more eagerly than ever. It was too soon to tell anything about the potatoes, but if the beans still looked good, he could probably be sure that they would live and grow and produce. And would the raspberries have any more buds today?

Luke reached his clearing and stopped short.

His garden was destroyed.

The raspberry branches were broken off at odd angles; the bean plants were trampled, smashed flat in the mud. There hadn't been any potato shoots to be ruined, of course, but the garden was so messed up, Luke couldn't even tell where he'd planted them.

"No," Luke wailed. "It can't be."

He wanted to believe that he'd accidentally walked into the wrong clearing. But that was crazy. There was the maple tree with the jagged cut in its trunk on one side of the clearing, the oak with the sagging limb on the other side, the rotting trunk in the middle—this *was* his garden. Or—it had been.

Who wrecked it?

His first thought was animals. Back home, back when his family still raised hogs, there had been a couple of times when the hogs had escaped and found their way to the garden. They'd rooted around like crazy, and Mother had been furious over the damage.

But there weren't any hogs in the woods. Luke hadn't seen anything bigger than a squirrel. And for all his shooings and worrying, he knew squirrels couldn't have done this kind of damage.

And squirrels didn't wear shoes.

Luke winced. He'd been too distraught to notice before: Instead of animal tracks, the garden was covered with imprints of the same kind of shoes Luke was wearing. Smooth-soled Baron shoes had stomped on his raspberries, trampled his beans, kicked at his potato hills. They had walked all over his garden.

For a crazy instant, Luke wondered if he himself was to blame. Had he been careless leaving the garden yesterday? Could he have stepped on his own plants by mistake? That was ridiculous. He'd never do such a thing.

What if he'd sleepwalked, and come out here in the night without even knowing it?

That was even more preposterous. He would have been caught.

And he didn't wear shoes to bed.

Anyhow, he could tell by stepping next to the other footprints: Some of the imprints were made by shoes that were bigger than Luke's. Some of the imprints were made by shoes that were smaller.

Lots of people had been in Luke's garden. Lots of people had been there destroying it.

Luke sank to the ground by the tree trunk. He buried his face in his hands.

"This was all I had," he moaned. Once again he was pretending to talk to someone who wasn't there. But it wasn't Mother or Dad, Jen or Mr. Talbot he appealed to now. It was Matthew and Mark, his older brothers. He had to apologize to them. He had to explain why he, Luke Garner, a twelve-year-old boy, was crying.

CHAPTER *SIXTEEN*

uke went back to school early that afternoon. What good would it do to stay in the garden? He'd only make himself more miserable. It wasn't worth trying to clean up, to replant. Whoever did this would only come back and destroy his garden again.

Washing his face in the creek before leaving, Luke tortured himself with questions. Who had done this? Who were the—vandals? The criminals? Luke couldn't even come up with a harsh enough word to describe them. Then he thought of the insults that had been hurled at him for the past month. Yes. The guilty ones were fonrols. Exnays. Leckers.

Luke wiped his face off on his sleeve, and it left a streak of mud. Who cared?

He circled wide leaving the creek so he didn't have to see his poor butchered garden again.

He didn't even bother running across the wide expanse of lawn back to the school. He trudged.

At the door, his brain woke again. He couldn't go back in now, in the middle of classes. He'd be noticed wandering the halls alone. How many people had yelled at him and

Rolly that first day? Luke looked at his watch and puzzled out the time. It was only one-thirty. It probably would be another half an hour before classes let out, and Luke could slip into the stream of other boys walking between rooms.

Luke leaned hopelessly against the rough brick wall beside the doorway. He almost welcomed the pain it brought, scraping his arm, pressing into his forehead. Maybe he should run back to the woods, where he could hide better, be safer. But he didn't care. He'd given up his name, his family—everything—for safety. Right now it didn't look like such a great deal.

Anyway, the woods didn't seem the least bit inviting anymore. They weren't his. They never had been.

Standing stoically before a closed door, Luke suddenly understood the clues he'd been too dense or blind—or hopeful—to notice before. Of course some of the other boys visited the woods. That's why the hall monitor had been so panicked that first night, when he saw Luke near the door. The monitor wasn't guarding the hall. He was guarding the door. Some boys had been planning to sneak out, that night, and the monitor was making sure it was safe. Probably they sneaked out to the woods all the time.

Luke could imagine how they'd acted, discovering the garden.

"Hey, look!" he could hear one boy calling to another. "Let's rip this up!"

And then they did—a horde of boys stomping the potatoes and yanking up the raspberries and hurling uprooted bean plants across the garden. Luke's garden.

"I'm going to find you," he whispered. "I'm going to get you."

CHAPTER *SEVENTEEN*

P romptly at two o'clock, Luke eased the door open a crack and peeked in. His timing was good—boys were walking to and from classes, their heads bowed, their eyes trained on the ground. But a hall monitor stood directly across from the door. Luke ducked back.

Look away, look away, Luke mentally commanded the monitor. Luke waited. Then, just when he moved over, ready to peek again, he saw the door slide shut.

Oh, no. Luke tried to figure out what had happened. Had the monitor seen the door open, thought that one of his marauding gang had forgotten to close it, and merely shut it to save his own skin?

Or did he know Luke was out there?

Stay calm, Luke commanded himself, uselessly. His panic boiled over. And his anger. He hated that monitor. He was probably one of the boys who'd trampled Luke's garden.

Luke could have looked for another door. He could have waited another hour, in hopes that a different hall monitor would be manning this spot, and not paying as much attention. He could have even gone back to the woods and waited until his usual time to come back.

But he didn't. He grabbed the doorknob and yanked.

As the door swung open, Luke saw that the hall monitor wasn't looking directly at the door just then. If Luke was sneaky enough, he could slip in without drawing attention to himself. But Luke let the door slam behind him. A cluster of boys with their eyes trained on the ground were jolted by the noise and even looked up briefly. Some of them started running, as panicked as if someone had fired a gun. Other boys didn't even glance Luke's way.

The hall monitor jerked his head around immediately. Luke quickly joined the slow-moving group of boys with their heads down. But just before he lowered his own head, Luke caught the hall monitor's stare. Their eyes locked for just an instant. Luke waited for the monitor to grab him by the collar, to yell, to haul him off to the headmaster's office. Luke could feel his shoulder hunching into a cower.

Nothing happened.

Luke shuffled forward with the other boys, and dared to look up again. The hall monitor was carefully looking past Luke.

He knows I was outside, Luke thought. *And he knows I know he knows. Why isn't he doing anything?*

It was like a chess game, Luke realized. He remembered one winter when Matthew and Mark had brought home a chess set from school. They'd had a blizzard after that, and they'd been snowed in for a long time, so Matthew and Mark spent hours playing chess. Luke had been a lot younger then, maybe only five or six. The game that fascinated his brothers only puzzled him.

"Why don't all the pieces move the same way?" he had asked, picking up the horse-shaped piece. "Why can't this one go in a straight line like the castle?"

"Because it can't," Matthew had replied irritably, while Mark squealed, "Put that down! You're messing up our game!"

Now Luke almost trod on another boy's heel. The boy didn't even turn around. If everyone at the school were a chess piece, Luke realized, most of the boys were pawns. The hall monitors and the other ones Luke thought of as starers were the big, important pieces. The bishops. And the king. Luke remembered that Matthew and Mark had treasured those pieces, sacrificing pawns and knights and castles to protect them. But Luke hadn't understood why. And he didn't understand the hall monitor now.

But he knew how to find out about him.

CHAPTER *EIGHTEEN*

When dinner was over that night, Luke slipped out of the dining hall behind all of the other boys. Instead of going into the evening lecture room like everyone else, he ducked down a dark hall. It wasn't a direct route to the door that led outside, but if Luke turned three corners and backtracked a bit, he'd get there.

I know the school really well now, Luke marveled. *If I had a note I needed to read in private now, it wouldn't be a problem at all.*

Luke felt decades older than the scared little boy who'd worried so over the note from Jen's dad. And gotten so upset when he read it.

It was just a scrap of paper. What did I expect?

Luke wondered: Would he ever look back on this day and regret getting so upset about his ruined garden?

No.

Luke had told himself it didn't matter if he ran into hall monitors. He could just start asking them questions: *Why did you destroy my garden? What if I told* the headmaster that you've been sneaking out? But now, creeping down the deserted hallway, he was glad he didn't have to test his bravado. As far as he could tell, the hall monitors only guarded the main route to the door. He'd suspected as much. The monitors didn't have to be very cautious, because most of the boys at the school behaved like sheep, only going where they were told. And all of the teachers seemed to be gone in the evenings.

Luke reached the final corner before the doorway, and stopped. The sound of his watch ticking seemed to fill the entire hall. Luke pressed his wrist to his chest to muffle it. Then it was his heart pounding that seemed too loud. His ears roared with listening.

Was this how Jen had felt, the night she left for the rally? Brave, reckless, crazy, courageous, terrified—all at once?

It didn't seem right to compare. Jen had been going to the rally—leading it, in fact—in an effort to win rights for third children all over the nation. Even her parents didn't know what she was doing. But she had believed so strongly that nobody should have to hide that she'd died for it.

Luke was mad about a garden.

Thinking that way, Luke felt foolish. He wondered if he should turn around. But just because Jen's cause had been enormous, that didn't mean Luke's was unimportant. Like Jen, Luke wanted to right a wrong.

Just then he heard the sounds he'd been waiting for: someone whispering, a muffled laugh, the click of the door latching. Luke waited a full five minutes—it was too dark to see his watch, so he counted off the tics. Then he tip-toed out of the shadows and followed the others out the door.

CHAPTER *NINETEEN*

The moon was out.

It had been so long since Luke had seen the night sky that he'd forgotten how mystical it could look. The moon was full tonight, a beautiful orb hovering low over the woods. Luke also recognized the same pinpricks of starlight he'd been used to seeing back home. But the stars seemed dimmer here, overshadowed by a glow on the horizon beyond the woods. Luke puzzled over that glow— it was in the wrong part of the sky to be the sunset. What else was that bright?

Luke remembered that Jen's dad had said the school was near a city. Could a city have lights that bright, that shone this far?

"I don't know anything," Luke whispered to himself. He'd thought that coming out of hiding would expose him to the world, teach him everything. But being at Hendricks seemed like just another way to hide.

A light flashed in the woods just then, and Luke realized he didn't have time to hesitate. He'd planned to creep across the lawn, but the moonlight was so bright, he worried about being seen. He decided to take his chances with running.

Nobody yelled. Nobody hissed, "Get away from here!"

Luke reached the edge of the woods and hid behind a tree. Then he cautiously moved up to the next tree. And the next one. The light swung erratically, just ahead.

Luke wished he'd taken the time to explore the woods, to get his bearings. He was terrified of walking straight into a tree, stepping in some big hole or tripping over a stump. He banged his shin and had to bite his lip to keep from crying out. He stepped in something squishy and almost fell. He wondered if he was traveling in circles.

Then he heard voices.

"—hate nature—"

"Yeah, well, you find a better place to meet—"

Luke crept closer. And closer. A strangely familiar voice was giving a long explanation: "—it's just your fear of the outdoors cropping up again. You've got to overcome it, you know?"

"Easy for you to say," someone else grumbled.

Luke was close enough now to see the backs of several heads. He dared to edge up to the next tree and peek out. Eight boys were sitting in a semicircle around a small, dim, portable lantern. Suddenly another light flashed on the other side of the group of boys. A twig cracked. Luke ducked back behind the tree.

"So what's with the emergency meeting?"

It was a girl's voice.

Luke inhaled sharply.

Jen . . .

It wasn't Jen, of course. When Luke dared to look out again, he saw a tall, scrawny girl with two pale, thin braids hanging on either side of her face. Jen had been shorter, more muscular, her brown hair cut short as a boy's. But just to hear a girl's voice again made Luke feel strange. It kept him from doing any of the crazy things he'd half-planned: leaping from behind the tree and screaming accusations, pretending to be a ghost haunting the woods, finding some way to exact revenge.

All he could do now was listen.

"Sorry to disturb the princesses of Harlow," a male voice was answering mockingly.

Luke knew he knew that voice. He peered out. Yes. Of course.

Jackal boy.

"It's the new kid," jackal boy was saying. "He's acting weird."

I should have known jackal boy was involved, Luke thought. *He probably planned the whole thing, led the charge on my garden. . . .* He glowered. Then he realized what jackal boy had said. "The new kid"? As far as Luke knew, there was only one new kid at Hendricks: himself. They were talking about him.

"Weird?" the girl's voice replied. "He's a boy, right? Isn't weirdness just kind of required?"

There were giggles. Luke squinted into the darkness. He

thought there were three or four other girls beside the girl with braids.

"Quit being such an exnay," jackal boy said.

"Exnay and proud of it," the girl retorted.

Luke listened harder, as though that would help him make sense of their words. Who would be proud of being an "exnay"? If he'd learned anything at Hendricks, it was that "exnay" was one of the worst insults you could hurl at anybody.

"Yeah, yeah. I don't see you announcing it anywhere but in the dark, in the woods, when nobody's around," jackal boy taunted.

"So you're admitting you're nobody?" the girl said.

One of the boys beside jackal boy made a frustrated grunt. "Why do we bother talking to them?" he asked.

Luke saw jackal boy dig his elbow into the other boy's ribs.

"I'll be noble and ignore that," jackal boy said loftily to the girl. "Naturally, we don't expect you to offer us any assistance in this matter. But we thought it was in everybody's best interest to keep you informed."

The girl sat down, and the other girls followed her lead. "So inform us."

"The new boy—" jackal boy started.

"Has he got a name?" the girl interrupted.

"He's registered as Lee Grant," jackal boy said.

Luke noticed how he said that. "Registered as . . ." Not, "His name is . . ." Did jackal boy suspect?

"I looked him up," jackal boy continued. "His dad's in charge of National Gas and Electric. Filthy rich. And he's switched schools a lot."

"That could fit," the girl said.

"But he doesn't seem like he has autism or any of the other disorders. I don't think he's even agoraphobic."

Luke didn't even try to puzzle out the unfamiliar words. Jackal boy was still talking.

"Trey over there saw him coming in from outside this afternoon."

"He was outside?" the girl asked. She sounded amazed, maybe even impressed. "Out here? In the woods? During the day?"

"Don't know," jackal boy said. Luke felt almost triumphant at the note of misery in the boy's voice. But Luke was confused. Had jackal boy and his friends destroyed the garden without even knowing it belonged to Luke? Or was jackal boy lying?

"Trey didn't see him until he was back inside," jackal boy continued. "He—you know—he doesn't like looking right at the door."

"Great guard system you got going there," the girl said.

"Shut up, Nina!" one of the boys yelled. Luke guessed it was Trey.

"Don't call me that!" the girl—Nina?—yelled back. Why would she have a name she didn't want to be called?

And then Luke understood. He, too, had a name he hated. He hated it because it was fake. And so was hers.

"Nina" was another former shadow child. She had to be.

Luke looked with new eyes at the group sitting in front of him in the dark woods. They must all be illegal third children using false identities. Luke's heart gave a jump. At last, he'd found others like him. He'd found a place to belong.

Luke started to move out from behind the tree, to reveal himself. Finally he'd found other kids to talk to about how hard it was pretending to be someone else. Finally he'd found other kids who would know how tough it was to come out of hiding. Finally he'd found other kids he could trust, as he'd trusted Jen. They could grieve for Jen with him.

Then he remembered: He was almost certain these were the ones who'd destroyed his garden.

Luke stayed put.

"All right, all right," jackal boy was saying. "Calm down. The point is, this kid, this 'Lee,' doesn't fit any of the profiles."

"Did you give him the test?" Nina asked.

"Um, well, there was a little problem—" jackal boy said hesitantly.

"Go ahead and say it!" Trey burst out furiously. "I flubbed the whole thing! I don't know why you make me guard that spot!"

"Because you're the bravest one," jackal boy said. Luke recognized that tone: It was the same sort of wheedling voice that Luke's brothers had used on him when they wanted him to do something unpleasant, like clean out the hog pen or spread manure on the garden.

Trey turned and faced Nina directly. "I left the door open, but I couldn't stand to be that close to it. I walked down the hall. Just for a minute! When I got back, this Lee kid was nowhere in sight."

Left the door open . . . Suddenly Luke understood. That first time he'd noticed the door, when it was ajar, it had been a test set up by jackal boy's gang.

But what were they testing him for?

"Maybe he went outside then, too," Nina said.

All the boys seemed to be shaking their heads in disbelief.

"I waited for three hours," Trey said. "I stared at that door the whole time, honest. Nobody'd stay out that long."

Why not? Luke wondered.

"So is he one of us or not?" Nina asked.

The question seemed to hang in the dark woods. Luke wanted to know the answer, too.

"Who knows?" jackal boy said. "The problem is, he's getting bold. Weird, like I said. We're scared he's going to get the rest of us in trouble. Blow our cover. This afternoon, he just stared back at Trey like he didn't care what Trey saw, or what Trey did. He was—"

"Defiant," Trey said.

Even Luke could see the baffled look jackal boy gave Trey.

"Sorry!" Trey said. "All I had to do when I was hiding

was read, remember? I didn't have a TV like the rest of you. I learned too many big words. 'Defiant' means, um— he was defying me, he was—"

"Offering a challenge," Luke said aloud.

And then he stepped out from behind the tree.

CHAPTER *TWENTY*

uke felt twelve pairs of eyes on him. Nina's mouth was frozen in a little "o" of surprise. Jackal boy's jaw dropped in astonishment.

But nobody was more astonished than Luke. *Why did I do that?* he wondered. He remembered thinking that most of the boys at Hendricks acted like pawns. *I'm a pawn, too, remember? Just plain old Luke Garner, who doesn't know anything about anything, who cowers in the attic while his best friend dies for the cause. Stepping out from behind that tree was something Jen would have done. Not me.*

But he had done it. Now what?

Luke longed to slide back behind the tree again or, given that it wouldn't be much of a hiding place now, to turn tail and run. But his legs were trembling so much that just standing still took all his strength.

Everyone was so quiet that Luke could hear his watch ticking again.

All right. He'd gotten himself into this mess by acting like Jen. What would she do next?

Talk. Jen could always talk.

"You destroyed my garden," Luke accused. "You'll have to make restitution."

Luke could use big words, too. He thought he saw a glimmer of appreciation in Trey's eyes. Everyone else stared blankly.

Would Jen bother explaining, or would she prefer letting them feel dumb?

"Garden?" jackal boy asked. "What garden?"

That wasn't what Luke had expected.

"What garden?" he repeated. "*My* garden. Over there." He pointed into the dark. "Last night, somebody trampled the whole thing, kicked over my beans, broke off my raspberry plants. *You're* the only ones I see out in the woods." Luke tried to let his anger carry him through. But all the faces in front of him looked vacant. Had he made a big mistake? Could they possibly be innocent? He finished weakly, "So you owe me."

Jackal boy shook his head.

"We don't know what you're talking about."

He didn't *seem* to be lying. But how good was Luke at judging liars?

"I'll show you," Luke said impatiently. He suddenly had the notion that if he saw them looking at the destruction, he'd be able to tell by their expressions whether or not they were guilty. He turned hastily and started walking. He was surprised when he heard footsteps behind him. They'd actually listened to him? *Obeyed* him?

They made a strange procession through the woods, Luke leading the way, the other boys following with their lantern, then the girls with a dim flashlight. Luke made a few missteps, and even had to backtrack once, but he circled around, hoping none of the others would notice. Finally they reached Luke's clearing. In the moonlight it looked desolate, just a stump and scraggly plants. It didn't look like it had ever contained a garden.

"There!" Luke said, trying to sound wronged and indignant. His voice came out in a squeak. "See these broken-off raspberry plants? See the squashed beans? But why do I have to show you? You know what you did."

No guilt showed on their faces. They still looked puzzled.

"He *is* crazy," jackal boy hissed.

"Wait a minute," Nina said. "Did you guys walk back to school this way last night?"

Trey shrugged.

"We might have," he said.

One of the other guys spoke up.

"It's not like we can tell any of the trees apart."

"So maybe you stepped on his garden by mistake," Nina said. "And didn't even know it."

"*I* certainly wouldn't know what a garden looks like," one of the other girls said. "Like this? What were you growing?"

"Nothing," Luke muttered. He was suddenly overcome with shame. He'd felt so brave stepping out from behind that tree. Just to make a fool of himself. Looking around, he could see how the other boys could have missed noticing his efforts, and trampled his garden by mistake. This had been a pathetic excuse for a garden. He'd been pathetic for ever thinking it was anything, let alone anything worth taking a risk for. He wished he could go back and hide behind a tree forever.

Jackal boy started laughing first.

"You thought this was a *garden?* You were sneaking out here to make a *garden?*" he asked.

The others began to snicker, too. Luke's shame turned into anger.

"So?" he asked, defiant again.

"So you are a lecker," jackal boy said. He was laughing so hard, he doubled over in mirth. "A *real* lecker."

"You always say that," Luke grumbled. "I don't even know what a lecker is."

"Someone from the country," Trey explained helpfully. "Like a bumpkin. That's what it really means. But now the word's just kind of a general insult, like calling someone a moron or stupid."

Luke thought Trey almost sounded apologetic, but that only made things worse.

"What's wrong with being from the country?" Luke asked.

"If you have to ask . . . ," jackal boy said, laughing again. He had to sit down on the rotting stump to catch his breath. Luke hoped he got mold smears on his pants.

"Want to know something even funnier?" jackal boy continued. "I'm betting you're really an exnay, too. So all those insults—lecker, exnay, fonrol—they're all true. I don't know that I've ever met someone who's all three before. We'll have to come up with a new word, just for you. What'll it be?"

Luke stared at jackal boy and the others laughing behind him. His faced burned. How could he have thought, even for an instant, that these might be kids he could trust? That he might belong with them?

"Leave me alone!" he shouted, and turned and ran.

CHAPTER *TWENTY-ONE*

L uke could hear someone crashing through the woods behind him, but he didn't look back. He'd run into the darkest part of the woods, and it took all his concentration to dodge the tree limbs that seemed to reach down out of nowhere. In fact, if Luke really wanted to terrify himself, he could think of those tree limbs as witches' arms, ghouls' fingers. He wasn't used to running through woods at night. Back home, when he'd gone outside after dark, it had mostly been for catching lightning bugs in the backyard, playing moonlight kick ball with his brothers— innocent fun.

He'd been so young, back then, back home.

He forced himself to run faster, but whoever was behind him seemed to be catching up. Luke zigzagged, because he'd read once that that was how rabbits escaped their predators. Then he slammed into a tree. He screamed in pain, and reeled backwards.

A dark shape pounced. Before he knew it, Luke was pinned to the ground.

Luke remembered another time he'd been tackled: the

first time he'd crept into Jen's house. He made a noise, and the next thing he knew, she had him facedown in the carpet. And they'd become friends.

This wasn't Jen.

"What do you think you're doing?" a voice hissed in his ear. Jackal boy's. "You go back now, during Indoctrination, and they'll catch you. They'll know. And then they'll come looking for the rest of us."

Indoctrination? Luke guessed that jackal boy meant the evening lecture. The name made sense—the lecture was always about how wonderful the Government was. But Luke hadn't even thought about what he was running toward. He was just running away.

"Who will catch me?" he asked. "The only ones who watch are the hall monitors. And they all report to you, right?"

"You got it," jackal boy said. He sounded pleased. "I worked hard setting up that system. The teachers didn't like hall duty, anyway. And now—"

"You can get away with anything, can't you?" Luke asked. "Unless I tell."

He didn't know what possessed him to make that threat. Maybe it was just habit—after twelve years of being the youngest brother, he knew the power of tattling.

And he knew how easily it could backfire.

"Make you a deal," Luke said quickly. "Let me up, and I won't go back now. Answer some questions for me, and I won't tell. I'll keep your secrets."

Jackal boy seemed to be considering. Finally, he said, "Okay."

Luke scrambled up and pulled away. He rubbed the side of his face. He wasn't sure if it was sore from hitting the tree or from being slammed against the ground. His hand came away wet.

"I'm bleeding," he said accusingly.

"You'll have to hide it," jackal boy said. "Are you good at hiding?"

Luke shrugged away the question. He knew jackal boy was really asking something else. But Luke wasn't ready to answer.

"What's your name, anyway?" Luke asked.

"Which one?" jackal boy asked. "If you look at the school records, I'm Scott Renault. Out here, I'm Jason."

"One of those names is fake," Luke said.

Somewhere in the woods, an owl hooted. Luke waited. Finally, jackal boy answered, softly, "Yes."

"Your friends all have fake names, too," Luke said.

"Yes." No hesitation.

"You're all third children who have come out of hiding with fake I.D. cards," Luke said.

"Exnays," jackal boy said.

"Is *that* what that means?" Luke asked.

"You didn't know?" jackal boy asked. "Where have you been all your life?"

Luke decided not to answer that question, either.

"And fonrols—" he started.

"—are any third children, hiding or not."

"Why does everyone at school call each other those names?" Luke asked. "Is everyone here an exnay?"

In the dark, Luke could barely see jackal boy shaking his head.

"Haven't kids called each other exnays and fonrols at the other schools you've been to? All the other places you've ever lived? Some say in the beginning the Government paid people to use 'fonrol' and 'exnay' as swear words. On TV, and stuff. Then those words were forbidden in public broadcast, which just meant that people used them more in private. They wanted to make sure that everyone thought of third children as terrible."

Luke wondered why Jen had never told him about that.

"Maybe I've never been to any other schools," Luke said cautiously. He'd said "maybe." He could still deny everything if he wanted.

Jackal boy laughed, openmouthed. His teeth glinted in the moonlight.

"Why don't you just come out and admit it?" he asked. "You're an exnay, too. I know it."

Luke dodged the question.

"Why do you harass me every night?" he asked. "When everyone else ignores me—"

"It's the procedure we developed for dealing with new boys," jackal boy said. "And new girls, over at Harlow School for Girls. We've discovered it's hard for shadow children when they first come out of hiding—they're overwhelmed, traumatized. Think about it. They've spent their whole lives thinking it's death to be seen, and suddenly they're expected to interact with others all day long, to sit through classes with dozens of other kids, behave normally. They freak out."

"Did you?" Luke asked, trying to picture jackal boy as the new kid, just come out of hiding, scared of everything. His imagination failed him.

"Me?" Jackal boy sounded surprised. "Sure. It was tough. The problem was, lots of exnays got so panicked, they'd do something really dumb—stand up and chant their real name, start screaming, 'Don't look at me! Don't look at me!'—you know, totally lose it. Now, Hendricks has a lot of disturbed kids, anyway—"

"It does?" Luke asked.

"Haven't you noticed?" Jackal boy sounded amazed. "The autistic kids—the ones who rock and won't look you in the eye—the phobic kids, we've got all sorts of troubled cases in there. Ever meet Rolly Sturgeon? *There's* a psycho for you. So exnays can get away with some pretty wacky behavior at Hendricks. But the Population Police still got in a few good raids. That's why a lot of us exnays got together and planned it all out. Every time a new kid arrives, we go into emergency mode until we can tell if he's an exnay or not. We watch. We protect." Luke remembered the hands pushing him down into the chair that first day, in his first class. "But we do it all in secret. We give the exnay plenty of breathing room. And we pick just one person to approach him. To be a friend."

Luke thought about having to chant, "I am a fonrol" fifty times, of having to do push-ups while everyone else laughed, of having to obey every single one of jackal boy's sarcastic commands.

"I thought friends were supposed to be nice to you," Luke said bitterly. "Maybe that's a word I don't understand, either."

"Being too nice to an exnay from the start only causes trouble," jackal boy said. "They break down. They get weepy. They're so happy to find a sympathetic ear that they tell everything, no matter who else can hear. No, exnays need the kind of friend who can toughen them up. Like I did for you."

Was that what had happened? Luke felt as overwhelmed and confused as he had his first day at Hendricks. Listening to jackal boy was like it used to be listening to Jen: They were both so sure of themselves, it was hard for Luke to figure out what he thought on his own.

"How can you tell if a new kid is an exnay or not?" Luke asked, stalling.

"We give them a test," jackal boy said. "When they're ready, we leave a door open and make sure they see it, we stare them right in the eye—we know exactly how an exnay would respond, compared with a typical agoraphobe, or a typical autistic kid."

"You've got everyone figured out, huh?" Luke said.

"Sure," jackal boy asked. "Can't you tell?"

Luke couldn't answer that question. He was feeling panicky again. In a minute, he was going to have to make a decision. With Jen, it had been easy—he'd trusted her right away. But he was older now, more suspicious. He knew that she had been betrayed.

And he could be, too.

"So you gave me the usual test," he said tentatively. "Did I pass?"

"Depends on what you call passing," jackal boy said. He sounded cagier now, like he wasn't sure whose side Luke was on.

Luke had run out of questions. Or—he had lots of questions, but none of them would help him decide whether to trust jackal boy and his friends with his secret. It would be so nice to be able to tell. But was it worth risking his life for?

Had he already risked his life by following them into the woods?

Luke didn't like thinking things like that. He missed Jen all of a sudden. She was always good at turning his fear into a joke.

"Did you know Jen?" he asked jackal boy abruptly.

"Jen?" jackal boy said, his voice suddenly exuberant. "Jen Talbot? You knew her, too?"

Luke nodded. "She was my, um, neighbor. I went over to her house whenever I could," he said.

"Wow," jackal boy breathed. "Come on!"

He grabbed Luke's arm and pulled him back through the woods, all the time marveling, "I can't believe you really met her. In person. It's incredible. She's legendary, you know—"

The low-hanging tree limbs didn't seem so frightening now. Luke and jackal boy simply ducked. Together. A couple times jackal boy held a branch out of the way so Luke could go first. A couple times Luke returned the favor. Jackal boy kept rushing Luke along. They burst back into the clearing where everyone else was still sitting, not even talking. They appeared to have nothing to do but wait for jackal boy.

"Listen, you all!" jackal boy announced. "This is unbelievable! He knew Jen. He went to her house and everything!"

There was a flurry of questions—"What was she like?" "Did she tell you about the rally?" "How did you know her?" Someone produced a bag of cookies and they all passed it around, like it was a party.

It was a party. It was a party where they were accepting Luke into their group. Just because he knew Jen.

Luke did his best to answer all the questions.

"Jen was—amazing," he said. "She wasn't scared of anything. Not the Population Police, not the Government, not anyone. Not even her parents." Luke thought about how strange it was that Jen's father worked for the Population Police. Mr. Talbot was like a double agent, trying to help third children instead of killing them. But he hadn't been able to prevent his own daughter's death. He'd just barely managed to keep the Population Police from finding out that she had been his daughter.

Luke didn't want to talk about Jen's death, just her life.

"She spent months planning the rally," he said. "It was her statement, 'I deserve to exist. We deserve to exist.' She wanted as many third children there as possible. Out of hiding. She thought the Government would have to listen. She took everyone to the steps of the president's house . . ." Luke remembered the fight they'd had when he'd refused to go. And how she'd forgiven him. He stopped talking, lost in grief.

"The Government killed everyone at the rally," Nina finished for him.

Luke nodded blindly. He couldn't ignore Jen's death. He choked out, "Jen was a true hero. She was the bravest person I'll ever know. And someday—someday everyone will know about her."

The others nodded solemnly. *They know how I feel,* Luke marveled. And then, in spite of his grief, he felt a shot of joy: I *am* one of them. I belong.

After that, somehow, he was able to tell happy stories about Jen. He had the whole crowd laughing when he described how Jen had dusted for his fingerprints the first time he'd gone to her house.

"She wanted to make sure I was . . ." Luke hesitated. He had been about to say "another shadow child, like her." But that wasn't how he wanted to reveal his secret, just letting it slip out like it didn't matter. He finished lamely, "She wanted to make sure I was who I said I was."

"So," jackal boy said, lounging against a tree. "Who are you, anyway? What's your real name, 'Lee'?"

Luke looked at the circle of faces surrounding him. Jackal boy's question had silenced the laughter. Or maybe it was Luke's sudden stammering. Now everyone was watching Luke expectantly. An owl hooted somewhere deeper in the woods, and it was like a signal. Finally. It was time to tell.

"L—" Luke started. But the word stuck in his throat. All those nights he'd whispered his name, all those times he'd longed to speak his name aloud—and now he couldn't.

Some of the dry cookie crumbs slid back on his tongue and he started coughing, choking. One of the other boys had to pound him on the back before Luke got his breath back.

"Lee Grant," Luke said, as soon as he could speak again. His urge to confess was gone. "My name is Lee Grant."

"Sure," jackal boy kidded him. "Whatever you say."

And then Luke felt foolish. Jackal boy had revealed his real name. Why couldn't Luke reveal his?

Because, Luke thought with a chill, *I didn't decide to belong. Jackal boy decided for me.*

CHAPTER TWENTY-TWO

Belonging to jackal boy's group made all the difference in the world. It began that night. Luke didn't have to creep back from the woods by himself, praying nobody noticed. He went with the others, as part of the crowd. They strutted down the hall, not even trying to be quiet.

"What if someone hears?" Luke ventured.

"Who cares?" jackal boy replied. "Indoctrination's almost over. If there are any teachers around, they'll just think we left early to man our hall monitor posts."

They were in a brighter end of the hall now. Jackal boy got a good look at Luke's face and whistled.

"You really did get all bloody. Come on. I'll take you to the nurse."

Jackal boy led Luke to an unfamiliar office, one he'd seen only once before, when he was searching for windows.

"My friend walked into the wall, coming out of Indoctrination," Jackal boy told the woman who answered the door. "Stupid, huh? Can you give him a bandage?"

"My, my, you boys. You never look where you're going,"

the woman fussed. She was old and wrinkled, like the pictures Luke had seen of grandmothers. She puttered around getting antiseptic and gauze and tape. Then she dabbed at Luke's cheek with a wet cloth. "This is an awfully rough abrasion. Which wall did you run into, dear?"

Jackal boy saved Luke from having to answer.

"Oh, he didn't get bloody from the wall," jackal boy explained. "He kind of bounced off the wall and fell down. Then he scraped his face on the carpet. Someone might have kicked him by mistake, too."

Luke's mother would have listened to an excuse like that and then said, "Okay. Now. What really happened?" But this woman only nodded and *tsk-tsked* a little more.

The antiseptic stung, and Luke had to bite his lip to keep from crying out. But the woman was quick, and his face was neatly bandaged before he knew it.

"Write your name and the time down in the log on your way out," the woman said. "And be more careful the next time, all right?"

Jackal boy even wrote Luke's name for him.

Up in their room, jackal boy stretched and yawned and proclaimed, "I don't feel like dealing with the new kid tonight. Let's just leave him alone. Okay, guys? He's getting boring, anyway."

Luke thought some of his other roommates looked disappointed, but nobody complained.

In the morning, jackal boy said, "You can have breakfast with us. We have our own table. Hall monitor privileges."

"But I'm not a hall monitor," Luke said.

"The teachers won't notice," jackal boy said. "And maybe you will be soon."

So Luke sat at a table with other boys. For once he didn't have to force himself to choke down his oatmeal. It practically tasted good. And for the first time, Luke got a good look around the dining hall without feeling like he had to glance quickly and furtively. With clean white walls and a peaked ceiling, it really wasn't such a bad place.

"Can I ask you some questions? Here, I mean," Luke said to jackal boy.

"As long as you're not acting like a real exnay," jackal boy said brusquely, as if he were truly swearing at Luke. But Luke caught the double meaning. It was a brilliant code.

"Why is this school like this?" Luke began. "I mean, with no windows, and the strange boys . . . and the teachers who don't seem to notice us unless we do something wrong. And even then, they just say, 'Two demerits.' I don't even know what that means."

Jackal boy pushed back his oatmeal and smirked.

"Confusing, huh?" he asked mockingly. But he started explaining, anyway. "Hendricks began as an educational experiment. Back when there were the famines, people had debates about whether the undesirables in society deserved food when so many were starving. They let all the criminals die, but a bunch of bleeding-heart, sympathetic types said it was cruel not to feed people with mental illnesses, physical disabilities, that kind of thing.

One man stepped forward and offered his family's estate to be two schools for troubled kids. Hendricks for boys and Harlow for girls. He said he'd feed them, too—you see how well he's doing." Jackal boy made a face at the oatmeal. "They built the schools without windows because Mr. Hendricks had the idea that kids with agoraphobia—the ones scared of wide-open spaces—would be better off not even seeing the outdoors. He thought they'd start longing for what they couldn't see. And he thought having windows would just overstimulate the autistic kids. But he also thought it'd be good to bring in some normal kids. Like role models."

Luke tried to absorb all of that. He thought about how differently jackal boy acted when he was explaining something, compared with how Jen had always been. Jen was always outraged, indignant over every little injustice. He could just hear her voice, rising in disgust: "Can you believe it? Isn't that terrible?"

Jackal boy just sounded secretly amused, almost haughty. Too bad. Poor kids. Who cares?

Luke swallowed another bite of lumpy oatmeal.

"And the teachers?" he prompted. "Why aren't they more ... um ..."

"Involved? Aware? Semi-intelligent?" jackal boy offered.

"Yeah. All the adults. Like, the nurse last night didn't seem very smart. And what's-her-name, in the office, when I was in there the first day, it was like all the students were just a pain to her."

"Think about it," jackal boy said. "If you were a grown-up, and you could get a job anywhere else, would you work here? We got the dregs, man, the real dregs."

Luke didn't know anything about grown-up jobs. He'd never thought he would be able to come out of hiding to have one.

Jackal boy was smirking again. "But it serves our purposes, all right, to have teachers who are just one step up from leckers. We can do just about anything we want. Got it?"

He looked around at his cohorts, the hall monitors, and soon they were all smirking, too.

Luke wanted to object to that word, "lecker." Just because someone came from the country, that didn't make him dumb. Did it?

Something else bothered Luke, too.

"But I wanted to learn a lot at Hendricks," he said. "Math and science and how to speak other languages. . . . I've been here a month and I haven't learned a thing. I don't even know if I'm going to the right classes. I wanted to—" he broke off at the last minute because he remembered he couldn't talk about being an exnay. He couldn't say that he wanted to learn everything he could to help make third children legal again.

Jackal boy was laughing anyway.

"Oh, right, we're all here to learn," he said, rolling his eyes. This made his friends laugh, too. "Just stick close to me," jackal boy continued. "That's how you learn what you need to know. Forget the classes. And if you're worried about grades—don't you think I know how to fix that, too? How do you think we all got on the honor roll?"

Luke didn't know. He didn't even know what the honor roll was.

But when the bell rang for the first class, he left the dining hall with jackal boy and his gang. He felt safe now, traveling in a pack. All the hall monitors he passed gave him knowing looks, with secret nods that nobody else could have noticed.

And when he hesitated between classrooms, jackal boy was quick to tell him where to go.

CHAPTER TWENTY-THREE

Luke didn't go back to his garden by himself anymore. But two or three times a week, jackal boy would whisper in his ear, "Tonight," and Luke's heart would jump. "Tonight" meant, "We're going to the woods. We're meeting the girls."

Each time he stepped outside, Luke would breathe in deeply, the same way a starving man gobbled down food. But he noticed that most of the others, all so brave and imposing indoors, positively cowered in the open air. They squeezed their eyes shut and took halting steps forward, like condemned men walking to their executions.

"You don't like the outdoors, do you?" Luke asked Trey once as they walked across the lawn to the woods.

Trey shook his head slowly, as if moving too quickly might make him throw up. He looked a little green already.

"It's better in the woods," he said through gritted teeth. "At least there we're covered."

"But—" Luke took another deep breath, savoring the smell of newly mowed grass and spring rain. He couldn't understand Trey. "Don't you hate being cooped up all the time?"

Trey gave him a sidelong glance.

"I spent thirteen years in the same room. I didn't step foot outside even once until I came here."

"Oh," Luke said. He suddenly saw that, for a third child, he'd been very lucky. Before the Government tore down the woods behind his house and built a neighborhood there instead, he'd spent most of his time outdoors. Except for not going to school, he hadn't lived that differently from his older brothers.

He couldn't imagine spending thirteen years in the same room.

"Jen went shopping on fake passes," he told Trey. "Her mother took her to play groups. I thought other third children lived like her."

"I wouldn't know," Trey said. "I—I wished—" He hesitated. "I miss my room."

Luke felt sorry for the other boy. How many of his other new friends had basically lived their entire lives in a box?

He watched jackal boy running ahead, then circling back to encourage the others.

"Jacka—I mean, Jason must have been like Jen," Luke said. "He must have gotten out a lot. He's not afraid of anything."

"No," Trey said. "He's not. He says he's overcome all his hiding-related phobias. And he's only been here a few weeks longer than you."

"He has?" Luke asked in surprise. He'd assumed jackal

boy was a long-timer, with years of experience at Hendricks.

"The rest of us only started last fall," Trey continued. "I think. No one talked much before Jason got here."

Before he could make sense of that, Luke had to remind himself all over again that "Jason" was really jackal boy. It was no wonder that Luke had been confused when he first started at Hendricks—the boys, at least the ones he hung out with now, did go by three or four different names. They might answer to the first or last part of their fake name at school, and the first or last part of their real name out in the woods. That was riskier. A few just went by initials.

Trey had explained that his name just meant "three." He wouldn't tell even jackal boy his real name.

They reached the woods, and what Trey had said finally sunk in.

"Wait a minute," Luke said. "You mean you weren't all friends before Jason came? You haven't been meeting in the woods all along?"

Trey flashed him a puzzled look.

"Just since April," he said.

Luke's mind was racing.

"The rally was in April," he said.

"Yeah," Trey said with a shrug.

The girls met them then, and they started the same kind of banter Luke had witnessed the first night. It sounded different to Luke now, not as if they were all worldly and experienced, but as if they were reading lines in a play, pretending to talk to each other the way normal boys and girls talked. Nina made jokes about how stupid boys were, and Jason made fun of the girls. Luke watched the faces of the ones who were quiet. They all looked scared.

"What's this meeting for?" Luke asked suddenly.

Jason turned to look at Luke in surprise.

"Why—we're planning ways to resist the Government over the Population Law. To follow up the rally."

"The rally," Nina echoed wistfully.

Luke's heart beat fast. This was what he'd wanted! He'd wanted to do something brave like Jen. It would be like apologizing to her for not going with her, for doubting her.

But could he be as brave as Jen?

Without dying, too?

"How?" he demanded. "How are we going to resist?"

Nina and Jason looked at each other.

"Well, that's what we're deciding," Nina said. "Just like a boy, asking dumb questions!"

But they didn't decide anything that night. They just joked around some more, made a game of guessing one boy's real name, and headed back to their schools.

Jason pulled Luke aside as they stepped back into the school building.

"Not everyone's as ready as you," he said. "You've got to give the others time. As long as they're trembling in their shoes every time they step outside, they'll never make good subversives."

Luke was flattered. It made sense.

"Okay," he said.

Jason playfully punched Luke's arm.

"Knew you'd understand. Hey—you ready for finals?"

"Finals?" Luke asked.

"You know, next week? End-of-term tests?" Jason said. "You pass, you get out of here, you fail, you're stuck for life?"

Luke stopped short.

"Oh, no . . . ," he breathed.

Jason laughed.

"Scared you, huh? Remember, you stay on my good side, I'll make sure your 'parents' get to look at a brilliant report!"

"I'm not even going to the right classes!" Luke said, panic coursing through his veins. "And I can't ask anyone now. It's been too long—"

"I'll find out for you!" Jason said, laughing again. He was already halfway down the hall.

CHAPTER *TWENTY-FOUR*

J ason was as good as his word. The next morning at breakfast, he handed Luke a computer printout that said, at the top, CLASS SCHEDULE FOR LEE GRANT. It had times, room numbers, teachers' names.

"Where'd you get this?" Luke asked.

"You think your only computer hacker friend is dead?" Jason said.

He meant Jen. Luke had a flash of missing her all over again. He could picture her sitting at the computer, typing fast. She'd created a chat room for third children, with the password of "free." She'd connected hundreds of third children, so they weren't just sitting in their little rooms, all alone. She'd hacked into the records of the national police, to make sure none of the kids going to the third-child rally were caught before they got to the capital.

But what good had all her hacking done?

"Earth to Lee," Jason was saying. "Or whatever your name is. You should know, your schedule really doesn't matter. I can change all your grades on the computer, anyhow."

But after breakfast, Luke determinedly marched off to his first class, listened closely, and took detailed notes. By the end of the hour, he knew something he'd never known before: Prime numbers could be divided only by themselves and one.

In his second class, he boldly grabbed a textbook off the bookshelf and read the poem whose page number the teacher had written on the board. He could even make sense of the fancy language—two people were friends, and one of them died, and the other one felt sad.

Luke figured he had an unfair advantage, understanding that.

In science and technology class, the teacher was talking about gasoline motors. Luke could just picture one, all grease-covered, in Father's tractor. And now he knew how they worked.

By lunchtime, Luke was ready to brag to Jason, "I *am* learning something now." He was even confident enough to tease, "Maybe I won't need your help with my grades."

"You're going to learn a whole term's worth in just a week?" jackal boy mocked. "Right. Next week, Friday, at five o'clock, you'll come begging, 'Please, please, I need help! I'll do anything!'"

Luke only set his jaw and pulled out a book to study.

CHAPTER *TWENTY-FIVE*

By the end of the week, all the teachers had test dates written in chalk on their blackboards. And Luke was spending every spare moment studying.

"Why?" Trey asked him one night as they were trudging out to the woods. "Jason can fix your grades. And it's not like your real parents are going to see them, anyway."

"When you were stuck in your room," Luke said, "didn't you ever want to know anything about the outside world? About whether other people were like you, or different, or whether grass grows the same way all over the world, or how a car runs?"

"Not really," Trey said.

Luke was sorry that he couldn't explain. It wasn't the grades themselves that mattered to him. But he felt like he had something to prove. Maybe that people from the country—leckers—weren't so dumb, after all. Maybe that Jen's dad hadn't risked his life for nothing, getting Luke a fake identity. Maybe that Luke wasn't wasting time just hanging out in the woods making jokes with the girls from Harlow while other third children still had to hide.

He was surprised that, with each day that passed, his classes made more sense to him. The teachers weren't really that bad, just distant. The history teacher, Mr. Dirk, could tell fascinating stories about kings and knights and battles, and they were all true. The literature teacher could recite whole poems from memory. Luke didn't always understand all the words, but he liked the cadence and rhyme. The math teacher said once, "Aren't numbers *friendly?*" and he really seemed to believe it. Luke wondered if the teachers were shy, too—if they had some of those phobias Trey and Jason had talked about, and were downright terrified of looking their students straight in the eye.

The night before his first test, Luke studied through dinner, and skipped going to the woods with all the others during Indoctrination so he could hunch over in a hallway, reading history. Jason mocked him—"What are you trying to do, bookworm? Learn as many big words as Trey?" and, "You could read all night and still not pass your tests. Come on."

"Leave me alone," Luke growled, eager to get back to the Trojan War.

Luke was surprised that Jason stepped back instead of insisting.

"Fine," he said. "Waste your time. See if I care."

The words sounded like the swaggering boy Luke was used to. But his tone seemed to say something else. So did the set of his shoulders as he walked away. He sounded wary, on edge.

Could Jason possibly be scared of Luke?

Luke was nobody. Jason was in charge. Luke decided he was imagining things, and went back to his book.

Still, after lights out, Luke couldn't sleep. He was too unsettled—worried about the test the next day, wondering what his family was doing back home, wishing Jen were there to figure out Jason for him. He even thought back to the advice Jen's dad had written for Luke: "Blend in." Who was Luke supposed to blend in with? The boys who trudged blindly through the halls each day? The ones who followed Jason? Or Jason himself?

Somewhere in the room, a bed creaked.

Luke thought it was just someone turning over in his sleep but he stiffened anyway, and listened hard.

There was a *pat-pat-pat* that could have been footsteps, or could have been Luke's imagination. And then, the hall light shone briefly into the room as the door was opened and closed.

Luke sat up. He crept over to the door and opened it a crack so he'd have light to see by.

All the beds were filled with sleeping boys except two. Luke's.

And Jason's.

CHAPTER *TWENTY-SIX*

L uke took time to grab one of his textbooks so he'd have an excuse if someone caught him out of his room after lights out. "I only wanted to study some more," he could say. "I'm worried about my tests."

But the only person who might catch him was Jason.

Out in the dimly lit hall Luke looked back and forth, not sure which way to go. Probably Jason had only needed to go to the bathroom, and Luke was foolish to follow him. Luke headed toward the bathroom first.

Why didn't I think to go to the bathroom after lights out, back when I was trying to find a place to read my note? Luke wondered. But Luke had been too terrified back then to think like that. He wouldn't have dared leave his bed. He had actually blended in quite well. *And if I'd read the note right away, I wouldn't have discovered the door to outdoors or the woods. I wouldn't have had those few days of setting up my garden.* He still missed his garden. He tried not to think about it. *And I never would have gotten to know anybody.*

But how well *did* he know his new friends? The only

friend he'd ever had before was Jen, and that friendship had been entirely different.

It wasn't fair to compare.

He sneaked quietly down the hall, feeling foolish. Of course Jason would be in the bathroom, and he'd only have rude comments and mockery for Luke when he saw him. "Can't even pee without your books, huh?" maybe, or even, "Hey, lecker, we've got toilet paper here and everything. You won't need to use that."

The bathroom was empty.

Luke backtracked, and glanced in his room again. Jason's bed was still empty. Luke went the opposite direction from the bathroom. All that lay down this hallway was the back stairs.

Maybe Luke wouldn't look for Jason anymore. What did he think he was going to do when he found him? But Luke was so thoroughly awake now that he decided he might as well study. The details of the Trojan War and the Peloponnesian War were blurring in his mind.

He went over to the stairwell and sat down on the top step. He leaned against the wall, opened his book, and began reading. "The Greeks fought battles for—"

Far below Luke, someone was murmuring.

Luke sat still for a minute, tempted to ignore it. It probably was Jason, but so what? If he was having a secret meeting without Luke, why should Luke care? It wasn't like Jason's gang ever planned anything real, anyway.

But Luke did care. If Jason's gang was going to help

third children, Luke owed it to himself—to his family, to Jen, to Jen's dad—to take part.

Luke eased down to the next step. And the next. And the next. He kept clutching his book because he didn't want to make any noise putting it down. Yet he wondered if he should be making noise, acting normal, so he could come upon the secret meeting casually, "Oh, hi, guys—didn't know you were down here. Can I help?"

There was nothing normal about walking around Hendricks in the middle of the night. Luke stayed quiet.

When he rounded the corner of the second flight of stairs, he could begin to distinguish words. The only person who seemed to be talking was Jason. Nothing new about that. Luke crouched behind the half-wall that surrounded the stairs. He listened closely.

"But it's too soon!" Jason was pleading.

Luke risked a peek over the banister. Maybe Trey was there, and would call out, "Hey, Lee! Glad you're here! I was hoping you would come!"

But Jason appeared to be alone.

He was talking into a small portable phone. At least, that's what Luke thought it was. He'd never seen one before, except in sketches in his science textbook.

Jason was facing the other way, so Luke kept watching and listening.

"I told you. There's no danger in waiting!" he exclaimed. "They're just sitting ducks!"

Jason was silent, listening. He turned slightly and Luke

caught a glimpse of the side of his face. Jason's expression was set, dead serious. Luke thought about all the times he'd seen Jason joking, joshing, prodding, mocking. Luke wouldn't have thought Jason could be 100 percent serious about anything. He seemed like a different boy.

Frightened, Luke ducked out of sight.

"I've got four and she's got two," Jason said. "But I could have more by the end of the week."

Four and two and more of what? Luke wondered.

"Well, I don't know about Nina," Jason said. "You'd have to ask her. But she says girls are harder to recruit."

Girls? Luke thought he'd solved his puzzle. Jason was making plans for some action against the Government—something like the rally, but safer, Luke hoped. He was telling someone how many boys and girls—how many exnays—were available to help. Except . . . the group that met in the woods had nine boys now, with Luke, and five girls.

Hadn't Jason told Luke once that the whole group wasn't brave enough yet to be subversives? Luke wondered whom Jason was counting and whom he was leaving out. Trey was pretty timid. So were several of the others.

What about Luke? What if Jason wasn't including Luke because Luke hadn't gone to the meeting in the woods that evening? Or because he knew that Luke was secretly the biggest chicken of all?

Luke started to stand up, to say, "Wait! Count me in!" His legs were quivering, but he could make himself be brave. He'd have to.

Jason had his back turned to Luke again. He was practically snarling into the phone now.

"You want names? All right, I'll give you the ones I have. Antonio Blanco, alias Samuel Irving. Denton Weathers, alias Travis Spencer. Sherman Kymanski, alias Ryan Mann. Patrick Kerrigan, alias Tyrone Janson."

Jason was saying the boys' real names. Luke was so thrilled, he couldn't speak. If only he'd told Jason his real name. He could just imagine hearing, "Luke Garner, subversive for the cause, coming to the aid of third children everywhere." Forget the alias. It didn't matter.

Jason shifted his portable phone in his hand, and Luke had a terrible thought. What if Jason's phone was bugged? Then Luke realized something even worse: Since it was a portable phone, the Population Police didn't even have to bug it. Luke had learned in science and technology class just last week that portable phones sent out messages indiscriminately. Didn't Jason know that? All the Population Police needed was a receiver.

And of course they had one. They had everything.

Luke rushed out from his hiding place and took the last flight of stairs in two leaps. He had to get the phone away from Jason before he accidentally betrayed another boy's identity. Jason still had his back to Luke. He was saying indignantly into the phone: "Of course I'll get the others to tell me their real names. They're just cagey. They do trust me. They don't have any idea I work for the Population Police."

CHAPTER *TWENTY-SEVEN*

Luke had his hand inches from the phone when Jason's words registered: " . . . I work for the Population Police." Luke's hand and arm kept going, even though his mind was suddenly frozen. He watched his hand as if it belonged to someone else. His fingers grasped the phone, jerked it out of Jason's grip, and threw it to the ground. Then someone's foot—no, Luke's foot, acting as independently as his hand—stomped on it.

Jason whirled around.

"You!" he spat.

Luke's frozen mind was struggling to thaw. Strange facts were emerging from the ice. Jason worked for the Population Police. That's why he hadn't cared about using a portable phone. He wasn't organizing subversive activity against the Government. He was turning in the exnays.

"You're an informer," Luke whispered.

Jason's eyes narrowed, calculatingly. Luke instantly saw his mistake. Why hadn't he played dumb? He could have pretended he hadn't heard Jason's last sentence. He could have acted hurt that Jason was leaving him out. He could have begged for a dangerous assignment.

It wouldn't have been too hard to act dumb. Until two seconds ago, he had been.

"Now, Lee," Jason said cautiously. He seemed to be trying to decide how to play things. Was Luke going to get, "Oh, don't be silly. What would make you think that? Why would I turn anybody in when I'm an exnay, too?" Or, "So you know the truth. That's it. You're dead"?

Jason took a step toward Luke. Luke clutched his history textbook like a shield. Jason came even closer.

And then, without thinking, Luke whipped the book out and swung it at Jason's head with all his might.

Jason crumpled. Knocked sideways, he tried desperately to regain his balance. Luke swung again.

This time, Jason fell backwards. His head hit the stairs with a loud *thunk*. His body rolled down to the landing.

He didn't move.

CHAPTER *TWENTY-EIGHT*

Luke hardly dared to breathe. He held his book high over his head.

Jason still didn't move.

What if Luke had killed him?

Luke knelt down and put his hand in front of Jason's nose. Very, very faintly, he felt bursts of air every few seconds. Jason wasn't dead, only knocked unconscious.

For how long?

Luke wasted time staring at Jason's motionless body. Luke wouldn't have wanted to be a murderer, but everything would be easier if Jason were dead.

Luke could kill him now.

Everything in Luke recoiled against that notion. Jason was the worst kind of fake—an informer, a traitor, someone who pretends to be a friend and then betrays. He probably had as good as killed four boys whose only crime was existing. Jason deserved to die.

But Luke couldn't kill him.

Luke was desperately trying to get his paralyzed brain to come up with another option, when the portable phone rang. The noise echoed in the stairwell as shrilly as a hundred roosters, all crowing at once. It sounded loud enough to wake the dead, not to mention the merely unconscious. Luke grabbed the phone, just to shut it up. It kept ringing. Luke stared at it stupidly. He'd never actually touched a phone before tonight. Didn't they stop ringing when you picked them up? He punched buttons on the phone at random. Finally, miraculously, the noise stopped.

Luke let out a sigh of relief. Why had the phone rung in the first place? Jason had been using it. Then when Luke pulled it away and stomped on it, that must have worked like hanging it up. But for it to start ringing again—

Someone was calling Jason.

Fearfully, Luke put the phone to his ear.

"Hello?" he whispered.

He had a sudden moment of hope. Maybe he'd misunderstood. Maybe Jason hadn't said that he worked for the Population Police, but that the exnays didn't trust him because they thought he *might* work for the Population Police. Or that the exnays didn't trust anyone, because of the Population Police. Maybe the person on the other end of the line was a good guy, working for the cause, worried that something had happened to poor, noble, misunderstood Jason.

"Hello?" Luke whispered again.

"Don't you ever pull that kind of a stunt on me again!" The angry voice on the other end came through the phone as forcefully as a tornado. "You hang up on the Population Police, you're a dead man. We'll kill you even

126   MARGARET PETERSON HADDIX

before we kill those four exnays you just turned in."

Luke's hope dissolved. He struggled to keep his mind from dissolving, too. Think, think . . . He'd heard Jen's dad fool the Population Police once. Mr. Talbot had lied so smoothly that even Luke, who knew the truth, was practically convinced.

Luke put his hand over his mouth. He had to make the man on the other end of the line think he was Jason.

"I'm sorry," Luke muttered. "It was a mistake. I accidentally dropped the phone and it shut off by itself." With a little help from Luke's foot.

"What? I can't hear you!" the man yelled.

"It's a bad connection," Luke said, speaking louder. He'd heard Mother and Dad say that all the time. He hoped portable phones could have bad connections, too. "I said I was sorry. I dropped the phone by mistake. I didn't hang up on you. Why would I hang up on you when I'm trying to convince you to give me more time?"

"Whatever," the man growled. Luke could tell: The man didn't care what had happened. He just wanted Jason to grovel. And Luke had done it for him. Luke was good at groveling.

"Here's how it is," the man continued. "We'll give you another day. Then that's it. And, Jason? You get those other boys or else. We've got a quota to fill, you know."

The phone clicked. Luke realized the man on the other end had hung up.

Luke had fooled him. And he'd bought some time. He had another day.

Or until Jason woke up.

CHAPTER *TWENTY-NINE*

L uke slid his hands under Jason's armpits and began dragging him down the stairs. Down was easier than up. And if Jason woke up and started screaming, he'd be less likely to wake somebody if he and Luke were on the first floor.

Of course, if Jason woke up and attacked Luke, there was also less chance Luke could get help on the first floor.

Luke made himself concentrate on pulling the bigger boy. Jason's feet slipped down the first step and hit hard. Jason moaned but didn't open his eyes.

Maybe he's just faking, Luke thought. *Maybe he's wide awake and he's just waiting for the right moment to attack.*

That thought made Luke sweat. But he pulled harder, and got Jason all the way to the bottom of the steps without waking him up.

Next, Luke dragged Jason down the hall. A right turn, a left turn, a right turn. Jason was heavy, and Luke's arms ached. His head ached, too, from trying to plan. He found the door he'd been looking for and forced himself to knock.

"Yes?" a sleepy voice responded.

Luke grimaced. He'd been half-hoping this idea would fail. *Be brave,* he told himself.

"Nurse!" he called out. "It's my—my friend. He's sick."

How could he have called Jason a friend?

Oh, well. He had a lot more lies ahead of him.

The door eased open. The nurse stood there in a ruffled dressing gown.

"Oh, my," she said dimly when she'd taken in the sight of Jason slumped on the floor. Luke tried to hold him up the way a concerned friend would, but it was hard. Luke would have enjoyed dropping him.

"He passed out," Luke said needlessly. "He was having a—a seizure, ranting and raving. He was . . . telling lies. Making up stories." That should help if Jason came to. "I think it's called delirium, what he had. I think staying unconscious is the best thing for him. Can you give him something that will keep him asleep?"

"Oh, my," the nurse repeated, frowning. "Usually, in these circumstances, we want to revive the patient."

It wasn't fair. Now the nurse seemed to know what she was talking about.

"Help me get him inside," she ordered Luke.

The nurse took Jason's legs, and Luke lifted. The strain on his muscles was terrible. Luke was panting by the time they got Jason to a bed in the nurse's office. She immediately began looking him over.

"Did he hit his head?" she asked Luke as she felt Jason's scalp.

Panic bubbled up in Luke's stomach.

"May-Maybe," he said. "He was, um, thrashing around a lot. In his sleep."

"I thought he was ranting and raving," the nurse said, fixing Luke with an unexpectedly sharp stare. "Was he doing that in his sleep, too?"

Luke gulped.

"No. He was thrashing about, and then he woke up, and acted delirious. And then he had a seizure and went unconscious. I think. It happened really fast. It was really scary."

Luke got another idea.

"You know, you should really strap him down in bed, so if he wakes up and starts acting weird again, he won't hurt himself."

"Thanks for the medical advice," the nurse said. She lifted one of Jason's eyelids and shone a flashlight into his eye. Luke held his breath. If Jason woke up now, he could tell the nurse anything he wanted, and she'd believe him. Jason was a much better liar than Luke. Jason's lips moved. Had he mumbled something that the nurse could hear but Luke couldn't? Luke tried to quell his panic. He watched with relief as Jason's eye rolled blindly back in his head. The nurse gently placed the eyelid back against the eye. Jason didn't move.

The nurse sat down at a desk and took up a pen.

"Now. What's your friend's name?" she asked.

"Ja—I mean, Scott Renault," Luke said.

The nurse peered at him doubtfully.

"And your name is—"

"Lee Grant," Luke mumbled.

The nurse was watching him carefully. Too carefully.

"Okay," she said. "Let me type your account of your friend's injury into the computer." She disappeared around a corner. Luke could hear the nurse muttering to herself. Then there was the *clickety-clack* of a keyboard. The sound made him miss Jen. He remembered Jason acting so excited when Luke had mentioned her name. But that had just been an act—an act contrived to get Luke to trust him, to reveal his real name, so Jason could betray him.

Luke's head spun. It was too hard to recast his memories with Jason as a traitor.

The nurse came back.

"Sign this," she said.

Disheartened, Luke signed without reading.

"Now. Why don't you go on back to bed?" the nurse said to Luke. "I'll take good care of your friend. I promise."

That's what Luke was afraid of.

But there was nothing else for him to do but back out of the door.

"Let me know how he is," Luke begged as he left. "And if he says anything crazy—"

"Don't worry," the nurse said. "I've heard plenty of crazy talk around here."

Out in the hallway, Luke wished he'd thought of another plan. Ropes! He could have tied Jason up, and

AMONG THE IMPOSTORS

131

gagged him, and . . . and put him where, exactly? Even the boys who stared at the ground all day would notice a bound and gagged boy lying around. And where was Luke supposed to get ropes and a gag? No, Luke had had to take his chances with the nurse. He just had to hurry even faster now. Who could tell what lies Jason might tell the nurse when he awoke? All Luke knew was, Jason wouldn't cast Luke as the heroic friend who'd carried Jason to help.

Actually, Jason wouldn't even have to lie. All he had to say was that Luke had hit him with a book and knocked him down. That was true, though not the whole truth. And if anyone wanted to investigate, they could examine Luke's book, and—

Luke's book. Stunned by his own stupidity, Luke realized: He'd left his book and Jason's portable phone back on the stairs.

Forgetting to go quietly, Luke raced down the hall, around corners, and back up the stairs. He saw the history textbook cast off in the corner of the landing, where he'd dropped it. He snatched it up and hugged it to his chest like a long-lost friend. Now, to find the phone—

The phone was nowhere in sight.

CHAPTER *THIRTY*

T he landing was barely a four-by-four square, flat and empty. But Luke walked around it again and again, as if he'd just missed noticing the phone and it was right there, in plain sight.

It wasn't.

Luke looked on each stair below, and even the stairs above the landing—as if the phone could fly. It took forever for his stubborn brain to accept that the phone was missing. Then he sank down on one of the stair steps, puzzling out who might have taken it.

Did Jason have an accomplice?

Luke thought about all the hall monitors, all the boys who'd met in the woods. Now that Jason's true nature had been revealed, Luke couldn't be sure of anyone. Maybe they all worked for the Population Police.

Except for the four boys Jason had betrayed.

Luke was desperately confused, but he could figure out one thing: The missing phone meant those four were in more immediate danger.

And so was Luke.

Luke's first instinct was to hide, to get the other four to hide with him. The woods wouldn't be safe because Jason would lead the Population Police straight there. Was there a safe place in the kitchen? Somewhere in an unused classroom? Some dormitory room off by itself, and unlikely to be searched?

Hiding was no good. In the end, they'd only be found.

Luke had to do something to prevent the Population Police from ever searching. But he didn't even understand what was going on. He had to find someone who knew more than Luke, who could lie better than Luke, who knew how to handle the Population Police.

Jen's dad.

But how was Luke supposed to reach him?

CHAPTER *THIRTY-ONE*

uke crept back down to the first floor with only the vaguest plan in mind. He needed Mr. Talbot's phone number. He needed a phone. The school office should have both.

The school office was locked.

Luke stood before the ornate door for what felt like hours. The door had a glass panel at the top, so he could see in easily. He could make out the shape of a phone on Ms. Hawkins's desk. He could see old-fashioned file cabinets behind it. Surely there was a file in there with Luke's name on it—his fake name, anyway. Would Mr. Talbot's phone number be listed in there, because he was the one who'd brought Luke to the school? Luke thought so. But it did no good unless Luke could get into the files. And no matter how much he jiggled the knob of the office door, the door held firm.

Desperately, Luke kicked it. But the door was thick, solid maple wood. Nothing flimsy at Hendricks. Even the glass was probably—

Glass. Luke couldn't believe how stupid he was being.

He slammed the glass panel with his textbook, and a satis-fying spiderweb of cracks crept across it. He hit it again, a little lower, smashing that portion of the panel.

"And Jason thinks books are useless," Luke muttered to himself. "Take that!"

Luke covered his hand with part of his pajama sleeve and pushed through the bottom of the glass. Only a few shards fell to the ground. The rest of the panel stayed in place. It was high-quality glass. Anything cheap would have shattered completely, and fallen to the ground with an enormous clatter.

Luke reached on through, until he could touch the knob from inside. He turned it—slowly, slowly—until he heard the click he'd been waiting for. He eased the door open and raced to the filing cabinet.

With only the dim light from the hall, Luke couldn't read any of the labels on any of the files. He had to carry them out to the door to see whose they were.

The first batch he pulled had Jeremy Andrews through Luther Benton. He replaced them and moved further back in the file. Tanner Fitzgerald through—yes, there it was. Lee Grant.

Luke was surprised by the thickness of his file, consid-ering how short a time he'd been at Hendricks. The first set of papers were school transcripts from other schools—evidently the ones the real Lee Grant had attended, before he died and left his identity to Luke. There were pictures, too, seven of them, labeled, KINDERGARTEN, GRADE ONE, GRADE

TWO . . . all the way up to grade six. Strangely, the photos really did look like Luke. Same sandy hair, pale eyes, worried look. Luke blinked, thinking he'd been fooled. But when he opened his eyes, the resemblance was still there. Had the real Lee Grant looked that much like Luke?

Then Luke remembered something Jen had told him once, about changing photos on the computer.

"You can make people look older, younger, prettier, uglier—whatever you want. If I wanted to make my own fake I.D., I probably could," she'd bragged.

But Jen had wanted to come out of hiding with her identity intact. She hated the thought of fake I.D.'s.

Staring at the faked pictures, Luke could understand. It was all too strange. He knew he should be reassured by how thoroughly his records had been doctored. But it frightened him instead. There was no sign of the real Luke Garner. Probably even his family would forget him eventually.

Luke didn't have time for self-pity. He turned the page, hoping his admission papers would be next.

They weren't. Instead, there was some sort of a daily log. Luke read in horrified fascination:

April 28—Student withdrawn, surly during entrance interview. Refuses to look interviewer directly in eye. Refuses to answer questions. Sullen behavior. Hostility believed connected to dissociation with parents. Can assume high risk of repeated attempts at running away. Treatment to commence immediately.

April 29—Sullenness continues. Attempts at interaction rebuffed. Teachers report disinterest, hostility.

The log continued in that vein, with an entry for every day Luke had been at Hendricks. There was repeated mention of therapy and treatment, and its success or failure. But Luke had had no entrance interview. He'd had no therapy, no treatment, no attention from the school officials at all. Obviously, this was another faked record.

But who had faked it? And why?

Thoroughly baffled, Luke turned the page. And there was the thick sheaf of his entrance papers.

Mr. Talbot was listed in the second column of the sixteenth page, as an emergency contact.

Luke grabbed the phone and started dialing.

CHAPTER *THIRTY-TWO*

A woman's sleepy voice answered.

"Is Mr. Talbot there?" Luke asked. "I need Mr. Talbot."

"It's three in the morning!" the woman hissed.

"Please," Luke begged. "It's an emergency. I'm a friend of—" He barely managed to stop himself from saying, "Jen's." Mr. Talbot's phone was probably bugged by the Population Police. Maybe the school's phone was now, too. Luke didn't know. But he tried again. "Mr. Talbot is a friend of my parents'."

There was only dead air in response. Then a man's voice, just as sleepy as the woman's.

"Hello?"

It was Mr. Talbot.

Luke wanted to spill out everything, from his first confusing day at Hendricks, to Jason's treachery, to the oddness of the file Luke still held on his lap. If only he could explain all his problems, surely Mr. Talbot could solve them all. But Luke had to choose his words carefully.

"You told me to blend in," he accused, hoping Mr. Talbot

would remember. "I can't. You have to come get me." *And four other boys,* he added silently, as if Mr. Talbot were actually capable of telepathy. If only Luke could just say, flat out, "You need to get four more fake I.D.'s for these friends of mine. And you'll need to protect their families, too." But Luke couldn't think of any code that would clue in Mr. Talbot, without clueing in the Population Police as well.

"Now, now," Mr. Talbot said calmly, sounding like an elderly uncle dispensing wisdom. "Surely school isn't that bad. You need to give it more of a chance. Is this finals week or something?"

Luke couldn't tell whether Mr. Talbot really didn't understand, or whether he was acting for the sake of the bug.

"That's not the problem!" Luke almost screamed. "It's— it's like a problem I had before."

"Yes, problems do seem to repeat themselves," Mr. Talbot said, still sounding untroubled. "Usually, there's some root cause. You need to attack that first."

Was Mr. Talbot speaking in code? Luke hoped so.

"It's all very well to say that," he protested. "But the problems are multiplying. There are four others, now, I have to think about. And they can't wait until the, um, root cause is fixed. This is an emergency. You have to help."

Luke was proud of himself. He couldn't be any clearer than that, not using a potentially bugged phone. Surely Mr. Talbot would understand.

"You children can be so melodramatic," Mr. Talbot said irritably. Now he sounded like a man ripped from sleep at three in the morning for no good reason. "I have every confidence that you can deal with your problems by yourself. Now. Good night."

"Please!" Luke pleaded.

But Mr. Talbot had hung up.

CHAPTER *THIRTY-THREE*

Luke stared at the phone. He'd tried so hard. It wasn't fair that he didn't even know if he'd succeeded or not.

No. He knew. He'd failed.

He'd heard the careless tone in Mr. Talbot's voice. Luke couldn't fool himself into thinking it was all an act, with each word carrying double meaning. It was three in the morning. He'd awakened Mr. Talbot out of a dead sleep. How could he possibly have understood what Luke needed?

Luke dropped the phone and put his face down on Ms. Hawkins's desk. The file he'd been holding on his lap spilled onto the floor, dumping out papers filled with lies. He didn't care. He didn't care that anyone walking by would catch him where he wasn't supposed to be. He was past caring about anything.

Had Jen ever reached this point, planning the rally?

Luke remembered the last time he'd seen her, the night she'd left for the capital. She'd seemed almost unearthly, as if she'd already passed out of the realm she shared with

Luke. And she had. He was still in hiding, and she was about to risk her life to be free.

It was simpler for you, Luke accused silently. *You weren't confused.*

It was hard having a dead hero for a best friend.

I just can't live up to you, Jen, he thought. *I'm not you.*

He wasn't Lee Grant, either. Slowly, just to get rid of them, he began picking up the faked papers and stuffing them back into the file. Moving like someone in a dream, he put the phone back on the desk and the file back in the filing cabinet, and shut the drawer. He walked out of the office and pulled the door closed behind him, making no effort whatsoever to hide the broken glass.

He'd have to run away, that's all there was to it. He could take the other four with him. They'd just have to take their chances. They could head to the city.

Luke had lost all track of time, now. Before he woke the others and terrified them out of their wits, he decided, he'd peek outside and see how much time they had left before daylight.

He went to the door they always used, the one that led to the woods and had once led to his garden. He tried to turn the knob, but his hand must have been weak with exhaustion. His fingers slipped right off. He gripped the knob again, and tried harder.

The door was locked. Locked from the outside.

Panicked, Luke ran to the front door, the one he'd come through with Mr. Talbot that first day.

It was locked, too.

What kind of a school kept its students locked in, at night?

No school. Just prisons.

Luke rushed around trying every door he could find, but it was hopeless. They were all locked. And none of them had glass panels for him to break.

Finally he sank to the floor outside his history classroom.

We're trapped, he thought. *Trapped like rats in a hole.*

Luke was not the least bit surprised when he heard footsteps coming down the hall. He hardly dared look up. But it wasn't Jason or someone from the Population Police standing over him. It was his history teacher, Mr. Dirk.

"Back to bed, young man," Mr. Dirk said. "I appreciate your dedication to history, but studying through the night is strictly prohibited. I'm afraid I'll have to give you—"

"I know, I know," Luke said. "Two demerits."

Under Mr. Dirk's stern gaze, Luke resignedly trudged back upstairs.

CHAPTER *THIRTY-FOUR*

L uke was overcome by guilt when he woke up the next morning. How could he have slept away so many hours? He'd had to come back to his room because Mr. Dirk was watching. But he could have sneaked out later. Why hadn't he at least warned the others?

Some rational side of his mind argued: What good would a warning do when they couldn't escape?

Around him, his other roommates were complaining about the exams they faced that day. One or two of them had books open on their beds and were studying as they got dressed. It seemed unreal that anyone could care about exams at a time like this.

Fearfully, Luke looked over at Jason's bed. It was empty. The sheets were rumpled the same way they'd been last night. The pillow still held an indentation. But Jason was nowhere in sight.

"Where's Scott?" Luke asked. His voice trembled despite his best efforts to sound casual.

His question was met with blank stares.

"Don't know," one boy finally mumbled, and went back to studying.

At breakfast, Luke sat with Jason's gang, but Jason was still missing. Luke peered around the table at the four boys Jason had betrayed: Antonio/Samuel, who had flashing dark eyes and a quick laugh; Denton/Travis, who knew hundreds of riddles; Sherman/Ryan, who talked with an accent Luke had never heard before; and Patrick/Tyrone, who had once claimed he got his fake I.D. by "the luck of the Irish." Luke couldn't have said he really knew any of them well. But it was agony to sit there watching them eat their Cream of Wheat, making jokes, totally unaware that they were doomed. Luke tried to lean over and whisper in Patrick's ear, "You're in danger—I need to tell you—" But Patrick only brushed him away with the words, "Quit it, lecker. You're bugging me." And then all the others stared at Luke. How many of them were on Jason's side, working for the Population Police?

Luke didn't dare give his warning out loud.

Breakfast time slipped away, with Luke's panic only growing. His thoughts ran in circles. He should go hide, by himself, if he couldn't save the others. But he couldn't just abandon the others. He had to save them. But how?

"If you're not going to eat your breakfast, I will," Patrick said when Luke's was the only bowl that wasn't empty.

Silently, Luke passed over his food.

"Hey, thanks," Patrick said, with a huge grin. "You're the greatest."

If only you knew . . ., Luke thought miserably.

Just then, the dining hall door banged open.

"Population Police!" a booming voice called out.

Luke froze. He'd known this was coming, but it still didn't seem possible. He tried to yell, "Run!" to Patrick and the others, but he opened his mouth and nothing came out. His legs were frozen, too. He could only sit and watch and listen in horror.

A huge man stepped into the room. Medals covered his olive green uniform. He clutched a sheaf of papers in his fist.

"I have a warrant here for the arrest of illegals who have compounded their crime by the use of falsified documents," he announced.

Luke closed his eyes, in agony. It was all over. He'd failed at everything. He hadn't saved the others, and he hadn't saved himself. He'd never done anything for the cause. He was going to die before he'd had a chance to accomplish a single thing.

The police officer peered at the papers in his hand. He cleared his throat.

"The sentence for those in violation of Population Law 3903 is death. The sentence for falsification of documents by an illegal citizen is death by torture, Government's choice."

One of the autistic boys was crying. Luke could hear him across the room. Everyone else sat in deathly silence. Luke hoped that he'd at least have the chance to apologize to the other four. The police officer continued.

"The first illegal I have come to arrest goes by the name of—"

"Relax, Stan. I found him," someone interrupted from behind.

Luke recognized the voice. A second later, Mr. Talbot came into the room.

And behind him, with his wrists in handcuffs and his ankles in leg-irons, was Jason.

CHAPTER *THIRTY-FIVE*

T he entire dining hall full of boys gasped.

"He was hiding in the nurse's office," Mr. Talbot was saying. "And the other one's over at the girls' school. Come on. I don't want to miss my golf game this afternoon."

"No!" Jason roared. Even in chains, he had a commanding presence. The police officer with the chestful of medals turned to look at him with something like respect. "I told you! I'm not an exnay. I can show you the exnays!"

Jason stepped forward, chains rattling. Mr. Talbot reached out to grab his arm, but the officer stopped him.

"Maybe he's right," the officer said. "I always love it when they betray each other. And I wouldn't mind getting a bonus for exceeding my quota this month."

Mr. Talbot shrugged and looked at his watch, as if all that worried him was showing up late for his tee time.

Jason hobbled slowly across the room, until he reached Luke's table. Luke felt faint. Everyone around him seemed to be holding his breath, too.

Jason pointed.

"Him. Antonio Blanco is his real name, but he goes by Samuel Irving. Him. Denton Weathers, alias Travis Spencer. Him. Sherman Kymanski, alias Ryan Mann. Him. Patrick Kerrigan, alias Tyrone Janson." Now Jason pointed to Luke. "And him. I don't know his real name, but he's pretending to be Lee Grant." He turned back to the Population Police officer, beseechingly. "And I know there are more. Just give me some time—"

Mr. Talbot started laughing. His guffaws rang out in the silent dining hall like bells after a funeral.

"Lee Grant an imposter? Now, that's a good one. I've known Lee since he was a baby. His whole family used to celebrate Christmas with mine, back when we lived in the city. Come to think of it, I've got one or two of those Christmas pictures in my wallet right now. Want to see them?" Mr. Talbot asked the police officer. He was already pulling the wallet out of his back pocket. "Hey, Lee, good to see you. Come look. Remember the year your parents made you wear the Santa Claus hat?"

Somehow Luke managed to make his legs carry him over to Mr. Talbot. Once before, Mr. Talbot had lied and said that he was a close personal friend of Luke's father's cousin. That was dangerous enough. Mr. Talbot could never back up this lie.

But the picture Mr. Talbot thrust at him was crystal clear. There was Mr. Talbot and three other adults, standing by a fireplace. Two boys that Luke recognized as Jen's brothers—Mr. Talbot's stepsons—sat on the hearth. And there, right between them, was Luke, in a flannel shirt and a Santa hat.

Mr. Talbot even flashed the photo in front of Jason's face.

"But I know—" Jason fumed. "He—I mean, I'm sure of the others. I'm positive!"

"Um-hmm," Mr. Talbot said. "I bet you just made up those names, trying to save your own skin."

Suddenly Patrick/Tyrone spoke up.

"He is, sir. My name is really Robert Jones."

"I'm Michael Rystert," Sherman/Ryan added.

The other two gave different names, too—Joel Westing and John Abbott. All four boys spoke in calm, even voices. Luke was stunned. What was going on? How could they possibly pull this off?

"They're lying! Look at their records!" Jason screamed.

"Good idea," Mr. Talbot said. "Is there a teacher or administrator who would be so kind—?"

At a far table, Luke's history teacher, Mr. Dirk, stood up.

"Just give me a minute," he said. Luke wondered how he could have ever found the man intimidating. He scurried out of the room like a mouse. In no time at all, he returned with four thick files. He handed them to the police officer. "Mind, please don't let any of the boys see. We like to keep their records private—"

But everyone was craning his neck, straining to see. Luke had the advantage because he was still standing next to Mr. Talbot. The police officer flipped quickly through the top file—Luke could see MICHAEL written again and again on each page. And in the next file, it was ROBERT, over and over and over.

"They're fake!" Jason howled.

"Aw, who could have faked these? In the two minutes we were standing here?" the police officer said in disgust. He threw the files down on the table and jerked on Jason's arm. "Come on. Out of here. Enough of your lies. We'd better go make that other pickup quick, or Mr. Talbot here will make me reimburse him for his lost greens time."

"But—but—" Jason sputtered, all the way out of the dining room.

And then he, and Mr. Talbot, and the Population Police officer were gone.

CHAPTER **THIRTY-SIX**

I t was strange, after everything that had happened, that the boys could shuffle off to their classes as usual. The hall monitors watched as usual. Once the bell rang, the teachers cleared their throats as dryly as ever and began lecturing about integral numbers or laws of thermodynamics or long-dead poets.

Luke took his history exam that afternoon, as scheduled. He was surprised that he could pencil in responses about Hercules and Achilles, Hannibal and Arthur, heroes of the distant past, even as his mind raced with questions about the present. He longed to ask Patrick/Tyrone—no, make that Robert now—for an explanation. Or any of the others. How had they known the right names to say? How had their records been changed? How was it that nobody in the entire dining room had stood up to challenge their stories? And—who had betrayed Jason?

But each time he saw the other boys, they only groaned about their exams, complained about the school food, told stupid jokes. They acted like their names had always been Michael, Robert, Joel, and John.

Nobody mentioned Jason.

"Are we going to the woods tonight?" Luke whispered to Trey as they were leaving dinner. "To talk about—you know."

Trey looked at him as though Luke was speaking a foreign language.

"Guess not, huh?" Luke said, unable to just let it go.

Luke felt an arm on his shoulder just then.

"I'd like a word with you, young man," a voice said.

With all his fears from breakfast-time rushing back, Luke had to force himself to turn around.

Mr. Dirk, his history teacher, stood there, looking stern.

"You are Lee Grant, are you not?" Mr. Dirk asked.

The other boys stepped past him. Luke watched the doors of the lecture hall close before he could bring himself to nod.

"Then come with me," Mr. Dirk said, and turned on his heel.

Luke followed a few paces behind. So Mr. Dirk was going to tell him how badly he'd failed the history exam. So what? Luke remembered that, with Jason gone, there was no one to doctor his grades. But Luke had never cared about the grades.

"I'll work harder next term," Luke started to say. "I didn't even start going to your class until last week—"

"Hush," Mr. Dirk said.

Luke fought the urge to giggle. It was so ridiculous that, after surviving the Population Police raid, he was getting in trouble because he had forgotten the names of a few dead guys most people had never heard of.

Mr. Dirk walked past his classroom. Luke started to protest, but Mr. Dirk was walking briskly now. Luke had to hurry to keep up. Mr. Dirk walked right up to the front door and turned the knob.

"Isn't it locked tonight?" Luke wanted to ask. But he was beginning to understand that Mr. Dirk wasn't going to scold him about ancient history. He kept his mouth shut.

The door opened easily. Luke and Mr. Dirk stepped outside together.

Tiers of steps lay before them in the twilight. Luke remembered his trepidation climbing these very stairs, his first day at Hendricks. They didn't seem quite so imposing now, probably because he was at the top looking down, instead of the bottom looking up.

"Where are we going?" Luke couldn't resist asking.

For an answer, Mr. Dirk put a finger to his lips.

They climbed down the steps and walked along the expansive driveway. June bugs sang, far off in the distance. They made Luke homesick. Back on the farm, his dad and brothers were probably just coming in for supper after a hard day of baling. Mother would just be getting home from the factory.

It didn't seem right that Luke had just had one of the most terrifying days of his life, and his own family would never know.

"Watch your step," Mr. Dirk said.

Luke had been so lost in thought, he hadn't even noticed that they had turned, and were now standing in front of a small cottage. No—not a cottage—the small scale had fooled him. This building had turrets and arches like a castle, but was nestled so neatly behind lilac bushes and rhododendron and forsythia that Luke could have walked right past without seeing it at all.

"Ring the bell," Mr. Dirk instructed. He turned to go.

Luke was swept with panic.

"Wait!" he cried. Mr. Dirk was hardly a comforting figure, but at least he was familiar. Luke didn't like being abandoned in a strange place, without explanation.

"I trust you can find your way back on your own, when you are finished," Mr. Dirk said, and disappeared into the shadows.

There was nothing for Luke to do but press the doorbell.

"Come in," a deep voice called from inside.

Luke gave the door a little push. It was made of the same kind of heavy wood as all the doors at Hendricks. It barely moved. Timidly, Luke edged it open and stepped inside.

A dim room lay before him. Prisms hung from old-fashioned lamps. Wood-framed couches curved between oddly shaped tables cluttered with dozens of framed pictures. Luke didn't even notice the man in the wheelchair until he cleared his throat.

"Welcome, young man," the man said. He was older than either Luke's parents or Mr. Talbot. He had thick white hair that swelled above his forehead like a snowbank. He wore crisp khaki pants and a pale blue shirt—the

same kind of Baron clothes Luke had almost become accustomed to wearing himself. "Would you care for a drink?
Bottled water, perhaps?"

Luke shook his head, baffled. Questions swarmed in his
mind.

"George," the man called.

Mr. Talbot stepped into the room from the back part of
the house.

Luke's knees went weak with relief. Finally! Someone
who could explain.

"Mr.—" Luke began.

But Mr. Talbot shook his head warningly. He waved a
long bar in front of Luke's chest and his legs, then behind
his back. Finally he leaned back and announced, "He's
clean. No bugs."

"I hate all this technology, don't you?" the man in the
wheelchair said, leaning back as though Mr. Talbot's
announcement had freed him to relax. He stirred a cup he
held in his hand. Luke thought he caught a whiff of something like the chicory coffee his parents had sometimes
drunk as a special treat. "But now I can introduce myself.
I'm Josiah Hendricks. You know my friend here, I presume."

Luke could only nod.

"Sit down, sit down," Mr. Hendricks said. "No need to
stand on ceremony."

Luke noticed that Mr. Talbot, always so much in charge
every other time Luke had seen him, obeyed instantly.
Luke quickly sank into an armchair as well.

Mr. Hendricks sipped his drink.

"You are an inquisitive young man," he said to Luke. "You wish some explanations. No?"

"Yes," Luke said eagerly. He looked over at Mr. Talbot, expectantly. But Mr. Talbot was staring pointedly at Mr. Hendricks.

"Once I was a very rich man," Mr. Hendricks said. "I spent my money foolishly—who doesn't when they have more money than they know what to do with? There is a long and not particularly attractive story about how I spent my younger days. But suffice it to say that I was given reason to develop compassion by the time of the Great Famines." He looked down quickly. Luke saw for the first time that both of his pants legs hung empty below the knee. "I am not disguising anything for you tonight," Mr. Hendricks said softly.

Luke shifted uncomfortably in his chair. What was he supposed to say? Evidently, nothing. Mr. Hendricks went on with his tale.

"You know the Government was considering letting the 'undesirables' starve, do you not?" Mr. Hendricks asked. "When there is not enough food, who deserves to eat? The blind girl? The deaf boy? The man missing his legs?"

The anger in his voice was unbearable. Luke stumbled over his own tongue, ready to say anything to move the story along.

"Jason—I mean, the one taken away this morning—he told me about that. At school."

"Indeed," Mr. Hendricks said. He seemed lost in thought, then roused himself to continue. "My family— and I—spent millions on bribes, to convince the Government to have a heart. They left the disabled alone. And passed the Population Law instead." He frowned, stirring his coffee. "And how compassionate had I been? I saved my own kind, knowing that others would likely be killed. So I set up the schools. As penance."

"Mr. Hendricks foresaw what others did not," Mr. Talbot said. "He understood that hundreds of illegal children would be born, and hidden. And he knew they'd need safe places to go if they were able to come out of hiding."

"But I thought your schools were for autistic kids, kids with phobias, the ones who—" Luke stopped. "Oh," he said.

Mr. Hendricks chuckled.

"So my charade fooled you?" he asked. "Who can tell if a child rocks because he has autism or because he is terrified out of his wits? Who can tell if agoraphobia is caused by oddities in the mind or lifelong warnings, 'Going outdoors is suicide'? In the beginning, yes, I accepted children whose problems stemmed from other causes. I nurtured a reputation as a schoolmaster who would take on any troubled child. And when the first illegal children began emerging, they came here, too."

Luke tried to grasp it all.

"So everyone's an exnay? And everyone knows?" he asked. "The teachers, Ms. Hawkins in the office, the nurse, all the other boys—"

"Oh, no." Mr. Hendricks shook his head emphatically. "My charade is complete. I don't even know for sure which boys are which. I don't want to know. There is the possibility of—"

"Torture," Mr. Talbot said grimly.

"Those I don't know, I can't betray," Mr. Hendricks said. "And I hire only employees who seem uniquely capable of ignorance. Teachers so enamored of their academic disciplines that they can't even recognize the students who sit before them for an entire year. Administrative staff whose incompetence is of such towering magnitude that they can't input records into computers, won't notice when files are faked or replaced. . . . There's a certain charm to my system, is there not?"

Luke remembered how Jason's portable phone had disappeared, how the doors had been locked, how the files under his four friends' new fake names had magically appeared.

"But *someone* knows," he insisted. "There has to be *someone* who oversees it all."

Mr. Hendricks shifted in his wheelchair.

"Oh, yes. I have my compatriots. Mr. Dirk, as you probably suspect, has been useful upon occasion, although his knowledge is limited. I will tell you no other names."

Luke should have felt relieved to finally get an explanation. For that matter, he should have been ecstatic to have an adult at Hendricks acknowledge his existence. But all he could think about, suddenly, was how lonely and isolated he'd felt his first few weeks at Hendricks, how invisible. How low he'd sunk, that he'd almost looked forward to Jason picking on him each evening. He felt a surge of anger.

"You think you're so great," he said before he could stop himself. "Don't you know how it feels to be an exnay? And then you just abandon us, among people who don't care. Or can't care. It's a wonder we don't all run back into hiding."

"Oh, no," Mr. Hendricks said, seeming totally unruffled by Luke's outburst. "You were never abandoned. I can assume you have never been deep-sea diving, correct?"

Luke shook his head, and resisted the urge to roll his eyes as well.

"But you understand the concept?" Mr. Hendricks didn't wait for a reply. "When a diver resurfaces, he has to go gradually, so his body can get accustomed to the change in pressure. Children coming out of hiding need that, too. They need places to adjust to the outside world. Somewhere that their extreme fear of the outdoors does not seem out of place. Somewhere that they can act antisocial and not stand out. Somewhere—well, like Hendricks. And then when they're ready, they move on."

"You mean—leave?" Luke asked, his voice squeaking in spite of himself.

"Yes," Mr. Talbot said. "And Mr. Hendricks and I agree: The events of the past twenty-four hours prove that your time has come. You're ready to go."

CHAPTER *THIRTY-SEVEN*

"**H**uh?" Luke said. He had not anticipated that turn in the conversation at all.

Mr. Hendricks leaned forward.

"My schools had never been infiltrated before," he said, with a sharp glance at Mr. Talbot.

Mr. Talbot frowned apologetically.

"The Population Police have always pretended that it's impossible for an illegal child to get a fake I.D.," Mr. Talbot added. "But after the rally—" His eyes clouded. Luke could see the effort he was making to continue without emotion. "After the rally, all the rules changed."

"So you see, we never expected betrayal," Mr. Hendricks said. "In the beginning, yes, we tiptoed and looked over our shoulders. And, fortunately, we kept habits of . . . strong security. But we were not prepared for the Population Police to plant impostors in our midst, to gather names, to encourage indiscretion."

Luke frowned.

"But Jason—he said there'd been raids before. He said—"

Mr. Talbot had a sarcastic smile on his face. Mr. Hendricks raised one eyebrow.

"My dear boy," Mr. Hendricks said. "He lied."

Luke grimaced. He didn't like them acting like he couldn't figure that out on his own. But he'd learned a lot from Jason. What was true and what was false? He remembered one of Jason's other explanations: *You can't be too nice to an exnay . . . exnays need the kind of friend who can toughen them up. Like I did for you.* Luke remembered how many times Jason had made him claim to be an idiot, do push-ups until his arms collapsed, make a total fool of himself. Jason hadn't been trying to toughen Luke up. He'd been trying to break him down.

But it hadn't worked.

Luke didn't know why. He felt breathless, thinking about what could have happened. Suddenly he was mad at Mr. Hendricks and Mr. Talbot, sitting there looking so condescending.

"Why didn't you know Jason was an impostor?" Luke said. "You should have. He acted so different from everyone else."

"Yes, and so did you," Mr. Hendricks replied quickly. "Should we have suspected you of working for the Population Police, just because you liked going outside?"

Luke blinked.

"Yes, we knew," Mr. Hendricks said. "Just as we knew Jason, as you call him, was forming a club of former hidden children. We'd never seen that happen before, and frankly, we viewed it as a positive development. Until you showed us the truth."

Luke remembered how frustrated and frightened and alone he'd felt, only the night before.

"I didn't do anything," he said. "I tried, but nothing worked. Mr. Talbot deserves all the credit."

"You stopped the infiltrator and knocked him out. Then you took him to the nurse who, under the school's protocol, had to alert me," Mr. Hendricks said. "She thought he was just another former hidden child, going through some very unusual trauma. But when he muttered, "my phone, my phone"—she got suspicious. We locked all the doors and made a search of the entire school building."

So that's what Jason had muttered to the nurse, Luke thought. He was kind of glad now that he hadn't heard. He had felt panicked enough, as it was.

"Once we confiscated his phone," Mr. Hendricks continued, "we found out that the last number he called was the Population Police. Meanwhile, your call made George here suspicious—"

"Without spilling everything for the bugs on my phone, thank you very much," Mr. Talbot said. "Because of your warning, I had time to double-cross the Population Police's efforts. So we arrested two traitors, instead of six former hidden children. A good trade, in my mind."

Luke felt dizzy. No matter how many explanations Mr. Talbot and Mr. Hendricks gave him, other questions sprang up in his mind like so many weeds. Both men were watching him.

"Nina," Luke said finally. "Nina was the other traitor."

"Yes," Mr. Talbot said.

Luke thought about how, just for a second, he'd mistaken Nina for Jen that first night out in the woods. He'd wanted to like Nina so badly. He'd liked the way she'd laughed. But she'd been a traitor, too.

"What will happen to them?" Luke asked. "Jason and Nina, I mean."

Mr. Talbot looked away.

"Sometimes it's better not to know," he murmured.

That meant they were going to be killed, Luke thought. Killed or tortured to death, which was even worse. He shivered. Was it his fault? Was there some way he could have saved the other exnays without destroying Jason and Nina? No—they were the ones who had chosen betrayal.

"This is a cruel business," Mr. Talbot said. "Don't dwell on it."

In a corner of the room, an old-fashioned clock ticked quietly. Luke gathered his thoughts for his next question.

"But why did the Population Police believe you instead of Jason? If he'd wanted to, that officer could have arrested us all," Luke said. He remembered how careful Mr. Talbot had had to be, ever since the rally, for fear that someone might connect him with Jen. "I thought you were out of favor at Population Police headquarters right now. No offense, of course," he added quickly.

Mr. Talbot shrugged, as though being out of favor was as insignificant as a mosquito bite.

"I had the evidence on my side," he said. "They like

evidence. And I have to say, it was a stroke of brilliance to computer-enhance that Christmas picture, to substitute your face over Jen's." He kept his voice even, saying Jen's name, but Luke noticed that Mr. Hendricks bowed his head, reverently, as though giving in to a moment of silent mourning. Had Mr. Hendricks ever even met Jen? Luke didn't know, but he found himself lowering his head as well.

"Jen would have liked that," Luke said. "Using her picture to fool the Population Police." He swallowed what might have been a giggle. Jen would have been very amused.

"And what better way to remember those we love than by doing what they like?" Mr. Hendricks asked.

Mr. Talbot nodded, silently. Mr. Hendricks took over the explanation.

"And, young man, you do not realize the power of the name you have been given. Lee Grant. Your father—the father listed on your school records—is a very important man in our society," he said.

"But he's not my father," Luke said, more forcefully than he intended. "I've never even met the man. And I'm not Lee Grant."

Mr. Hendricks and Mr. Talbot exchanged glances. Luke wondered if they were deciding he wasn't so ready, after all.

"But you know how to pretend to be Lee Grant," Mr. Hendricks said. "That is what matters."

Luke shook his head impatiently. He'd suddenly had it

with all this double-talk. None of this was real, not the way planting potatoes was, or growing beans. It was easier to be a farmer, to know by looking whether your crops were good or not. Still, another question teased at the back of his mind.

"Why did they do it?" he asked. "Jason and Nina—why did they betray their friends? Their fellow exnays?"

"They were never your friends," Mr. Hendricks said harshly. "They came to Hendricks and Harlow schools with one purpose, and one purpose only: to seek out and betray all the former hidden children they could. They preyed upon all the exnays' secret desire to speak their real name, because the Population Police needed the real names to complete the betrayal. Jason and Nina had never been hidden children. They were just plants. Impostors."

"But the Population Policeman said they were illegals with false documents—" Luke said.

"The Population Police can lie, too," Mr. Hendricks said grimly. "It suits the Government's purposes to say they are arresting third children rather than traitors."

Luke tried to absorb this. Nina, who spoke so passionately about the third children's cause; Jason, who talked about protecting exnays at Hendricks—they had never been in hiding themselves? They only wanted to harm the ones who trusted them most?

This was a level of evil Luke never could have imagined before, back on the farm.

And now Mr. Hendricks and Mr. Talbot wanted him to

go to another new place, someplace even more challenging than Hendricks?

"With all due respect to my friend here," Mr. Talbot nodded toward Mr. Hendricks, "we don't really know how Jason and Nina came to work for the Population Police, or why they came to these schools. We're mostly guessing. They're just kids, after all."

"'Just kids?'" Mr. Hendricks protested. "You think only adults are capable of such villainy? Naturally, adults must have put them up to it, but—"

"I'll be interrogating both of them tomorrow," Mr. Talbot interrupted quietly. "Let's just say I intend to discover facts that my Population Police colleagues probably don't want me to know. It's likely that those two kids were offered substantial bribes for their work. Or"—he laughed bitterly—"maybe they were true believers devoted to their cause. Who knows?"

Luke wondered about that. Long ago, when he'd first met Jen, he'd wondered if the Population Law *was* correct, if maybe he really didn't have any right to exist, to eat food that might go to others. But Jen had convinced him that wasn't so, that everyone had a right to live. No matter what. But what if Jason and Nina had truly believed in what they were doing, even among their enemies—just as Mr. Talbot believed in what he was doing, double-crossing the Population Police, even as he worked in their head-quarters every day?

Luke rubbed his temples. This wore his brain out even

more than the history test had. He wished everyone could just be what they were, and not have to pretend.

The clock in the corner began donging, giving off distinguished, silvery peals. Luke read the time effortlessly, without having to count dongs: eight o'clock.

"Well," Mr. Talbot said, rising, "you'll need to get your things out of your room before the other boys come out of—what do you call it? Indoctrination? And then I can drive you to your next school tonight. I'll tell you about it on the way."

"No," Luke said.

Mr. Talbot and Mr. Hendricks looked at him in bafflement. Then Mr. Hendricks chuckled.

"Oh, so you boys have come up with another name for it besides Indoctrination?"

Luke understood the old man's confusion. He could go with that, make up some silly name for Indoctrination, pretend that that was all he'd been objecting to. But it wasn't.

"No," Luke said firmly. "I mean, I don't want to leave Hendricks."

Now Mr. Talbot and Mr. Hendricks absolutely gaped at him, thoroughly aghast. Luke could tell what they were thinking: *We gave him a new identity. We gave him a place to hide. We saved his skin today. And now he tells us "no"? How dare he?*

Luke gulped. He wasn't so sure how he dared, either. Only two months earlier, when he'd left home, he'd been a scared little kid afraid even to speak. He'd had a borrowed name and borrowed clothes—nothing but memories to call his own. But those memories were worth something, and so was he. He wasn't some pawn to be moved across a chessboard, according to other people's plans.

Luke thought about what he'd accomplished at Hendricks—not just what he'd done to help outsmart Jason, but what he'd done making his garden, trying to make friends, studying for his tests. *Jen, you'd be proud,* he thought. He tried to figure out how to explain to Mr. Hendricks and Mr. Talbot.

"I'm glad you want to help me," Luke started softly. "And I'm, um, honored that you think I'm ready to leave. But I don't think I'm done here. When I came out of hiding I told my parents that I wanted to help other third children. Only, I didn't know how. But now I do. I want to help them *here.*"

Mr. Talbot and Mr. Hendricks exchanged glances. Then Mr. Talbot sat down.

"Tell us more," he said.

CHAPTER *THIRTY-EIGHT*

The sun was barely over the horizon, but it was already a steamy day. Luke brushed sweat out of his eyes and pushed another seed into the ground. It was late in the season to plant a garden, but they'd had to wait until after exams. Luke could only hope for a late frost in the fall.

Behind Luke, four other boys clutched a sturdy rope stretched across the garden rows. One boy dipped quickly toward the ground, dropping a seed before he straightened up.

"Good, Trey," Luke said, laughing. "But it's easier if you open your eyes."

"I might see something that way," Trey grumbled. "Everything's so bright out here."

"Just smell, then," Luke suggested.

Trey breathed deeply.

"It's so fresh," he said in a marveling voice.

"Wait until you taste the peas you're planting," Luke said.

Luke was still surprised that Mr. Hendricks and Mr. Talbot had agreed to his plan.

"I never intended to run an *agricultural* school," Mr. Hendricks had grumbled. "Some of these boys are from the richest families—or supposedly from the richest families—"

"Then they need to know how food grows, as much as anyone," Luke answered, surprised at his own tone of authority.

Sometimes Luke wondered if he was just taking the easy way out—staying at Hendricks because it was familiar, growing a garden because that's what he liked. But the Population Law had started over food, so nobody could say that growing food wasn't important. Or maybe that was the problem—that people had started believing it wasn't important.

Luke watched Trey plant another seed, this time with his eyes open.

"This little thing is really going to grow?" Trey asked incredulously.

Luke nodded.

"It ought to," he said. "And it'll be yours."

He hadn't been able to tell Mr. Hendricks and Mr. Talbot how much longer he wanted to stay at Hendricks school. Last week's exams had pointed out plenty of holes in his education, and he knew now that he could learn here. And, no matter what, he knew it had to be good for the other boys to get outside.

"Are you some kind of a teacher?" one of the boys behind Trey asked Luke. He spoke hesitantly, like a little kid just learning how to talk. "What's your name?"

"Just call me 'L,'" Luke said, without thinking.

Now, where had that come from? It wasn't Luke, it wasn't Lee—it was, somehow, both identities at once.

Just like Luke himself.

Here's a peek at Margaret Peterson Haddix's *Found*, which launches her new series, The Missing.

Jonah has always known that he was adopted, and he was never really interested in his birth parents. But when he and his friend Chip start receiving threatening messages, they start to investigate—and what they find shocks them. Thirteen years ago an airplane appeared mysteriously at an airport—the only passengers were thirty-six infants—and then disappeared. When Jonah, his sister Katherine, and Chip start digging, they find an FBI cover-up, people who appear and disappear into thin air, and a vast conspiracy that has its roots in the distant future. And Jonah and Chip are pawns in a battle between two forces that both want to control their lives—for very different reasons.

PROLOGUE

It wasn't there. Then it was.

Later, that was how Angela DuPre would describe the airplane—over and over, to one investigator after another—until she was told never to speak of it again.

But when she first saw the plane that night, she wasn't thinking about mysteries or secrets. She was wondering how many mistakes she could make without getting fired, how many questions she dared ask before her supervisor, Monique, would explode, "That's it! You're too stupid to work at Sky Trails Air! Get out of here!" Angela had used a Post-it note to write down the code for standby passengers who'd received a seat assignment at the last minute, and she'd stuck it to her computer screen. She knew she had. But somehow, between the flight arriving from Saint Louis and the one leaving for Chicago, the Post-it had vanished. Any minute now, she thought, some standby passenger would show up at the counter asking for a boarding pass, and Angela would be forced to turn to Monique once more and mumble, "Uh, what was that code again?" And then Monique, who had perfect hair and perfect nails and a perfect tan and had probably been born knowing all the Sky Trails codes, would grit her teeth and narrow her eyes and repeat the code in that slow fake-patient voice she'd been using with Angela all night, the voice that said behind the words, *I know you're severely mentally challenged, so I will try not to speak faster than one word per minute, but you have to realize, this is a real strain for me because I am so vastly superior. . . .*

Angela was not severely mentally challenged. She'd done fine in school and at the Sky Trails orientation. It was just, this was her first actual day on the job, and Monique had been nasty from the very start. Every one of Monique's frowns and glares and insinuations kept making Angela feel more panicky and stupid.

Sighing, Angela glanced up. She needed a break from staring at the computer screen longing for a lost Post-it. She peered out at the passengers crowding the terminal: tired-looking families sprawled in seats, dark-suited businessmen sprinting down the aisle. Which one of them would be the standby flier who'd rush up to the counter and ruin Angela's life? Generally speaking, Angela had always liked people; she wasn't used to seeing them as threats. She forced her gaze beyond the clumps of passengers, to the huge plate glass window on the other side of the aisle. It was getting dark out, and Angela could see the runway lights twinkling in the distance.

Runway, runaway, she thought vaguely. And then—had she blinked?—suddenly the lights were gone. No, she corrected herself, *blocked.* Suddenly there was an airplane between Angela and the runway lights, an airplane rolling rapidly toward the terminal.

Angela gasped.

"What now?" Monique snarled, her voice thick with exasperation.

"That plane," Angela said. "At gate 2B. I thought it—"What was she supposed to say? *Wasn't there? Appeared out of thin air?*"—I thought it was going too fast and might run into the building," she finished in a rush, because suddenly that had seemed true too. She watched as the plane pulled to a stop, neatly aligned with the jetway. "But it . . . didn't. No worries."

Monique whirled on Angela.

"Never," she began, in a hushed voice full of suppressed rage, "never, ever, ever say anything like that. Weren't you paying attention in orientation? Never say you think a plane is going to crash. Never say a plane could crash. Never even use the word *crash*. Do you understand?"

"Okay," Angela whispered. "Sorry."

But some small rebellious part of her brain was thinking, *I didn't use the word* crash. *Weren't you paying attention to* me? *And if a plane really was going to run into the building, wouldn't Sky Trails want its employees to warn people, to get them out of the way?*

Just as rebelliously, Angela kept watching the plane parked at 2B, instead of bending her head back down to concentrate on her computer.

"Um, Monique?" she said after a few moments. "Should one of us go over there and help the passengers unload—er, I mean—deplane?" She was proud of herself for remembering to use the official airline-sanctioned word for unloading.

Beside her, Monique rolled her eyes.

"The gate agents responsible for 2B," she said in a tight voice, "will handle deplaning there."

Angela glanced at the 2B counter, which was silent and dark and completely unattended. There wasn't even a message scrolling across the LCD sign behind the counter to indicate that the plane had arrived or where it'd come from.

"Nobody's there," Angela said stubbornly.

Frowning, Monique finally glanced up.

"Great. Just great," she muttered. "I always have to fix everyone else's mistakes." She began stabbing her perfectly manicured nails at her computer keyboard. Then she stopped, mid-stab. "Wait—that can't be right."

"What is it?" Angela asked.

Monique was shaking her head.

"Must be pilot error," she said, grimacing in disgust. "Some yahoo pulled up to the wrong gate. There's not supposed to be anyone at that gate until the Cleveland flight at nine thirty."

Angela considered telling Monique that if Sky Trails had banned *crash* from their employees' vocabulary, that maybe passengers should be protected from hearing *pilot error* as well. But Monique was already grabbing the telephone, barking out orders.

"Yeah, Bob, major screwup," she was saying. "You've got to get someone over here. . . . No, I don't know which gate it was supposed to go to. How would I know? Do you think I'm clairvoyant? . . . No, I can't see the numbers on the plane. Don't you know it's dark out?"

With her free hand, Monique was gesturing frantically at Angela.

"At least go open the door!" she hissed.

"You mean . . ."

"The door to the jetway!" Monique said, pointing. Angela hoped that some of the contempt on Monique's face was intended for Bob, not just her. Angela imagined meeting Bob someday, sharing a laugh at Monique's expense. Still, dutifully, she walked over to the 2B waiting area and pulled open the door to the hallway that led down to the plane.

Nobody came out.

Angela picked a piece of lint off her blue skirt and then stood at attention, her back perfectly straight, just like in the training videos. Maybe she couldn't keep track of standby codes, but she was capable of standing up straight.

Still, nobody appeared.

Angela began to feel foolish, standing so alertly by an open door that no one was using. She bent her head and peeked down the jetway—it was deserted and turned at such an angle that she couldn't see all the way down to the plane, to see if anyone had opened the door to the jet yet. She backed up a little and peered out the window, straight down to the cockpit of the plane. The cockpit was dark, its windows blank, and that struck Angela as odd. She'd been on the job for only five hours, and she'd been a little distracted. But she was pretty sure that when planes landed, the pilots stayed in the cockpit for a while filling out paperwork or something. She thought that they at least waited until all the passengers were off before they turned out the cockpit lights.

Angela peeked down the empty jetway once more and went back to Monique.

"Of course I'm sure there's a plane at that gate! I can see it with my own eyes!" Monique was practically screaming into the phone. She shook her head at Angela, and for the first time it was almost in a companionable way, as if to say, *At least you know there's a plane there! Unlike the other morons I have to deal with!* Monique cupped her hand over the receiver and fumed to Angela, "The incompetence around here is unbelievable! The control tower says that plane never landed, never showed up on the radar. The Sky Trails dispatcher says we're not missing a plane—everything that was supposed to land in the past hour pulled up to the right gate, and all the other planes due to arrive within the next hour or so are accounted for. How could so many people just lose a plane?"

Or, how could we find it? Angela thought. The whole situation was beginning to seem strange to her, otherworldly. But maybe that was just a function of being new to the job, of having spent so much time concentrating on the computer and being yelled at by Monique. Maybe airports lost and found planes all the time, and that was just one of those things nobody had mentioned in the Sky Trails orientation.

"Did, uh, anybody try to contact the pilot?" Angela asked cautiously.

"Of course!" Monique said. "But there's no answer. He must be on the wrong frequency."

Angela thought of the dark cockpit, the way she hadn't been able to see through the windows. She decided not to mention this.

"Should I go back and wait? . . ."

Monique nodded fiercely and went back to yelling into the phone: "What do you mean, this isn't your responsibility? It's not my responsibility either!"

Angela was glad to put a wide aisle and two waiting areas between herself and Monique again. She went back to the jetway door by gate 2B. The sloped hallway leading down to the plane was still empty, and the colorful travel posters lining the walls—"Sky Trails! Your ticket to the world!"—seemed jarringly bright. Angela stepped into the jetway.

I'll just go down far enough to see if the jet door is open, she told herself. *It may be a violation of protocol, but Monique won't notice, not when she's busy yelling at everyone else in the airport. . . .*

At the bend in the ramp, Angela looked around the corner. She had a limited view, but caught a quick glimpse of a flight attendants' little galley, with neatly stowed drink carts.

Obviously, the jet door was standing wide open. She started to turn around, already beginning to debate with herself about whether she should report this information to Monique. Then she heard—what? A whimper? A cry?

Angela couldn't exactly identify the sound, but it was enough to pull her on down the jetway.

New Sky Trails employee saves passenger on first day on job, she thought to herself, imagining the praise and congratulations— and maybe the raise—she'd be sure to receive if what she was visualizing was real. She'd learned CPR in the orientation session. She knew basic first aid. She knew where every emergency phone in the airport was located. She started walking faster, then running.

On the side of the jet, she was surprised to see a strange insignia: TACHYON TRAVEL, it said, some airline Angela had never heard of. Was that a private charter company maybe? And then, while she was staring at it, the words suddenly changed into the familiar wing-in-the-clouds symbol of Sky Trails.

Angela blinked.

That couldn't have happened, she told herself. *It was just an optical illusion, just because I was running, just because I'm worried about whoever made that cry or whimper. . . .*

Angela stepped onto the plane. She turned her head first to the left, looking into the cockpit. Its door also stood open, but the small space was empty, the instruments dark.

"Hello?" Angela called, looking to the right now, expecting

to see some flight attendant with perfectly applied makeup—
or maybe some flight attendant and a pilot bent over a prone
passenger, maybe an old man suddenly struck down by a heart
attack or a stroke. Or, at the very least, passengers crowding
the aisle, clutching laptops and stuffed animals brought from
faraway grandparents' homes, overtired toddlers crying, fragile
old women calling out to taller men, "Could you pull my luggage
down from the overhead for me? It's that red suitcase over
there. . . ."

But the aisle of this airplane was as empty and silent as its
cockpit. Angela could see all the way to the back of the plane,
and not a single person stood in her view, not a single voice
answered her.

Only then did Angela drop her gaze to the passenger seats.
They stretched back twelve rows, with two seats per row on
the left side of the aisle and one each on the right. She stepped
forward, peering at all of them. Thirty-six seats on this plane,
and every single one of them was full.

Each seat contained a baby.

ONE

"You don't look much like your sister," Chip said, bouncing the basketball low against the driveway.

Jonah waited to answer until he'd darted his hand in and stolen the basketball away.

"Adopted," he said, shooting the ball toward the backboard. But the angle was wrong, and the ball bounced off the hoop.

"Really? You or her? Or both?" Chip asked, snagging the rebound.

"Me," Jonah said. "Just me." Then he sneaked a glance at Chip, to see if this made a difference. It didn't to Jonah—he'd always known he was adopted, and as far as he was concerned, it wasn't much more of a deal than his liking mint chocolate-chip ice cream while Katherine liked orange sherbet. But sometimes other people got weird about it.

Chip had one eyebrow raised, like he was still processing the information. This gave Jonah a chance to grab the ball again.

"Hey, if you're not, like, related by blood or anything, does that mean you could date her?" Chip asked.

Jonah almost dropped the ball.

"Yuck—*no!*" he said. "That's sick!"

"Why?" Chip asked.

"Because she's my sister! Ugh!" If Chip had asked him that question a few years ago, Jonah would have added, "And she's got cooties!" But Jonah was in seventh grade now, and seventh graders didn't talk about cooties. Anyhow Jonah hadn't known Chip a few years ago—Chip had moved into the neighborhood just three months ago, in the summertime. It was kind of a new thing for Chip to come over and play basketball.

Carefully, Jonah began bouncing the ball again.

"If you think me and Katherine don't look alike, you should see my cousin Mia," he said.

"Why?" Chip asked. "Is she even cuter than Katherine?"

Jonah made a face.

"She's only four years old!" he said. "And she's Chinese. My aunt and uncle had to go to Beijing to adopt her."

He could remember, the whole time Aunt Joan and Uncle Brad were arranging to adopt Mia—filling out the paperwork, sending away for the visas, crossing dates off calendars, and then buying new calendars to cross off new dates—his own mom and dad had spent a lot of time hugging him and exclaiming, "We were so lucky, getting you! Such a miracle!"

Katherine had been jealous.

Jonah could just picture her standing in the kitchen at age five or six, wispy blond pigtails sticking out on both sides of her head, a scowl on her face, complaining, "Weren't you lucky to get me, too? Aren't *I* a miracle?"

Mom had bent down and kissed her.

"Of course you're a miracle too," she said. "A big miracle. But we had nine months to know you were coming. With Jonah, we thought it would be years and years and years before we'd get a baby, and then that call came out of the blue—"

"The week before Christmas—" Dad added.

"And they said we could have him right away, and he was so cute, with his big eyes and his dimples and all that brown hair—"

"And then a year later, lovely Katherine came along—" Dad reached over and put his arm around her waist, pulling her close, until she giggled. "And we had a boy and a girl, and we were so happy because we had everything we wanted."

Jonah's parents could be so sappy. He didn't have too many gripes about them—as parents went, they were pretty decent. But they told that story way too often about how excited they'd been, getting that call out of the blue, getting Jonah.

Also, if he was listing grievances, he often wished that they'd had the sense *not* to name him after a guy who got swallowed up by a whale. But that was kind of a minor thing.

Now he aimed carefully and sent the ball whooshing through the net. It went through cleanly—the perfect shot.

Chip flopped down onto the grass beside the driveway.

"Man," he said. "You're going to make the basketball team for sure."

Jonah caught the ball as it fell through the net.

"Who says I'm trying out?"

Chip leaned forward.

"Well, aren't you?" he asked. "You've got to! That's, like, what everyone wants! The basketball players get all the chicks!"

This sounded so ridiculous coming out of Chip's mouth that Jonah fell into the grass laughing. After a moment, Chip started laughing too. It was like being a little kid again, rolling around in the grass laughing, not caring at all about who might see you.

Jonah stopped laughing and sat up. He peered up and down the street—fortunately, nobody was around to see them. He whacked Chip on the arm.

"So," he said. "Do you have a crush on my sister?"

Chip shrugged, which might mean, "Yes," or "Would I tell you if I did?" or "I haven't decided yet." Jonah wasn't sure he wanted to know anyway. He and Chip weren't really good friends yet, but Chip having a crush on Katherine could make everything very weird.

Chip lay back in the grass, staring up at the back of the basketball hoop.

"Do you ever wonder what's going to happen?" he asked. "I mean, I really, really want to make the basketball team. But even if I make it in seventh and eighth grades, then there's high school to deal with. Whoa. And then there's college, and being a grown-up. . . . It's all pretty scary, don't you think?"

"You forgot about planning your funeral," Jonah said.

"What?"

"You know. If you're going to get all worried about being a grown-up, you might as well figure out what's going to happen when you're ninety years old and you die," Jonah said. Personally, Jonah didn't like to plan anything. Sometimes, at the breakfast table, his mom would ask the whole family what they wanted for dinner. Even that was way too much planning for Jonah.

Chip opened his mouth to answer, then shut it abruptly and stared hard at the front door of Jonah's house. The door was opening slowly. Then Katherine stuck her head out.

"Hey, Jo-No," she called, using the nickname she knew would annoy him. "Mom says to get the mail."

Jonah tried to remember if he'd seen the mail truck gliding through the neighborhood. Maybe when he and Chip were concentrating on shooting hoops? He hoped it wasn't when they were rolling around in the grass laughing and making fools of themselves. But he obediently jumped up and went over to the mailbox, pulling out a small stack of letters and ads. He carried the mail up to Katherine.

"You can take it on in to Mom, can't you?" he asked mockingly. "Or is that too much work for Princess Katherine?"

After what he and Chip had been talking about, it was a little hard to look her in the eye. When he thought about the name Katherine, he still pictured her as she'd been a few years ago, with pudgy cheeks and those goofy-looking pigtails. Now that she was in sixth grade, she'd . . . changed. She'd slimmed down and shot up and started worrying about clothes. Her hair had gotten thicker and turned more of a golden color, and she spent a lot of time in her room with the door shut, straightening her hair or curling it or something. Right now she was even wearing makeup: a tiny smear of brown over her eyes, black on her eyelashes, a smudge of red on her cheeks.

Weird, weird, weird.

"Hey, Jo-no-brain, can't you read?" Katherine asked, as annoying as ever. "This one's for you."

She pulled a white envelope off the top of the stack of mail and shoved it back into his hands. It did indeed say *Jonah Skidmore* on the address label, but it wasn't the type of mail he usually got. Usually if he got mail, it was just postcards or brochures, reminding him about school events or basketball leagues or Boy Scout camp-outs. This envelope looked very formal and official, like an important notice.

"Who's it from?" Katherine asked.

"It doesn't say." That was strange too. He flipped the envelope over and ripped open the flap. He pulled out one thin sheet of paper.

"Let me see," Katherine said, jostling against him and knocking the letter out of his hand.

The letter fluttered slowly down toward the threshold of the door, but Jonah had already read every single word on the page.

There were only six:

YOU ARE ONE OF THE MISSING.